SUZANNE COLLINS

GREGOR AND THE CODE OF CLAW

> THE UNDERLAND CHRONICLES BOOK 5

SCHOLASTIC

Published in the UK by Scholastic Children's Books, 2020
Euston House, 24 Eversholt Street, London, NW1 1DB, UK
A division of Scholastic Limited.

London – New York – Toronto – Sydney – Auckland
Mexico City – New Delhi – Hong Kong

First published in the US by Scholastic Inc, 2007

ISBN 978 0702 30329 6

A CIP catalogue record for this book is available from the British Library.

Printed by CPI Group (UK) Ltd, Croydon, CR0 4YY
Papers used by Scholastic Children's Books are made
from wood grown in sustainable forests.

1 3 5 7 9 10 8 6 4 2

www.scholastic.co.uk

For Kathy, Drew, and Joanie

PART 1

THE CODE

CHAPTER

1

Gregor's back pressed into the cold stone floor as he stared up at the words on the ceiling. His eyes and skin were still stinging from the volcanic ash that had engulfed him hours ago. Between the burning in his lungs and the rapid beating of his heart, it was hard to get a full breath. To steady himself, he tightened his grip on the hilt of his newly claimed sword.

As soon as he had retrieved the sword from the museum, he had run to this room. Every inch of it —walls, floor, and ceiling — was covered in prophecies about the Underland, this gloomy warring world far beneath New York City, which had consumed Gregor's life for the past year. Bartholomew of Sandwich, the man who had founded the human city of Regalia, had carved the prophecies some four centuries ago. While most of his words were for the benefit

1

of the Regalians, they also made reference to many of the giant creatures who lived in the neighboring lands down here — the bats, the cockroaches, the spiders, the mice, and, most often, the rats. Oh, and Gregor. Several were about Gregor. But they didn't call him by his name. In the prophecies, he was known as "the warrior."

Gregor hadn't allowed anyone to enter the room with him. He'd wanted to be completely alone when he first read this prophecy. Everyone had taken such pains to keep its contents from him in the last few months that he had known it must say something awful. And he had wanted to be able to react to the awfulness without anyone watching him. Cry, if he needed to cry. Scream, if he needed to scream. But it turned out it didn't really matter, because he'd barely reacted at all.

"You've got to face this thing. You've got to understand it," he told himself. So he forced himself to focus on the precisely chiseled letters again.

As he reread the words, it was as if he could actually hear a clock ticking along with the lines. It was, after all, "The Prophecy of Time."

Tick, tick, tick, tick, tick, tick, tick, tick, tick, tick, tick, tick, tick, tick, tick . . .

THE WAR HAS BEEN DECLARED,
YOUR ALLY BEEN ENSNARED.
IT IS NOW OR IT IS NEVER.
BREAK THE CODE OR DIE FOREVER.

TIME IS RUNNING OUT
RUNNING OUT
RUNNING OUT.

TO THE WARRIOR GIVE MY BLADE..
BY HIS HAND YOUR FATE IS MADE.
BUT DO NOT FORGET THE TICKING
OR THE CLICKING, CLICKING, CLICKING.
WHILE A RAT'S TONGUE MAY BE FLICKING,
WITH ITS FEET IT DOES THE TRICKING.
FOR THE PAW AND NOT THE JAW
MAKES THE CODE OF CLAW.

TIME IS STANDING STILL
STANDING STILL
STANDING STILL.

SINCE THE PRINCESS IS THE KEY
TO UNLOCK THE TREACHERY,
SHE CANNOT AVOID THE MATCHING
OR THE SCRATCHING, SCRATCHING, SCRATCHING.
WHEN A SECRET PLOT IS HATCHING,
IN THE NAMING IS THE CATCHING.
WHAT SHE SAW, IT IS THE FLAW
OF THE CODE OF CLAW.

TIME IS TURNING BACK
TURNING BACK
TURNING BACK.

When the monster's blood is spilled,
When the warrior has been killed,
You must not ignore the rapping,
Or the tapping, tapping, tapping.
If the gnawers find you napping,
You will rot while they are mapping
Out the law of those who gnaw
In the Code of Claw.

The ticking stopped with the words.

Gregor closed his eyes as that one phrase hammered in his brain:

When the warrior has been killed

That was it, obviously. The part that nobody had wanted to tell him.

When the warrior has been killed

Not even Ripred — and you had to figure that rat was used to breaking bad news to people after all those years of fighting in wars.

When the warrior has been killed

Not even Luxa — who was only twelve, yet seemed much older because she was a queen and had lost her parents and all. What was it that she had said to him on the edge of

4

the cliff a few hours ago? "If you were to return home after you read the prophecy, I would not hold it against you."

"Really, Luxa?" thought Gregor. "You wouldn't hold it against me? Because if the tables were turned . . . I'd never forgive you in a million years."

WHEN THE WARRIOR HAS BEEN KILLED

In theory, sure, Gregor could still go home. Pack up his three-year-old sister, Boots, get his mom out of the hospital, where she was recovering from the plague, and have his bat, Ares, fly them back up to the laundry room of their apartment building in New York City. Ares, his bond, who had saved his life numerous times and who had had nothing but suffering since he had met Gregor. He tried to imagine the parting. "Well, Ares, it's been great. I'm heading home now. I know by leaving I'm completely dooming to annihilation everyone who's helped me down here, but I'm really not up for this whole war thing anymore. So, fly you high, you know?"

Like that would ever happen.

WHEN THE WARRIOR HAS BEEN KILLED

It simply didn't feel real. Any of it. Maybe it was because he was so tired. Gregor hadn't slept in days. Not since before he'd watched the rats murder hundreds of mice in a pit at the base of a volcano in the Firelands. He'd fallen unconscious for a while from the poisonous fumes the volcano had emitted when it erupted. Did that count as sleep? Maybe. But it had been only a short time before he'd come to and waded through deep ash in search of his friends. Before he could even experience the joy of finding them, he'd learned that Thalia, the sweet little bat who had mistakenly been caught up in the ill-fated trip, had suffocated as she tried to escape the volcano. Hazard, Luxa's seven-year-old cousin who had planned on bonding with Thalia, had been so distraught they'd had to sedate him. Later, when they had finally found some clean air on a cliff overlooking the jungle, Gregor had volunteered to keep watch while the others rested. On the flight home, packed onto Ares's back with Boots, Hazard, their cockroach friend, Temp, and a heavily drugged mouse, Cartesian, he had been unable to sleep. Now he was numb. . . .

WHEN THE WARRIOR HAS BEEN KILLED

And unable to muster any real emotional response to the prophecy. "What's wrong with me?" Gregor thought. "Shouldn't I be freaking out?" He should, of course, he should. Only after all that had happened, he just didn't have it in him. "It'll hit me later, I guess. Maybe in a couple days. If I last that long . . ."

Rotten as the prophecy was, Gregor supposed it could have been even worse. On the good side, Boots and his mom might make it out of the Underland alive. It looked like Boots, who was known to the giant cockroaches as "the princess," had some important role to play in breaking this

6

Code of Claw thing. But the prophecy didn't call for anyone else's death.

Wait, yes it did.

WHEN THE MONSTER'S BLOOD IS SPILLED

After what Gregor had witnessed in the last few days, he couldn't imagine anyone being the monster but the Bane. The enormous white rat, whose life Gregor had spared as a baby, had grown up to be a vicious leader consumed with hatred and was at least somewhat insane. Life had twisted and tormented that fragile rat pup into a monster, but there was no helping the Bane now. He had given the order to wipe out the mice and there was no telling what he would do next. He had to be stopped. In the Overland, he might be imprisoned for life or something. But that wouldn't be an option in the Underland. Down here, he would have to be killed.

"I guess I should get started. Eat something at least," he thought. An army of rats would be here soon. Ares had flown over them on their way back to Regalia. Gregor should be getting ready. He knew he had to fight.

But he seemed frozen in place, as if he had become part of the stone, too. He remembered something he'd seen on a field trip he'd made to the Cloisters in New York City. It was an old museum filled with medieval stuff. One room held tombs. On top of each tomb was a life-size image of the dead person carved in stone. There was this one guy — had it been a knight? —who'd had his hands folded over

7

the hilt of his sword. In fact, he'd been lying in almost the exact position Gregor was in now. "That's me," thought Gregor. "That's me. I've turned to stone and I'm as good as dead." How perfect for Sandwich to have put "The Prophecy of Time" smack in the middle of the ceiling so that Gregor would have to be lying just like this to read it. How perfect that the sword under Gregor's hands had once belonged to Sandwich and would now carry out his visions. How perfect and horrible the whole thing was.

The door swung open softly and footsteps crossed to him.

"Gregor? How fare you?" said Vikus. The old man's voice sounded as exhausted as Gregor felt. He probably hadn't had much sleep, either. As head of the Regalian council, Vikus was overworked, anyway. His wife, Solovet, who'd been in charge of the Regalian army until recently, was about to go on trial for ordering research that had created a plague, and Luxa, his granddaughter, was in terrible danger in the Firelands. No, Vikus couldn't be getting much rest.

"Me? I'm good," said Gregor evenly. "Never better."

"What think you of 'The Prophecy of Time'?" asked Vikus.

"It's catchy," said Gregor, and slowly, painfully got to his feet. He'd messed up his knee on this last trip.

"I came in to remind you how easy it is to misinterpret Sandwich's prophecies," said Vikus.

Gregor pulled his sword from his belt and tapped the line about his death with the point of the blade. "This? You think it's easy to misinterpret this?"

Vikus hesitated. "Possibly."

"Well, it seems pretty clear to me," said Gregor.

"Believe me, Gregor, if there was any way I could take your place, fulfill this prophecy myself . . . I would do it in a moment. . . ." Vikus's eyes filled with tears.

Despite his own situation, Gregor had to feel sorry for him. Life had not been particularly kind to Vikus, either. "Look, I could've died fifty times down here already. It's a miracle I've lasted this long." If Vikus was this upset, how would Gregor's family react? He didn't ever want to find out. "Just don't tell my mom about it. Or my dad. No one in my family can know. Okay?"

Vikus nodded in agreement.

As Gregor slid the sword back in his belt, Vikus reached for it. Gregor instinctively covered the handle. "It's mine. You gave it to me," he said brusquely. How quickly he'd become protective, even jealous of the weapon.

Vikus's face registered surprise, then concern. "I had no thought of taking it, Gregor. Only you must wear the sword so." He placed his hand on top of Gregor's and gave the handle a twist. "At this angle, you will avoid cutting your leg."

"Thanks for the tip," said Gregor. "Well, I'd better go get this stuff off of me." Although he had washed as best he could at a spring on the cliff, much of the volcanic ash was still eating away at his skin.

"Go to the hospital. They have a salve for that," said Vikus.

Gregor started for the door but Vikus stopped him with

his voice. "Gregor, you have demonstrated an extraordinary ability to kill. But a year ago, you refused to even touch that weapon. Remember that even in war there is a time for restraint. A time to hold back your sword," said Vikus. "Will you do that?"

"I don't know," said Gregor. He was too tired to make any noble promises. Especially when once he began to fight, he usually lost control of himself. "I don't know what I'll do, Vikus." He sensed the answer was insufficient, so he added, "I can try." Gregor left the room quickly to avoid any further discussion of what he might and might not do.

Down in the hospital he was immediately sent to soak in a tub bubbling with some kind of herbal mixture designed to remove the ash from his skin. As the steam from the concoction filled his lungs, Gregor began to cough up a lot of junk he had inhaled over the last few days. It took not one bath but three until the doctors were satisfied that he was free of the ash, both inside and out. Then they covered his skin in a pleasant-smelling lotion. By the time the process was over, Gregor could barely keep his eyes open. He drank the broth in a bowl held against his lips. He thought he swallowed some medicine, too. And then fatigue began to take over. Gregor grabbed the nearest doctor's sleeve. "I have to go fight!"

"Not like this," said the doctor. "Do not worry. Wars are not fleet. There will be much fighting left when you awaken."

"No, I . . ." said Gregor. But somewhere inside himself,

he knew the doctor was right. The sleeve slipped from his hand and he gave in to sleep.

When Gregor opened his eyes it took him a minute to realize where he was. His hospital room was so clean and well lit after his days on the road. He drowsily took stock of his body. His skin had absorbed the lotion and felt soothed and cool. His knee, which he had injured falling from a rock, had been wrapped and was less painful. Someone had trimmed his ragged nails. He was dressed in fresh clothes.

Suddenly he sat bolt upright, his right hand clutching the empty space on his left hip. His sword! Where was his sword? He saw it almost at once, propped in the corner of the hospital room, the sword belt dangling from it. Of course they had not put him to bed with it. That would have been dangerous. And no one had stolen it. Still, even the twelve feet that separated him from the weapon caused him unease. He did not like it to be out of his reach.

Gregor was swinging his stiff legs to the floor to retrieve the sword when a nurse came in with a tray of food and ordered him back in bed. He didn't want to argue with her, so he obeyed. But after she left, he slid the tray onto the sheets, got the sword, and propped it right against the side of his bed. Now he could eat.

Food had been scant over the last days of the journey. Some fish, a few mushrooms. He was so hungry he ignored the utensils and scooped up the food with his hands, stuffing it into his mouth. The bland meal —bread, fish chowder, and pudding — tasted wonderful and he ate every bite. He was wiping his finger around the pudding bowl, trying to get out the last bit, when his old friend Mareth came into the room.

"You are allowed to have seconds," said the soldier with a smile. He called down the hall for them to bring Gregor more food. Then he limped to a chair by the bed. Gregor noticed he was doing a lot better with his prosthetic leg, but he still needed the help of a cane to walk. "You slept for a full day. How do you feel?" he asked Gregor, giving him a significant look.

"Fine," said Gregor. He hadn't been injured badly on this trip. Mareth didn't need to look so concerned. Then Gregor realized he was referring to the prophecy calling for the warrior's death. "Oh, you mean . . ." Dread began to seep into his brain. He pushed it away, still unable to deal with it. "I'm okay, Mareth."

Mareth gave his shoulder a squeeze but didn't pursue it. Gregor was glad they didn't have to have some big talk about it. "How's Boots and Hazard and everybody?"

"Well. They are well. They have all been purged of ash. Hazard is confined to bed until his head wound has healed fully. But Howard's medical training has paid off. He did an excellent job of stitching it," said Mareth.

His friend Howard and his bat, Nike. Luxa and her bat, Aurora. Ripred. They were not safe and clean in the hospital but fighting to free the mice who were still alive in the Firelands. "Any word from them?" asked Gregor.

"None," said Mareth. "Two divisions of soldiers have been sent after them. We hope to hear soon. But our normal

12

channels of communication are somewhat disrupted now that Luxa has declared war."

Luxa . . .

Gregor felt the back pocket of his pants, but it was empty. His old clothes had probably been destroyed. He felt slightly panicked. "I had a picture. In my pocket —"

Mareth lifted a photograph off of the bedside table and handed it to him. "This?"

There they were. Luxa and Gregor. Dancing. Laughing. Captured in one of the few really happy moments they had shared. Just a few weeks ago at Hazard's birthday party. Gregor slid the photo into the pocket of his shirt. "Thanks."

Mareth did not make him explain that, either. Which was good because Gregor was not sure how to put into words what had begun to happen between himself and Luxa. How their rocky friendship was transforming into an entirely different relationship.

"My parents?" Gregor asked.

"Your father has been told of your safe return. A bat was sent to the Overland with the news as soon as you arrived. He said to tell you that your grandmother and sister Lizzie are well," said Mareth. Then he paused.

"And my mom?" Gregor prompted him.

"She has had a relapse," said Mareth.

"You mean the plague came back?" said Gregor anxiously.

"No, no, but an infection of her lungs," said Mareth. "She will mend but it has weakened her greatly."

This was not good. Whatever else happened, Gregor

needed to get her home. If he had to die, he had to die. But that made it a hundred times more crucial for his mom and Boots to get back to New York City safely. His parents and grandma and sisters had to have one another.

The nurse brought another serving of pudding and left. Gregor no longer felt so hungry. He poked at the pudding with his spoon.

"Where are the rats now? The ones Ares and I saw headed for Regalia on our way back?" asked Gregor. "Have they attacked the city yet?"

"No. The rats turned back to the Firelands when they saw our troops fly over," said Mareth.

"What?" said Gregor in surprise.

"I am sure they mean to bolster the Bane's defenses," said Mareth.

"You mean . . . there's no one here to fight?" Gregor's mind suddenly cleared. He had completed this phase of his mission. He had brought back the kids and the wounded to Regalia. He had read "The Prophecy of Time." And most of all, he had taken possession of Sandwich's sword. His next step, he'd assumed, would have been to help defend Regalia from a massive rat attack. But there was no attack on Regalia. "This is bad," he mumbled. A rat army waiting at the walls of a well-fortified city was scary, but a rat army descending out in the open was much worse. So what was he doing here, lying in bed stuffing his face with pudding, while his friends were caught in a battle in the Firelands?

Gregor shoved his tray off of his legs so quickly that the

bowls clattered to the floor. He jumped out of bed and grabbed the sword belt.

"What are you doing?" said Mareth.

"I'm going back," said Gregor. "I'm going back to fight those rats."

CHAPTER

2

Mareth rose to block his way. "Wait, Gregor. It is not so simple now. We are at war."

"Yeah, that's what I'm talking about," said Gregor. His fingers fumbled in their eagerness to buckle on the belt. "Is Ares still in the hospital?" He knew his bond would be as anxious as he was to rejoin their friends.

"Yes, down the hall. But listen a moment —" Mareth began.

"Great, then we can get going," said Gregor. He moved for the door only to find he was being lifted in the air and thrust back against the bed. Mareth might have lost his leg, but he could still toss Gregor around, no problem.

"Listen!" said Mareth. "During wartime, you are a soldier. Perhaps the most valuable one we have. You cannot

16

go running off when the mood strikes you. You will be expected to follow orders."

"Whose orders?" asked Gregor.

"Solovet's," said Mareth.

"Solovet's?" said Gregor, genuinely thrown. As far as he knew, she was no longer in a position to give anyone orders. "I thought she was locked up in her room and had to go on trial for causing the plague."

"The trial was put on hold once it was known that Luxa had declared war," said Mareth.

"But . . . why? That doesn't change what Solovet did," said Gregor. "She still ordered the doctors to make the plague into a weapon. She still killed all those people and bats. She almost killed my mom."

"By accident. Her plan was to kill rats," said Mareth. "Now that we are at war with them, a person who thinks of little but killing rats is of great value. So the council has reinstated her as head of the Regalian army."

"The head of — no way!" exclaimed Gregor. He'd thought that maybe they'd made her the leader of his squadron or something. But now she was back in charge of everything? "Couldn't they get someone else?"

"There is no human, save yourself, who the rats fear as much," said Mareth. "Solovet is both cunning and ruthless in war. It was felt we needed her to survive."

"But — that trial will never happen now!" said Gregor bitterly. It wouldn't. The war would erupt and blank everything else out. As the hatred against the rats built, the humans would think that Solovet had had a good idea in

17

turning the plague germs into a weapon. Despite all of the deaths she had caused to her own people, she would be seen as heroic, not criminal. Gregor thought of his mom struggling to breathe somewhere in the hospital. The purple scars that Ares's fur still could not quite cover. All of the people and bats and rats who had died. "That's not right, Mareth," said Gregor. "Do you think it's right?"

Mareth sighed and averted his eyes. He released Gregor and took an awkward step back. "Whatever my private opinion of the situation is, it is of no matter. Solovet is now in command."

"Not of me," said Gregor. Of one thing he was certain. He was not going to go to his death on Solovet's terms; he was going to go on his own.

"Be careful to whom you say that, Gregor," said Mareth quietly. "Not everyone here is your friend." With that, the soldier limped out of the room.

Gregor took a few deep breaths to get a handle on himself, then unbuckled his sword belt and placed the blade back in the corner of the room. He wiped up the pudding he'd knocked to the floor and neatly reset the tray. Then he lay back down in bed to look like a model patient while he worked things out in his head.

Mareth was right. Not everybody in Regalia was Gregor's friend. Plenty of people would be more than happy to spy on him for Solovet. Gregor didn't know what she had in store for him, but it was unlikely it involved him hopping on Ares and flying straight back to the Firelands. Probably he would be part of some master plan. Whatever Gregor wanted would be of no consequence. She would view him as a weapon to be used at her discretion. If he was going to get back to the Firelands, he would have to do it in secret. And he would have to do it carefully.

"What's your plan?" he heard Ripred's voice in his head. The rat was trying to break him of the habit of flying off the handle and taking action without thinking of its consequences. "What's your plan?"

"First of all, I can't let anyone else guess that I want to go back," Gregor thought. He was pretty sure Mareth wouldn't tell anyone. But he couldn't count on other people's loyalty. Gregor's initial impulse had been to run straight to Ares, but that would be odd. If he were not obsessed with returning to the Firelands, if he were planning to stay in Regalia like a good little soldier, wouldn't he ask to see his mom first? He felt a flush of shame. Shouldn't he have asked to see his mom first either way? Yes. Only the truth was, if she was well enough to see him, she was going to be both furious about his trip to the Firelands and adamant that he return immediately to New York City. Which he wasn't going to do. So he would either have to fight with her, openly defy her, or lie to her. All three options were lousy. Underneath it all, though, he was still aching to see her.

When a doctor came by a few minutes later, Gregor asked if he could visit her and was given permission to do so. Briefly. "It is fine to use your knee, good even. But take it slowly for the first few days," said the doctor, helping him into a pair of sandals.

"Got it," said Gregor, and made a big show of walking

19

carefully down to his mom's room. He had to wear a mask, not for his own protection but for hers.

Gregor had underestimated what a relapse could be. His mother was as sick as she'd been when he'd first seen her with the plague. Sicker, maybe. Then, at least, she'd had the energy to order him home. Now she was too weak to even speak. All of her effort went into breathing. When he held her hand, the skin was hot and dry from fever. Her eyes had a distant look.

"This isn't the plague, right?" Gregor asked the doctor.

"No, this is a lung infection. I believe you call it 'pneumonia' in the Overland," said the doctor.

"But she could go home, if she was well enough to travel?" said Gregor.

"If she was well enough to travel, but she is not," said the doctor.

Gregor stroked his mother's cheek. "Don't worry, it's going to be all right. It's going to be all right." He couldn't tell if she understood him or not.

Outside the room, the doctor took Gregor aside and spoke in a whisper. At first Gregor assumed it was for his mom's sake, but then he realized the doctor was afraid of anyone hearing his words. "Warrior, if she were my mother, I would use whatever influence I have to get her back to the Overland. Your hospitals could treat her as well as ours now. And with the war commencing, the palace may come under attack. She may even have to be moved to the Fount."

"But you said she was too sick to travel," said Gregor.

"That is what I must say. And it is true. For a time of

peace," said the doctor. "But now you must weigh the dangers of her staying here during a time of war." He looked nervously around. "Please, keep my counsel to yourself." Then he walked swiftly away.

For a moment, Gregor felt torn as the desire to get to the Firelands fought with the need to get his mother to safety. His mother won. His friends in the Firelands had one another and an army to lean on. His mother had no one but himself.

Gregor left the hospital without permission and found Vikus in the room off of the High Hall. "When are you sending the next message to my father?" he asked.

"I was about to do so now, Gregor. Is there something you wish me to include?" asked Vikus.

"Yeah, my mom," said Gregor.

Vikus rubbed a hand over his eyes. "I have tried, Gregor. Three times already. The council has denied the requests."

Gregor knew Vikus couldn't officially move his mom without the council members' authority, but he couldn't help being frustrated by the way the old man constantly deferred to them. "But she can't stay here during the war. What if the rats attacked the palace? You'd have to move her somewhere else, anyway." Gregor thought he could say that much without getting the doctor in trouble.

"I have made this argument," said Vikus. "But the council does not accept it. They refuse to let her go. My wife has convinced them that your mother's health will not bear the move."

Suddenly Gregor understood what was going on. "It's not

about her health. It's about me. It's about keeping me here," he said. Solovet was holding his mother hostage down here. She knew Gregor would never leave without his mom.

Vikus's silence confirmed his words.

"You tell the council they'd better keep her alive. If she dies, you just lost a warrior!" said Gregor.

"Are you sure you wish me to say this?" asked Vikus.

"Why wouldn't I?" said Gregor.

"It gains you nothing and it reveals much of your hand," said Vikus. "I myself find it wiser to keep certain thoughts to myself until they can be to my advantage."

Vikus was right. The doctors in the hospital would do their best to heal his mother. Threatening the council members would only increase their suspicion of Gregor at a time when he was trying to appear tractable. "I see what you mean. Thanks," said Gregor. At least Vikus was still looking out for him.

He headed back to the hospital, gripped by fear for his mother. Could he move her on his own? No, she was way too sick. That would take a whole team of doctors. When she got home she'd have to go straight to the hospital and then the questions would begin. Even so, Gregor would rather gamble on his dad and Mrs. Cormaci coming up with some crazy story to explain his mom's condition than to risk having her down here during the war.

It was all a moot point, though, because of Solovet. She would never let his mom go until she was through using Gregor. A voice came out of the past: "I was just thinking, it did not take long for my mother to get her claws into you." Hamnet. That's what Hamnet had said on their first meeting in the jungle, before he had been Gregor's guide, before the ants had killed him. Hamnet, a famous warrior himself, had fled Regalia because his conscience would no longer allow him to fight, and he knew his mother, Solovet, would try to force him. Who would know better than Hamnet what it felt like to have Solovet's claws in him? Well, they were digging into Gregor now, in a whole new way. But it only increased Gregor's resolve to defy her.

He returned to his hospital room to find that another meal had showed up. He ate it to keep up appearances. Probably needed it, anyway. He might be back on a diet of fish and mushrooms pretty soon. Then he went to find Ares. Since he'd seen his mom, this would not raise any red flags.

Ares was just finishing up his meal when Gregor came in. A nurse was gathering up the platters that had held the bat's food.

"How you feeling, man?" asked Gregor.

"A bit stiff, but I am well," said the bat. His voice, which was usually a low purr, was hoarse from the volcanic ash.

"Think you'd be up for a game of chess later?" asked Gregor. This was entirely for the nurse's benefit. Gregor and Ares had never played chess before. Never even spoken about it. But Gregor had seen a lot of people and bats playing in the hospital while they were recovering. It seemed like something the nurse would be in favor of.

"The question is, are you up for it?" asked Ares.

"That sounds like a challenge," said Gregor with a grin.

The nurse seemed to approve. "I will see if we have a board available." She collected the dishes and left the room.

Gregor and Ares waited a few moments, then spoke in urgent whispers.

"We must get back to the Firelands," said Ares.

"I know. But Mareth says we're under Solovet's command now," said Gregor. "Can you meet me at the place?" "The place" was a pretty general term, but he knew Ares would understand he was referring to the spring-fed lake known as the Spout. There was a secret passage that led to it from a stone turtle in the old nursery.

"In one hour," said Ares. "The nibbler pups are still in the nursery. If your sister is not with Hazard, she will likely be there, too."

"I'll find a way," said Gregor. Although persuading Boots, a litter of mouse babies, and probably their nanny, too, to look the other way while he flipped open that big stone turtle shell and climbed through it was going to be some trick.

The nurse came in holding a chessboard. "I have a board but no pieces at the moment. Some will be available soon."

"You know, I think there's a set in the museum," said Gregor. "I'm supposed to exercise this knee some, anyway. I'll get it." There actually was one of those little magnetic travel chessboards complete with pieces in the museum. It was the perfect excuse.

Gregor stopped by his hospital room and buckled on his sword belt. If anyone asked, he could always say he was just trying to get used to the feel of wearing it. But he still waited until the hall was free of doctors and nurses to slip out of the hospital. He took a less-traveled route to the museum as well, and managed to avoid running into anyone but a group of schoolchildren.

When he got to the museum, the first thing that caught his eye was a brown cardboard box that was sealed with masking tape. The words FOR GREGOR had been printed neatly across the top in red marker. He recognized the handwriting as Mrs. Cormaci's. When had this box come? Today? Yesterday? Or during his week or so of absence in the Firelands? Gregor ripped open the box and found a note right on top. As he read the words, he could hear Mrs. Cormaci's voice in his head.

Dear Gregor,

Well, this is a fine how-do-you-do. Everyone's in a state because you've disappeared on some picnic, but I feel certain you've got yourself mixed up in some kind of funny business down there. I know it's strange, but I'm not even worried. Not about you or Boots. Although your parents . . . well, that's another story. Do you realize, I wonder, what it does to your family when you go off?

Gregor felt like someone had hit him in the stomach. Yes, he realized! Of course he knew! Hadn't he been the one waiting for his dad for two and a half years? Didn't his family's situation gnaw away at him every time he was on some mission?

Now you're in Regalia because you're reading this. So it's a good time to step back and take a hard look at things. I know most of what happens to you down there is out of your control. I know you're only doing what you feel you have to do. But your family is hurting right now. All I'm saying is, don't let yourself get killed, or you'll have an awful lot of explaining to do.

Love,
Mrs. Cormaci

Why had she written that about him being killed? It was almost as if she had read the prophecy. But if she had, she would also know that his death was one of those things out of his control. As for explaining things once he was gone . . . well, that didn't even make sense. Why was she even saying this stuff to him? Maybe she meant it as a joke. Of course, it being Mrs. Cormaci, maybe she didn't. Wait, there was something at the bottom. . . .

P.S. Lizzie helped make the cookies. She says to share them with the rat.

So Lizzie was home from sleepaway camp. He knew she'd be a wreck. Even when things were going fine, his sister was anxious. He could see her face now, her brow furrowed the way no eight-year-old kid's should ever be. Skinny, little, nervous, way-too-smart-for-her-age Lizzie. Worrying about him and Boots. Worrying about his mom and dad. Even worrying about cranky old Ripred.

"Next time I see Lizzie —" Gregor thought. And then he realized he would never see her again. Or any of them back home. Because he was never leaving the Underland. He was going to die down here. . . .

Gregor watched as the note floated from his hand and came to rest gently on the floor. And that's when Sandwich's words finally hit him.

WHEN THE WARRIOR HAS BEEN KILLED

The room spun around and he clutched a shelf to keep from falling. He felt an immense pressure in his chest, as if he were in danger of breaking into a thousand pieces, and was unable to draw a breath. "No! I don't want this! I don't want to die!" he thought. His entire body began shaking as he tried to push the threat from his mind, but it was too powerful. "I can't do this. I can't. I've got to get home." Luxa was right. It was too much to ask of him. To give his life, his future, to give everything he had for the Underlanders. "I'm getting out of here. Going to get Boots and my momand get home and — never — look — back!"

For an instant, he thought he really might do it. But then what? What? What happened to everyone he loved down here? They would all die as the prophecy foretold. He could never let that happen. Would never let that happen. So then —

Gregor sank to the floor, panting, as the waves of tremors ran through him. He struggled to get ahold of himself. This had to stop! He couldn't flip out every time he thought

27

about what lay before him. Of all the people he would never see, or all the things he would never do. He would be worthless. Of no use at all. He had to have something in his mind to hold on to. Something that gave him strength. Images flew through his head, of his family, of his friends, of places and things he loved. None of them were of any help.

Then he remembered the stone knight in the Cloisters. Cold, hard, unyielding, long since removed from anything in life that could hurt him. A long time ago, the knight had fought . . . maybe died in a horrible battle, too . . . everybody had to die even-tually . . . but now he was invulnerable. Sleeping on his marble bed. Safe. Peaceful even. Somehow the thought of this other soldier from another time comforted Gregor in a way that nothing living could. He had gone through something awful, but it was over, and he was now in a place where no one could ever harm him again. The shaking began to subside. Gregor inhaled and the pain in his chest lost its grip. "That's me. I have to remember that's me from now on," he thought. "I'm that knight, I'm made of stone, and in the end nothing can touch me. Okay. Okay, then. That's how it is."

As he calmed down, he remembered that Ares was waiting for him. He had things to do. People to help. And time was short.

Gregor retrieved the note and pulled himself to his feet. He saw a foil-wrapped package that had to be the cookies. But the box was too deep to hold only cookies. He lifted out the foil package and his heart skipped a beat. Two flashlights.

A big stack of batteries. And a brand-new pair of sneakers. The good kind. Mrs. Cormaci. How did she know? How did she always seem to know what he needed? The waterproof flashlight she had given him before he'd crossed the Waterway. The work boots that had saved his toes from being destroyed by acid in the jungle. Could she see the dangers he would encounter in those tarot cards of hers, even though Gregor would never let her do a reading on him? Or was she just a good guesser?

Gregor added a new roll of duct tape and two water bottles to the box. The bottles were the kind joggers used in Central Park. They were empty, but he could fill them up at a stream along the way to the Firelands. He looked for a new backpack, but all he could find was a small pink one with thin cords for straps. He emptied out a lady's wallet, a makeup case, a book of maps of Manhattan, and a hairbrush, and stuck it in his box. It didn't look like something a warrior would carry, but it would hold his supplies and that was all that really mattered. Then he placed the cookies back on top of the whole thing. He wouldn't get ready to travel until he was in the secret passageway that led to the Spout. Remembering his story to the nurse, he placed the magnetic chessboard on top of the cookies. He probably wouldn't see her again, but he wanted to cover all of his bases. Now he had to get to the old nursery and into that passageway.

Gregor picked up the box. He walked out of the museum and down the hall. "Taking your time. Looking natural," he thought. "You can do this."

Then he turned the corner and pulled up short.

Solovet was standing in front of him. Behind her were two men.

The last time Gregor had seen Solovet was months ago, when he had arrived back from the jungle. She had been in the council meeting where they had arrested Dr. Neveeve. By the time Gregor had been treated for his injuries and come out of the anesthesia, Dr. Neveeve had been executed and Solovet confined to her rooms. Gregor had been glad she'd been taken away to a place where he couldn't see her. Where he didn't have to deal with what she'd done to his mom and Ares and Howard and countless others. But here she was. The woman who wouldn't think twice about letting his mom die if it meant holding on to Gregor. In one second, he realized both how much he hated her and how careful he had to be. She was now in command of him.

"Gregor," she said with a warm smile.

He smiled back. "Hey, Solovet. How've you been?"

"Very well. And yourself?" she asked.

"Doing all right," he said.

"What have you there?" she asked, nodding at the box.

"Mrs. Cormaci sent me some cookies. Thought I'd take them back up to the hospital. Spread the goodness around," said Gregor. "Want one?" He peeled back the foil on the cookies and the delicious smell of oatmeal raisin filled the hallway.

"Why not?" Solovet accepted a cookie and took a bite. She chewed it thoughtfully and nodded her approval. "Excellent."

"So, I need to talk to you pretty soon, right?" asked Gregor as he shifted the box to his hip. "See what you want me to do. Mareth says you're running the war."

"Yes. Yes. And you are, of course, very precious to me. Know you Horatio and Marcus?" Solovet casually gestured to the men behind her.

"Hi." Gregor gave them a wave and they nodded back. For the first time he noticed how they were dressed. They each wore protective gear made of leather and metal on their chests, legs, and arms. Helmets covered their heads. Wicked-looking swords and daggers were at their belts. "Are they, like, generals or something?"

"No, Gregor. They are your personal guards," said Solovet. "We are very concerned with your safety."

"My personal guards? Great." Her real meaning was beginning to dawn on him, but he just laughed. "I sure could've used them a few days ago. Doesn't seem like I'd need them in here, though. Aren't even any rats around."

"The guards are not to keep the rats out," said Solovet pleasantly. "They are to keep you in."

CHAPTER

3

Gregor just stared at her as his options flipped through his head. Run. Fight. Laugh. Protest. Act offended. Lay his cards on the table. Do nothing.

Do nothing won out.

"I cannot afford to have you running off on any more picnics," said Solovet. "Come to see me in an hour. We will discuss your future then."

She walked off, leaving Gregor with the two formidable soldiers. He sized them up and determined it had been a good decision not to start a fight. They were tall with rippling muscles and hardened looks on their faces. Solovet's men through and through. Gregor had no idea if he would have stood a chance against them if they had all drawn their weapons. Maybe, if his rager side kicked in. When Gregor became what the Underlanders called a rager, he transformed into an accurate and deadly fighter. But he could never count on that happening. Better to be on good terms with his guards.

"Cookie?" said Gregor, holding out the package. They both shook their heads no. "Well, my sister will want some. She's probably with the mice. Come on. This way." Gregor gestured for them to follow him and started for the old nursery. He limped a lot, to show his knee was really badly injured and there was no way he could run. "Now what?" he thought. "How on earth am I going to lose these guys?"

He took his time getting up to the nursery, hoping for some brilliant plan to strike him like a lightning bolt. None did. He was just going to have to do his best with whatever circumstances he found.

The nursery was in an almost deserted wing of the palace. As far as he could tell from the glimpses he caught through doorways, most of the other rooms in the hall seemed to be used for storage.

A warm light shone out of the nursery door. He stepped inside and heard a pleased squeak. "Gre-go!" Boots ran over and flung her arms around his knees. He set the box down and lifted her up into his arms for a real hug.

"Hey, Boots," he said, pressing his face into her curly head. She smelled like an herbal bath and milk and her own sweet self. It was a comforting smell, and for a minute, he almost felt okay. Then he caught a glimpse of the stone turtle at the far end of the room, its face in a vicious snarl. "What's going on?"

"I helping Dulcie take care of the baby mouses," Boots said. She pointed over to the alcove where the nanny, Dulcet, had made a nest out of blankets. Dulcet sat among the blankets now with the six baby mice crawling around her.

Cartesian, the adult mouse Gregor had brought back from the Firelands, lay in the nest as well. Both of his front legs were in casts. He was still very weak. But he looked far better than he had when Gregor had first seen him, left for dead at the base of a cliff, surrounded by scores of mice who had not survived the fall. One of the baby mice climbed up on Cartesian's back. It must have hurt, but he made no move to stop it.

"Greetings, Gregor," said Dulcet. She raised her eyebrows slightly. "I see you have brought company."

Gregor looked behind him and saw that Horatio and Marcus were standing on guard at the doorway. "Yeah, these are my new bodyguards."

"Horatio, Marcus, would you mind very much standing outside of the door? I am afraid you may frighten the nibbler pups," said Dulcet.

"We have orders to attend the Overlander at all times," said Horatio doubtfully.

"I promise he shall be safe in my hands," said Dulcet with a laugh.

For a moment, Horatio's face lost its hard edge, and Gregor realized he had a soft spot for Dulcet. "Man," he thought. "Is it that easy for people to tell I like Luxa now?"

"I suppose we may risk standing outside of the door,"

conceded Horatio. "Come, Marcus."

"Thank you, Horatio," said Dulcet. Gregor examined her face for any sign that she returned Horatio's feelings. She didn't. Or else she was just a lot better at hiding it. He wondered briefly if he might be able to get her to distract the guards while he sneaked through the turtle shell, but then abandoned the idea. He didn't want to get Dulcet in trouble with Solovet. Somehow, he was going to have to get her out of the nursery before he made his escape.

Boots got down and climbed into the nest. "I rock the babies." She picked up the nearest mouse pup and cradled it in her arms. It let her rock it for a bit, then wiggled free, placed its front paws on her shoulder, and played with one of her curls. Boots giggled. "Mouses like my hair."

Gregor squatted beside the nest and stroked one of the velvety pups. "Do you remember me?" he asked Cartesian. The mouse had been either so delirious or so heavily drugged in the Firelands that Gregor didn't think he'd made much of an impression. But he was wrong.

"You are the warrior," said Cartesian. "Yes, I remember you. Have you any word of our friends in the Firelands?"

"No, Mareth said they sent two divisions to help. Haven't heard back yet," said Gregor, not letting himself imagine what might be happening on that battlefield now. "Do you know these pups?"

"They are my sister's children," said Cartesian. "She felt they would fare better on the river than under the gnawers' control."

"She was right," said Gregor, remembering the mouse

pups he had seen suffocating to death in the volcanic pit. "Did their mother — ?"

"I do not know. I do not wish to speak of this before them," said Cartesian, indicating the pups with one of his casts. "They are beginning to understand English and they have enough fodder for nightmares already."

"I'm sorry," said Gregor, feeling bad he had even brought up the subject. "Hey, Boots, you want to give the babies a treat?"

Boots trotted over to the box with him and was delighted to find the cookies. She stuck one in her mouth right off. "Mmm," she said.

"Good, huh? Why don't you give one to everybody?" suggested Gregor. He piled cookies into her hands, careful not to remove the foil package from the box and reveal his travel supplies underneath.

"I have treats!" crowed Boots, spraying crumbs everywhere. She excitedly passed around the cookies to everyone in the nest.

The pups made happy smacking sounds as they munched away on the cookies. Gregor plastered a smile across his face as he watched the scene, but inside his mind was racing. "I've got to get out of here. Now!" he thought. Ares was probably flying around the Spout at this moment. But how could he get everybody out of the room? Suggest a visit somewhere in the palace? That would be weird because Cartesian couldn't travel far with those legs. Pretend to accidentally knock over a torch and start a fire? No, bad idea. That would only bring in more people. And if the fire got out of hand someone could get hurt. The babies might get scared and try to hide and — wait! That was it!

"Who wants to play a game?" asked Gregor, clapping his hands for attention. The pups did seem to understand that much, because they gathered around him, hopping up and down expectantly.

"Me! Me!" said Boots.

"What should we play, Boots?" asked Gregor. Boots could almost always be counted on to pick one game.

"Hide-and-seek! Hide-and-seek!" she squealed, and Gregor exhaled in relief.

"All right, great. Hide-and-seek. Do the mice know how to play?" he asked.

"Oh, yes," said Dulcet. "We have played many times in here. You will be hard-pressed to find a hiding spot they have not already discovered."

"That's no good. Maybe we could use some of the other rooms out in the hall," said Gregor.

"Yes, I had considered that, but with only myself to watch them I felt it too unmanageable," said Dulcet. "Perhaps with you and Cartesian here, we could do it. I know they are becoming bored with this room."

"Sure, I'll help," said Gregor. "Wait, let me take this thing off." He removed his sword belt and set it on the box. It was hard, letting go of his weapon.

"Oh, and we have Horatio and Marcus!" said Dulcet. The guards were in the doorway the moment they heard their names. "We are to play hide-and-seek. Can you help us?"

The guards did not want to at first, but soon Dulcet had them positioned at either end of the hallway. That way, the others could play the game using six rooms, but no one could leave the area without going by them. Or so everyone but Gregor supposed.

Gregor and Dulcet did a quick check of the rooms, but there was nothing particularly dangerous in any of them. A couple held old furniture. Blankets, baskets, and coils of rope were stored in some of the others. One had once been a bathroom, but there was no water flowing through it now, so it was more like a stone playground. Lots of good safe places to hide.

Cartesian hobbled out in the hallway to watch. First Boots was "It," then a couple of the pups, then Dulcet. While the others hid, whoever was It sat by Cartesian. He was in charge of making sure no one peeked, and he helped the little ones count slowly to twenty. Gregor went into the nursery twice, hoping for a chance to escape, but both times a mouse pup hid in there as well. Time was running out. The game would end soon. Even if Ares had managed to slip out of the hospital unnoticed, they might be looking for him now.

Tick, tick, tick, tick, tick, tick, tick, tick, tick, tick, tick, tick, tick, tick, tick . . .

"Okay," Gregor announced at the end of Dulcet's round. "My turn to be 'It.' "

He placed himself as close to the nursery as he could, to discourage anyone from hiding there, covered his eyes, and began to count to twenty. "One, two, three, four . . ."

Gregor could hear the scampering of mouse feet, Boots's sandals, giggles, and hushed squeaks. No one hid in the nursery. ". . . eighteen, nineteen, twenty. Ready or not, here I come!"

Gregor surveyed the hall. Horatio and Marcus were in their places, arms crossed, eyes trained on him. He looked in one room, then pretended to hear something from the nursery and crossed into it. The second he was out of his guards' sight lines, Gregor grabbed the box and sword belt and sprinted for the stone turtle. He shoved his hand in the thing's mouth and found the latch that popped open the shell. He lifted it, quickly climbed inside, and closed it quietly behind him. Afraid any light might be seen shining from the turtle, he went down the first flight of steps in total darkness. There were still no footsteps from above. He pulled out a flashlight from under the cookies and snapped it on. "Go," he thought. "Go as fast as you can." His feet flew down the stairs. He didn't even try to be quiet anymore. Once he'd turned up missing, there'd be confusion, and then Solovet would have that room turned inside out until she found the stairway. He wished he could have kept the secret longer, for Luxa's sake, but it was for her sake that he had needed to use it.

At the bottom of the stairs, he almost ran into the second turtle, the one with the awful leer. As he opened the shell, he could barely make out the shouts coming from several floors above his head. He leaned his head into the damp air over the Spout.

"Drop, Overlander," he heard Ares say in an urgent tone,

and Gregor jumped into the void. Ares caught him instantly and took off at warp speed.

"Barely got out," said Gregor, putting his box behind him as he fastened on his sword. "You?"

"The doctors gave me fifteen minutes to exercise over the river. That has long passed," said Ares. "They will be after us."

"Oh, yeah," said Gregor. "No one saw me go through the turtle, but they saw me go into the room. They'll find the passage now."

"Maybe this is a good thing. If all who know the secret should perish in the Firelands, someone should know of it," said Ares. "It may provide a means of escape if the castle is under siege."

"That's true," said Gregor, thinking of his mom and Boots.

Gregor immediately organized himself. He secured one flashlight on his left forearm with duct tape and hooked the other to his belt. The tape, batteries, shoes, water bottles, and remaining cookies went into the pink backpack. He stuck the chess set in, too, although he couldn't think what use it might be. Then he tossed the box into the darkness and flattened himself on Ares's back to provide as little wind resistance as possible.

Ares took a completely new route back to the Firelands. They did not fly through the usual wide caverns but through a series of smaller, twisting tunnels. At one point Gregor had to dismount so they both could squeeze through a crack in a rock wall. Then they took off down a whole new set of tunnels.

"How did you find this way?" asked Gregor.

"With Henry. We spent many hours finding alternative paths. It was essential, since much of what we did was unsanctioned," said Ares.

Henry was Luxa's cousin and Ares's old bond. He had betrayed them all to the rats on Gregor's first trip to the Underland. Neither Luxa nor Ares spoke about him very often. At first, Gregor had supposed this was because they now hated him so much. Later, he'd understood it was because they still loved him so much, too. When Henry came up, their voices would become tight, their eyes pained. That was the hard part. Still caring. Not being able to simply write Henry off.

"So this route is pretty safe?" asked Gregor.

"No one will find us," said Ares. "Sleep if you can."

Although Gregor didn't think he would sleep with his mind so full, he stretched out, anyway. But he must have still been really tired because the next thing he knew, Ares was waking him. They were back on the cliff overlooking the jungle where they had said good-bye to their friends a couple of days ago. The trip must have taken six or seven hours. Ares was beat.

"I must sleep," said the bat. "But it will not be for long."

Ares went right out while Gregor kept watch. He cleaned the water bottles and filled them at the spring. Put on his new shoes and laced them up. Practiced making cuts in the air with Sandwich's sword. What a weapon! It was almost as if he had only to think of a motion and the sword was already there. At first he gave the sword all of the credit. Then he realized he had to give himself some credit as well. Although he was in no danger at the moment, the rager sensation was humming quietly deep inside him. He stopped practicing and it turned off. He started practicing and it came back to life. Could it be that he was finally getting a small amount of control over it? The idea gave him confidence but it was tempered by the memories of past failures. Still, if he could learn to turn that rager switch on and off . . . that would be amazing.

Ares awoke after a couple of hours. He caught a fish that they ate quickly. They both drank their fill at the spring.

"Ready?" asked Gregor. He tried to feel as impervious as the knight back in the Cloisters.

"Yes," said Ares. "I am ready for whatever lies ahead. Shall we go back to the Queen?" This is what the previous prophecy had called the volcano that had been the death of the nibblers. It was the last place they had seen both the mice and their rat captors.

"Yeah, let's start there," said Gregor, taking his place on Ares. Ares retraced their path back to the volcano, flying through the tunnels still covered in deep layers of ash. When they came out at the Queen, she was quiet. The mice and the little bat Thalia, whom Ares had laid to rest in the pit where the mice had died, had all been buried under the lava flow. There was no trace of them at all.

It didn't take Ares long to hone in on a destination. He jetted across the large cavern and into a long, low tunnel. Gregor's ears began to catch sounds as well. Screams, shrieks, metal against stone. The air thickened with dust.

Gregor drew his sword, wanting to be prepared for what awaited him. But as they burst out of the tunnel, he gasped and almost lost his grip on his weapon.

Nothing in his experience had prepared him for the sight of a battle between the humans and the rats.

CHAPTER

4

Ares had blasted straight into the war zone. Gregor's senses were assaulted by what lay before him, beneath him, and all around him.

They were in one of the Firelands' enormous caverns. The battleground was brighter than Gregor had expected because the walls were studded with burning torches held in globs of something. Clay, maybe? He saw an Underlander woman toss a burned-out torch to the ground and replace it with a new one.

Despite the extra light, it was still difficult to see because the army of rats had churned the volcanic dust on the floor into a choking cloud that rose to the ceiling. Bats swirled around Gregor, carrying their human bonds. Most of the humans had drawn swords. Something obscured the faces of the people and the bats.

A person flew by and a packet hit Gregor on the chest. "Don you this!" he thought he heard them shout, but he wasn't sure because the cavern was filled with a din of voices. Gregor unrolled the packet and found two face masks, one for him and one for Ares. That's what everybody was wearing. He quickly positioned the bat mask on Ares and slipped his own over his mouth and nose. The mask was stuffy, but using it sure beat inhaling that junk in the air — and it cut down on the reek of blood.

Blood seemed to be everywhere. Dripping off of people, staining bats' fur, pouring out of rat bodies on the ground. It dawned on Gregor that the main goal of each side was to relieve the other of its blood, thereby eliminating it. For a moment, he felt sickened; then he remembered why he was here.

"Do you see Luxa?" he asked Ares.

"No!" replied the bat.

It was next to impossible to find anyone in this mess. It wasn't just the masks that made it difficult. Where they weren't bloodstained, the rats, bats, and humans were coated in dust, making everyone largely unrecognizable. He could fly around for hours looking for Luxa and still not find her. Then his thoughts turned the Bane. Even in the dust he might be able to see that monstrous figure. But he could not spot any rat that was larger than average.

Gregor was just going to have to keep an eye out and hope for the best. In the meantime, he didn't exactly know how to join in the battle. Should he report to someone? Was there some plan being executed? Because if there was, he couldn't see it. The whole thing just looked like some big free-for-all.

"What do we do?" Gregor said. "Can we jump in anywhere?"

"Anywhere," said Ares.

But even now, even after all he had been through and witnessed, something in Gregor balked at the idea of simply going down and running his sword through a rat. His ambivalence was interfering with his ability to connect with his rager side. He concentrated hard for a second to establish his place in all of this chaos. The reason he must kill the rats, the reason they must die had to do with . . . had to do with . . . the gasping mice in the pit and his mother lying in the hospital and Boots and those baby mice in the nursery — and Luxa, who must be, had to be somewhere out in this mayhem. It had to do with what had happened, and would happen, not only to him but to those who were not warriors, if these rats were not stopped.

"Down there! By the right wall!" cried Ares.

Gregor could see a woman trying unsuccessfully to rise from the ground. Blood poured from a gash in her leg. A bat hovered over her, slashing at an oncoming rat with its claws.

The buzzing began in Gregor's veins. "Go," he said.

They had never flown in a battle together, Gregor and Ares. The one real battle Gregor had fought in had been with the ants in the jungle. At that time, Ares had been struggling to survive the plague in the hospital in Regalia. But they had trained for hours and hours in the arena and

46

had been in enough tight spots together to know they could count on each other completely.

Ares dove for the charging rat, tipping sideways to allow Gregor the closest possible range. The rat was leaping for the injured woman just as Gregor's sword made contact. His blade severed one of the rat's ears. The rat turned on him with a ferocious hiss.

"That got its attention," said Gregor, as Ares looped back for another attack.

A look of shock crossed the rat's face as it recognized them. Even in this mess, it would be hard to overlook a bat as imposing as Ares with an Overlander rider. "It's the warrior! The warrior!" the rat screamed.

Gregor could hear the phrase rippling through the army of rats as word of his presence spread. He knew the rats had been laughing at him of late because of an encounter he'd had a few weeks ago under Regalia. Twirltongue, the hypnotically persuasive rat who advised the Bane, had sicced two of her buddies on him. Gregor had been fighting very well until one of the rats had smashed his flashlight, leaving him in darkness and reducing him to helplessness. He had crawled around on the tunnel floor like a mouse cornered by a couple of alley cats and barely escaped with his life.

"Good," thought Gregor. "Let them laugh." Because now, with the numerous torches, there was no danger of being without light. Now he had seen what they had done to the mice. Now everything was different.

The bat they had come to aid had swept up the wounded

woman and flown off, so Gregor redirected his attention to the scene below him. A group of about eight rats had gathered beneath him, no doubt eager to claim him as a prize. Ares could easily fly elsewhere, but Gregor wanted to see how high the rats could jump. Ares dipped down and the entire pack leaped up. The most athletic made it a good fifteen feet in the air. Gregor's sword made contact with a pair of claws that was just about to shred a spot on Ares's left wing.

"Watch your wings," said Gregor.

"That is the trick," said Ares. "To fight them we must be close, but if we are too close, I cannot evade them. When things move quickly, you will have to trust my choices."

Gregor understood what Ares meant. In the heat of battle, they could not stop and have some detailed conversation over what target to attack next. Ares was going to have to make most of those decisions, and Gregor was just going to have to go with them.

"Whatever you think, I'm with you," said Gregor.

And with that, Ares threw them into the battle. Wherever they turned, a group of furious rats awaited them. It was less a question of attacking than of countering the attacks of the mobs of rats. He was surrounded by a blur of razor-sharp claws and deadly teeth that all seemed bent on tearing open one of his main arteries. But he had no intention of dying. Not while the Bane was still alive. If he was going out, he was determined to fulfill the prophecy and take the white rat with him.

The rager sensation was pulsing through him but he was

managing not to give in to it completely. Perhaps all of the hours of training in the arena were helping him stay focused. The movements were so familiar. Mareth had put Gregor and Ares through their paces a thousand times this summer — dive attack, feint right, wing block, loop back — but in the arena, Gregor's sword had been encountering air or strategically placed sandbags. Sometimes they had worked with cow carcasses that were headed for the kitchen. Mareth had wanted him to get the feeling of driving his sword into a real body. It was a lot harder than it looked. The blade had to pierce the hide, then muscle, and then sometimes ran into bone before it could reach the vital organs inside. It took a lot of power. The lessons with the dead cows had always made Gregor somewhat queasy, but he was grateful for them now. Grateful, too, for the superiority of the sword he had inherited from Sandwich. Sandwich's sword was to a common Underlander sword as a steak knife was to a butter knife. It moved like lightning and slid far more easily across a throat, between ribs, through the joint above a foreleg. It could even cleanly cut off a row of rat teeth in one stroke. At least it could in Gregor's hand.

Soon Gregor was covered in blood, and Ares's fur had become damp and sticky with the stuff, but neither of them had more than scratches. He didn't have to think about how to wield his sword; it moved instinctively from target to target. And every time it connected, Gregor became more confident, more powerful. He injured many rats, some of them fatally, he thought, although he couldn't be sure, but the numbers attacking him only increased. If he had needed the images of the mice and his loved ones to propel himself into battle, they were rapidly replaced by the desire for self-preservation. "You really have no idea how much they hate you, do you, Overlander?" Luxa had said to him when they'd been arguing about her starting the war. Well, he did now.

"Man, these rats want me dead!" Gregor remarked to Ares when they had lifted above the fighting to take a breather. On the ground, a snarling group of two dozen rats ran to stay directly under Ares.

"Has this only just occurred to you?" asked Ares, and Gregor could hear the rare *Huh-huh-huh* that meant Ares was laughing. Gregor laughed, too. They were both in uncharacteristically good moods.

In fact, Gregor felt better than he had in ages. "It's the rager thing," he thought. The last time he had fought — it had been against snakes in the jungle — he had apparently been grinning his head off, which had upset him at the time. But here, with the battle around him, he didn't care.

And as for Ares laughing . . . for the first time Gregor had to wonder if his bat might not have a little rager blood in him, too. Or maybe it was just the relief of finally doing something, something real. Of obliterating that feeling of intense frustration they had experienced as they watched the mice suffocate to death while they were helpless to stop it.

At any rate, they were both flying high.

"Ready for more?" asked Ares.

50

"Yeah, go for it," said Gregor. Then something caught his eye. "No, hang on a minute, Ares!"

For the first time, the action on the ground seemed to have taken on some kind of order. Gregor and Ares were among a group that was dealing with the rats along one front. But there was a second line of intense fighting on the far side of the cavern, nearly blocked out by the dust cloud it caused. "What's happening over there?"

As Ares flew toward the cloud, Gregor began to make out more of the scene. A long shelf of rock jutted out of the cavern wall about twelve feet from the ground. Under the edge of the shelf, a wall of humans was on the ground trying to hold off an intense rat attack. Their bats were performing some kind of strafing maneuver from the air, diving down on the rats and literally ripping chunks of flesh off of their bodies.

"It is the nibblers! Our army is trying to get them to safety!" said Ares.

Gregor squinted into the dust and could just make out a line of mice. The humans were protecting them as they scurried from a cave along the cavern wall to a tunnel opening some twenty yards away. But it was a very dangerous task, since the humans were at a complete disadvantage fighting on the ground. There was no choice, though. Gregor could see that. The stone shelf made aerial fighting unthinkable. The rats would be picking the bats off right and left at that altitude.

At the mouth of the tunnel, the onslaught was the heaviest. Both human and rat bodies were piling up at an

51

alarming rate. The humans had formed one of their standard defenses, an arc. But holding down the center point, the key position in the formation, was a rat. Ripred. He was spinning so fast that a funnel cloud of dust had risen up around him. Any rat that came into his reach was instantly killed. Gregor did not know how long he had been holding that position, but he did know that even Ripred had a breaking point. What was it he had said once? "I start to crack at about four hundred to one."

Just then, Ripred's spin was thrown off as an enormous rat drove straight into him. Ripred still managed to tear its throat out, but he was knocked backward hard and seemed stunned.

"I've got to get down there!" Gregor shouted.

Ares didn't question him, but as he angled in, Gregor heard him call, "I am here!"

The rats had immediately sensed the opening made by Ripred's incapacitation. Seven gathered into a pack, obviously preparing to charge the cave entrance.

Gregor landed squarely in the spot where Ripred had been standing, sinking up to his ankles in the muck of dust and blood. He slashed his blade across the air and then hit a defensive position.

For a moment, the rats hung back, surprised by the appearance of their new opponent. Then the leader let out a growl, and the entire pack went for Gregor's throat.

CHAPTER

5

Gregor's feet automatically began to pivot. He just had time to turn once before the rats were within sword's reach. He'd gathered enough momentum to damage the two coming in on his left — one in the neck and one in the eyes — with the first cut. The person fighting to his right drew off another pair. But a trio of nasty-looking rats was still coming at him.

He dug his sneakers into the grit and stood his ground. These three made Twirltongue's buddies seem like cream puffs. They were larger for one thing, nearer to Ripred's size. A combination of drool and blood dripped off of their fangs. Their scarred faces indicated years of fighting. But it was the look in their eyes, the pure viciousness that told Gregor that he was dealing with a whole new level of opponent.

They knew how to fight as a team, too, coming at him with multiple attacks, so that it was nearly impossible to fend off both blows at once. He did, though, he did, because now the rager effect was in full gear, splintering his vision, allowing him only to perceive the deadly teeth and claws and, in rare moments when he was not simply defending himself, get glimpses of their vulnerable eyes and necks where he could counterattack.

The sort of white-noise roar that sometimes accompanied his rager state was there, but a voice was managing to cut through it. Although it was hoarse almost beyond recognition, it could only belong to one creature.

"Oh, look who's decided to show up! Smelling like pudding and bubble bath. *Mmm-mmm*. So glad you could make it. Had a nice little vacation, did you? While the rest of us were out here breathing sulfur and eating . . . well, not *eating* exactly. Howard had the idea of cutting off the leather pocket on your old backpack. That gave us something to chew on for a while, but I can't really call it filling. No, not satisfying in the way one might have hoped. Oh, and then there's been the little matter of freeing the nibblers. As you can see, the rats didn't especially go for the idea."

Gregor wanted to tell Ripred to shut up, tell him he was being distracting. But he didn't have a breath to spare and forming words at the moment seemed very difficult. Like when he was trying to talk to someone in a dream but no sound came out. A claw came within inches of his throat and he took off the rat's foreleg at the joint. It fell back with a scream of pain. Two to go.

"You know, I've been getting to know that girlfriend of yours," Ripred continued almost lazily, as if they had all the time in the world to chat.

"She's not my girlfriend!" Gregor wanted to yell at Ripred, but the words wouldn't come. Besides, Ripred already knew his feelings about Luxa. Denying it would only bring on another speech.

"She's got grit, I'll give her that. You should have seen her taking those nibblers right out from under the Bane's nose. Would have made her grandmother proud," said Ripred.

The last thing Gregor needed now was to think about Solovet, who was Luxa's grandmother, and how she might be reacting to his running off.

"But frankly I'm a bit concerned about her," said Ripred.

Gregor caught one of the rats in the windpipe and it retreated. But now Ripred's words had his attention. Why was he concerned about Luxa? Was she sick? Injured? "What?" he managed to bark out. The last rat was a huge brute with teeth gnawed into razor-sharp points.

"She needs some clean air. We didn't have masks until the army showed up and by then she'd been breathing this stuff for days," said Ripred. "I'm not wearing a mask, of course, could hardly fight in the thing. But as a rodent, my lungs are tougher than hers."

"She's sick?" Gregor got out. His opponent was relentless. Gregor had stabbed him twice, but it only seemed to enrage him.

"Sick? Well, yes. Frankly, I'm not even sure she's still alive," said Ripred.

Gregor's hand faltered, and the rat he was fighting nailed his head with its tail. He fell to the right, pinning his sword arm beneath him. The rat immediately lunged for him. Gregor braced himself for the teeth when suddenly the rat was yanked up into the air, howling in rage. Ares had sunk his claws into the thing's rump and he carried it high into the cavern. The rat tried to twist around to attack the bat, but it was hopeless. When Ares released it, it screamed all the way to the ground, and then was still and silent.

Ripred stepped over Gregor, cuffing him upside the head with a paw as he went. "You're going to have to have a little more mental discipline than that, boy. Now get up!"

Gregor rubbed his head in confusion. Was this Ripred's idea of on-the-job training? Had that thing about Luxa been just a test? Was she really okay? Gregor wanted to ask, but he was pretty sure Ripred would knock him into next week if he did.

"Get up!" Ripred repeated with even less patience.

Gregor sprang to his feet. Ripred had the center point of the arc again. On his left was a woman Gregor recognized, Perdita. She had almost been killed the very first night Gregor had fallen to the Underland. He had tried to escape, ran into two rats on a beach, and was rescued by a party of humans and bats. Perdita had been badly injured that night. But she'd recovered from her injuries since then, and Gregor had trained with her. She fought with a sword and a dagger and could hit almost as many bloodballs during drills as Gregor could, which made her one of the Regalians' top fighters. On Ripred's right was a man who Gregor had never seen before. He would have remembered him, too, because he must have been close to seven feet tall. With both hands he wielded a thick broadsword that would easily have come up to Gregor's shoulder. He hollered a lot when he fought.

"By me!" Ripred ordered and flicked his tail to indicate where Gregor should fight next to Perdita.

"She lives, Overlander!" said Perdita as he stepped into place, and she managed to shoot him an encouraging look between attacks.

"Thanks," said Gregor. He was at first grateful, then embarrassed because he realized Perdita now knew about him and Luxa. Maybe everybody knew. But Ripred was right. He couldn't think about that now. He had to focus on the battle.

Gregor wasn't the only one joining up with the forces at the tunnel mouth. Both the humans and the rats seemed to be directing all of their soldiers there. There was no time to ask for an explanation of the battle orders. It was all he could do to keep alive.

He knew Ares was an excellent fighting partner, but the bat was proving to be quite remarkable in his own right. Since so many of the humans were now fighting on the ground, their bats were executing a full-scale aerial attack on the rats. Mainly they would dive down, rip a clawful of flesh from a rat's backside, and whip quickly back into the air to escape damage to their wings. But Ares was one of a handful of bats with the strength to lift a full-grown rat off of the ground and drop it to its death. Again and again he picked off the deadliest fighters, saving many humans besides Gregor. And as the battle continued, Gregor could hear desperate people begin to call out, "Ares!" hoping for a last-minute rescue from a rat attack. Despite the grim circumstances, Gregor could not help taking satisfaction that his much maligned bond was finally getting some appreciation.

It was hard to tell how much time had passed —thirty minutes, maybe forty-five — when people began to call, "The nibblers are in! The nibblers are in!" He guessed this meant that all of the nibblers had made it into the tunnel. He'd yet to get a good look at them, so he had no idea what condition they were in. Pretty bad, probably.

A few minutes later, an order was given to retreat into the tunnel. Ripred took a second out to growl, "Not you, boy!" at him, so Gregor just held his position. This was getting trickier by the moment because he was now up to his knees in bloody ash, and keeping a foothold was harder than ever. Around him, humans and bats carrying wounded began to make for the tunnel. He heard repeated cries of "No torches! No torches inside!" and could only wonder what that was about. Those carrying torches hurled them like javelins into the army of rats, causing some welcome disruption.

Retreat seemed to be something the humans and bats could execute quickly, because in a matter of minutes, only twenty or so were left defending the tunnel mouth. Then they, too, under the tremendous pressure of the rats, began to slowly fall back. Soon, even the front line, still composed of Perdita, Gregor, Ripred, and the giant man Gregor didn't know, was forced into the tunnel.

"Fliers, go!" Perdita called. Ares and the last two bats swept across the rat army, peppering them with torches, and then dove into the tunnel.

Gregor had backed only a few steps into the tunnel when he knew he was going to run into trouble. "Why no torches?" he yelled, but no one had time to respond. Maybe there was some plant in the tunnel that was flammable. Some weird moss or something. The light from the cavern was growing faint. That meant he was going to have to rely entirely on the flashlight taped to his arm to see. He clicked the switch to turn it to high beam and was reassured by the amount of visibility it restored. But what about the others? Ripred didn't need light to fight. He could "see" by echolocation if need be, as could the oncoming rats. Perdita could probably get by on what his flashlight was putting out. But that big guy with the broadsword on the other side of Ripred, he was going to have problems.

"Retreat! It's too dark for you!" Ripred said to the man, whose only response was a string of curses.

Gregor yanked his spare flashlight off of his belt and turned it on. "Hey! You on the end!" he yelled. No response.

"York," Perdita prompted him.

"Hey, York!" said Gregor. The man looked over and Gregor tossed him the flashlight. "In your teeth!" he instructed. There was no time to tape it to York's arm or even explain what the flashlight was. But York seemed to get the idea. He yanked off his mask, crammed the end of the handle between his teeth, and kept hacking away.

Somewhere behind him, Gregor supposed, were backup soldiers, but he never saw them. As the rats drove them deeper into the tunnel, all of the light disappeared except the beams from the flashlights. And between handling his own rats and trying to keep Perdita from falling into darkness, there was no time to turn his head. He was still managing, but in this gloom, could it be that some of his confidence was slipping away? A rat's tail came frighteningly close to taking out his flashlight, cracking the glass. A claw caught the duct tape, almost ripping it free. Gregor realized they were targeting his light. They must know, after his humiliating encounter with Twirltongue and her pals, that he was worthless without it. He ripped off his mask, pulled the flashlight free, and stuck it between his teeth as he had instructed York to do, just barely blocking a tail that came straight for his mouth. The bulb was beginning to dim. He could feel the power draining out of him and the seeds of fear beginning to grow. What should he do? Tell Ripred? Keep fighting? Cut and run? Because frankly, if his rager abilities left him he was just another twelve-year-old kid who'd had a few sword lessons. And, as he was realizing, a really tired one at that.

A rat claw got through his defenses and opened up a cut on his calf. The tip of a tail made contact with his flashlight and knocked the beam sideways. As Gregor straightened it, another claw tore through the laces on one of his shoes.

"I can't hold on!" Gregor wanted to scream, but the flashlight made it impossible to talk, anyway. But he had to at least let someone know that he was fading, that they

60

couldn't count on him, that —

"Hey!" Gregor yelped as his feet flew out from under him. He landed on his back in a pool of thick, slippery liquid and came up sputtering.

"Run! All of you!" snapped Ripred, and began a spin attack.

What was going on? Gregor scrambled to his feet and saw — by the light of York's flashlight, his own having dropped somewhere into the pool when he cried out — that York and Perdita had not hesitated to follow Ripred's instructions. So Gregor ran after them as well.

That is, he tried to run, but he was doing more wading than anything else. The floor sloped down and the liquid rose up to his chest. It was all he could do to sort of bob forward. York's light showed they were in a shiny, black pool that filled the floor of the tunnel. "Oil," he thought. What else could it be? Gregor held his sword high over his head as he went along, hoping the stuff wouldn't get any deeper. Moving forward, moving forward, until there it was. The light at the end of the tunnel. Literally.

The pool became shallower and now Gregor could run, but carefully, carefully because the stuff was so slick. He went toward the light, breaking out of the tunnel but still up to his knees in oil. Before him lay a huge cavern, at least a quarter-mile long, that was much less dusty than the one they had battled in. At the far end were lit torches but they were placed very high on the walls. Huddled far below on the ground lay hundreds upon hundreds of mice.

Gregor didn't know exactly what was happening, but he

got a grip on the blade of his sword and began to sprint. This was one thing he could do, whether he was raging or not. He could hear his track coach's voice coming from what seemed like another lifetime, calling pointers to him. The oil disappeared, his sneakers hit cinders, and he accelerated.

Humans on bats were flying by, picking up mouse stragglers and wounded. Ares flew in for him but Gregor waved him toward the mice, some of whom were unable even to get to their feet. Suddenly the cinders vanished and he was wading again, this time through a shallow river with a current. He plucked a struggling mouse pup from the water and hoisted it onto his shoulder. Fortunately it was able to cling there on its own because his arms were soon full of a second pup. As he came to the bank at the far side, hands reached for the pups and pulled him up onto a beach.

Gregor collapsed, gasping for breath. He looked back across the cavern. The last few mice were being lifted from the ground and flown here. Three humans on bats were jetting toward the tunnel with the black pool. They each carried a bow in one hand and a flaming arrow in the other.

"Shall I give the signal, Your Highness?" shouted a voice.

"Not yet." Gregor could barely make out the hoarse voice. He turned and there was Luxa, just a few yards behind him, eyes fixed on the tunnel. She was drenched in oil and so weak she had to support herself on a rock.

"Now, Your Highness?" The voice was tense with urgency.

"Just give him a few more moments," said Luxa. "There!"

Gregor looked back, straining to see the tunnel opening. A large, glistening form barreled out of the mouth and made for them. Ripred. Any second now, the army of rats would be after him.

Behind him, Gregor could hear Luxa whispering, "Wait for them, wait for them." Then, as the first rat heads appeared, he heard her say quietly, "Now."

A signal must have been given because the three archers shot their flaming arrows into the pool of oil spilling out of the cave. As the first made contact, a ball of flame burst toward the ceiling, igniting the rat army. Gregor knew it must have blasted back into the tunnel, across the pool, incinerating everyone in its path. For a moment, he couldn't help thinking of what that must have meant, the rats burned alive, the black smoke suffocating those who had been far enough up the tunnel to escape the fire, the horror of it all.

Then another danger arose. So much oil had been dragged across the cavern that the fire spread toward them as well. Although it was not as fierce, it would be deadly if it caught on any of their oil-soaked bodies.

Gregor sprang to his feet. "Ripred? Where's Ripred?" he shouted, only to see the big rat splash into the river before him. He looked up to where Ares was circling overhead.

Ripred slowly dragged himself onto the beach and surveyed the scene. There was no trace of the rat army, only a roaring fire before the tunnel. The flames had stopped at the far side of the river, cut off by the water. They were safe. "Now whose idea was this?" he croaked out.

"Queen Luxa's," said a nearby Underlander.

Ripred turned his head, spotted Luxa leaning against the rock, and glared at her a moment. Then he gave her a nod of approval. "Good plan."

Luxa opened her mouth to answer but instead began to cough into her hand. It was a horrible, rasping cough that shook her entire body. When she removed her hand from her mouth, it was covered in red. She stared at the blood for a moment, as if faintly surprised, and then collapsed to the ground.

CHAPTER

6

A dozen people ran for her but Gregor reached her first. "Luxa? Luxa?" He could not keep the desperation out of his voice. He rolled her onto her back and gently propped her head up on his lap. She was still conscious, but barely. Another wave of coughing racked her body and fresh blood ran from the side of her mouth.

An Underlander, dressed in white to signify that she was a doctor, uncorked a bottle and held it to Luxa's lips.

"Look at her! She should have been sent home days ago!" bellowed a man. Gregor looked up and saw York striding toward them.

"We could not make her go," another voice rasped out. Howard, who seemed nearly as bad off as Luxa, crouched down to wipe his cousin's face with a cloth.

"You are still here as well?" asked York in exasperation.

"I was needed," said Howard faintly. "So many wounded, Father."

Father? So this giant of a man was Howard's dad? Gregor tried to remember what he knew of him. He was the governor at the Fount. He had been kind to the mice. Not much else.

"You are no help like that. The pair of you! To Regalia! Now!" He raised his head in the air. "I need a flier with some life in it!" shouted York.

Ares fluttered to the ground. "I have life," said Ares. "I have been in the ash but a few hours."

"We can take them," said Gregor. "He's really fast."

York gave them each a piercing look and then handed Gregor back the flashlight he'd used in the cave. "Load them up!" he ordered, and lifted Luxa in his arms as if she weighed no more than a doll.

Gregor scrambled onto Ares's back before anyone could say he couldn't go.

"It would be best if she could remain sitting up," said the doctor. "Easier for her to breathe."

York placed Luxa in front of Gregor. "Can you keep her upright?"

"Yeah," said Gregor. He wrapped his arms around her waist and pulled her back so her head was resting on his shoulder. "I can do it."

"Give her sips of this when the coughing resumes," said the doctor, and pressed the corked bottle in Gregor's hand. "Howard will advise you. Other than that, her hope lies in getting to the hospital in Regalia."

As Howard was being lifted onto Ares's back, Luxa began to struggle. "Aurora . . ." she said.

"On my own flier, niece. She will be right behind you," said York, smoothing back Luxa's hair.

"Ripred," Luxa got out. The rat appeared and stuck his nose up to hers.

"Right here," he said.

"The nibblers. If I die . . ." said Luxa.

But Ripred cut her off. "You? Die? You're too mean to die." Luxa actually managed a smile. "But don't worry, Your Highness, I'll look after them." Ripred nudged Ares with his head. "Fly you high and fast."

Ares lifted into the air and shifted his powerful wings into high gear. They did not need to take the secret, winding tunnels that had brought them here. But even though they flew through the main thoroughfares, the trip was excruciatingly long.

Nothing Gregor had experienced in the battle came close to filling him with the terror he experienced on the flight home. Luxa was so ill — barely able to breathe, wounded in several places, burning up with fever — that at times he truly doubted she would make it home alive. At one point, in fact, when she became very still, he thought he had lost her. "Luxa!" he cried out and gave her a shake, and she began to cough again, bringing up more blood but still with him, still there.

"Talk to her, Gregor," said Ares. "As you did to me in the currents."

Once, when they had been caught in a web of powerful

67

air currents, Ares had nearly gone insane. Gregor had launched into a nonstop monologue to distract the bat and keep his spirits up. And so he began to talk to Luxa about anything and everything he could think of. New York City, funny things Boots had done, a paper he had written on spiders, what winter was like, Mrs. Cormaci's recipe for spaghetti sauce — anything — anything to keep her from drifting away.

Somewhere behind him, Howard lay in the darkness. Gregor was reminded of his presence by an occasional cough or an order to dose Luxa with more medicine. But as poor as Howard's condition was, he was able to stay conscious, unlike his cousin.

After what seemed like an interminable amount of time, Gregor began to recognize the landmarks around Regalia. They were flying down the wild river that ran from the Fount past Regalia to the Waterway. Only it didn't look as wild as Gregor remembered it. The surface was not churned to a white froth — it was several feet lower than usual. The earthquake that had altered the landscape by the mouse colony near the Fount must have affected the river flow as well.

"Almost there now," he told Luxa. "Almost home." She made no response. She hadn't even coughed in probably an hour. But he could still feel her chest rising and falling.

Ares flew directly to the dock on the river. Even before they had landed, Gregor was yelling, "Help! Doctor! Medic! Help! Help!" Underlanders unloaded Luxa and Howard directly off of Ares and onto stretchers. They tried to place

Gregor on a stretcher as well but he pushed them aside and ran after Luxa. She was whisked into some kind of emergency room, surrounded by a team of doctors snapping orders. Gregor tried to see what was going on but was unceremoniously shoved out of the room. A stone door swung closed in his face.

He stood in the hall, panting and trembling, brushing aside the doctors who tried to treat him. It was not until Mareth appeared and grasped him firmly by the arms that he began to come back to himself. "Gregor," said Mareth. "You have need of medical assistance as well. You must come with me."

"Is she going to live?" asked Gregor.

"I cannot say. But she is getting the best treatment we are able to give. You do not help her, or anyone, by letting your wounds inflame," said Mareth. "Come."

Then Gregor was in one of those herbal baths again, soaking the oil and ash from his skin. The rats had gotten him good in a few places, particularly the one who had cut his calf open in the cave. He was stitched up and rubbed down with salve but he pushed away the medicine that he knew would make him sleep. Mareth took care to see that the photograph of Gregor and Luxa made it into the pocket of his new shirt, that his sword was propped up against his bed. But Gregor insisted on getting up. Ordinarily, that would not have been allowed, but the hospital was becoming flooded with human and nibbler casualties and no one had time to deal with him. He prowled up and down the halls, trying to get news of Luxa but hearing very little. Periodically he stood at the window to his mother's hospital room — she looked better at least — watching her sleep. Then he'd pace the halls again.

Finally Mareth took charge of him. "They are overwhelmed in the nursery with pups from the Firelands. We are only in the way here. Let us see if we cannot put ourselves to use."

After exacting a promise from a doctor that he would be sent updates on Luxa's condition, Gregor followed Mareth to the old nursery. It was total chaos. The mouse pups had been among the first to be airlifted out of the Firelands. While those in the worst state had been sent directly to the hospital, the others had been assigned to the nursery while they awaited care. The shell of Sandwich's hateful turtle was open —Solovet had found the secret passageway as Gregor had predicted — and the babies were being carried in from the Spout. The nursery could hold only a fraction of them, so the entire wing was swarming with sick, frightened pups.

Attempts were being made to accommodate them. In the bathroom in which Gregor had played hide-and-seek less than a day ago, every tub had been filled with herbal bathwater, and a marathon session to clean the pups was under way. Two other rooms that had held supplies had been fashioned into giant nests made of great piles of blankets. Another room was completely devoted to feeding the starving creatures.

Dulcet rushed by them, carrying a screaming pup wrapped in a towel, then did a double take. "Gregor!

Mareth! Can you help in the baths?"

"You got it," said Gregor, glad for some way to occupy himself. In another minute he was up to his waist in water in one of the deep tubs, receiving a mouse pup. The baby was trembling so hard its teeth were chattering. Separated from its parents, ill and starving, of course it was a wreck.

"You're okay. You're all right, little guy," said Gregor soothingly. The pup's fur was caked with oil and dust, and it was no easy matter getting it clean. Eventually, with the help of some kind of shampoo and a comb, Gregor got its coat to its normal gray color. As soon as he passed the pup on to be dried, another was placed in his arms.

There were scores waiting to be cleaned and more arriving all the time. Gregor worked tirelessly, bathing the pups, calming them with his words. But his mind was in the hospital with Luxa, willing her to keep breathing. Once, when a doctor came through, he got a piece of real news. They were trying to rid the ash from her body, but it was a delicate process since her lungs were damaged by days in the foul air. At least she was still alive.

Periodically Dulcet or Mareth would try to make him leave his post in the bath, but he couldn't, wouldn't. Then, as he was handing off another mouse pup, he realized Boots was crouching at the edge of the tub with a plate, waving at him.

"Hey, Boots," said Gregor, and crossed to her. "What's going on?"

"I helping Dulcie feed the babies," said Boots. "Now she says I feed you."

On the plate were a slice of meat, some bread, and a mug of tea. Gregor ate, more to please Boots than anything, but he did feel a little better with something in his stomach. "Thanks, Boots."

"I'm going to feed the babies more," said Boots.

"Good work," he said.

"You give baths," she reminded him.

"Right," said Gregor, and reached for another pup. And so it went on for several hours, until Dulcet tapped him on the shoulder.

"Gregor, you are being called to the hospital," she said.

Without hesitation, Gregor gave the mouse pup he was holding to a nearby Underlander and hoisted himself from the water. His skin was wrinkled and tingling from the hours in the herbal bath and his legs felt slightly numb. "Is she all right? Can I see her?" he asked.

"I do not know," said Dulcet. "Only that you were summoned." Her eyes darted over to the doorway and back again significantly. In the entrance stood Horatio and Marcus.

"Oh, my bodyguards are back," said Gregor, buckling on his sword belt. He didn't care. As long as he got to go see Luxa. He walked right past them without a word but he could hear them fall into step behind him. Through the crowds of mouse pups, along the hallways, down the steps that led to the hospital, they followed him. He chose a shortcut, a little-used staircase for the last flight. At the bottom was a small stone door that gave access to the hospital. But Gregor never reached the door. About ten

72

steps from the bottom, Horatio suddenly slammed him into the wall and before he could recover, Marcus had bound his hands behind his back. He started to holler and they tied a gag around his mouth. Then he was being lifted, carried back up the steps, along narrow passages, and then down deep under the city of Regalia. He fought like crazy, but they were too strong for him. Eventually they tossed him onto a stone floor and backed away with their weapons drawn. Gregor was in a small room with a low ceiling. He had just gotten to his knees when Solovet stepped into the doorway.

"You and I must come to an understanding," she said.

The door swung shut, a key turned in a lock, and Gregor was left in complete darkness.

CHAPTER
7

Gregor gave a cry of fury that was muffled by his gag. He made it to his feet and ran blindly toward the door to his cell, slamming into it. This was no good. It was a thick slab of stone; the only thing damaged was his shoulder. For a while he continued to yell but eventually gave that up as well. There was no sound outside of his cell. If there were guards, they were silent and unresponsive. He slumped against the door and tried to control himself. But it wasn't easy. The rager sensation had begun to brew in him from the moment the door had swung shut. Without a way to focus the bizarre feeling — like, say, battling rats — he felt out of control. He could not keep himself from straining against the leather strap that held his wrists behind his back, from making growls of frustration. From wanting to kill someone.

"Calm down," he ordered himself. "Calm down!" He took deep breaths while he tried to assess his situation.

"What's your plan?" he imagined Ripred's voice again. Somehow it helped him to focus.

"The first thing I need to do is get my hands free!" he snapped back in his head. They had not taken his sword, so there had to be a way. Gregor scooted his foot along the wall until he came to a corner. He inched his sword belt around so that the weapon was behind him. He wedged the point of the sword into the corner of the floor and braced the hilt with his back. The blade was very sharp, and by rubbing the leather strap against it, he was able to saw through his bonds in a matter of minutes. Next he cut through the gag and flung it away. He could scream now for real. But he didn't bother. He knew no one was going to come to his rescue.

It was pitch-black. They hadn't left him with so much as a candle. The flashlight York had returned to him . . . where was it? Lost somewhere in the confusion of the hospital. The door fit so tightly into the walls around it that not even the faintest shaft of light leaked around its edges.

Gregor felt his way around the cell. It was small, about ten feet by ten feet. If he stood up straight, the ceiling brushed his hair. There was nothing to be found in it. Not a bench to sit on. No food or water. No place to pee. No blanket to keep him warm, which was his most immediate concern, because it was cool in the cell and he was soaking wet from bathing the mice. He slumped down in the corner and pulled his arms inside his shirt to conserve body heat.

Why had Solovet done this? Probably to punish him for running back to the Firelands. To show him that she was in charge and, if he disobeyed her, she could toss him in the dungeon anytime she wanted to. But that wasn't exactly the message Gregor was getting. If she had really been in charge she wouldn't have needed Horatio and Marcus to abduct him secretly and spirit him down to this cell. He had been arrested one other time, when he had placed the baby Bane in Ripred's care instead of killing him. But there had been an official, public arrest and a trial to follow.

Gregor had an unsettling feeling that now no one but Solovet and a few of her soldiers knew where he was. Who else could know? Who would come to his aid or even notice he was gone? Dulcet had seen Horatio and Marcus take him away, but they could easily say they had escorted him to the hospital and then he'd slipped off again. If Dulcet even had time to think about it, because she definitely had her hands full in the nursery. Mareth usually kept an eye on him, but again, with the general confusion going on in the palace, it would be easy to think Gregor was in another place dealing with another problem. Even Boots would be too busy to miss him. His mother was sick, his dad back in New York City. Luxa and Howard were barely hanging on to life. Ares? No doubt Ares was expending every bit of energy he had helping to airlift the nibblers out of the Firelands and back to Regalia. A job like that could take days. That pretty much left Vikus. Would he realize Gregor had been imprisoned? With the war starting, he was probably working around the clock, too. And Gregor felt certain Solovet hadn't told him about this. They were married but they didn't always confide in each other. Take the development of the plague as a weapon. If Solovet had hidden that from Vikus, then concealing that she had locked up Gregor was nothing.

Hours passed. Gregor huddled in the corner trying to stay warm. His clothes barely seemed to be drying at all. He was hungry and exhausted. The lack of light weighed on him. His thoughts turned to "The Prophecy of Time," to his death, to how he was meant to kill the Bane. He didn't see how he was going to get a chance to do that in here. What would happen if he didn't? And what was going on with that Code of Claw thing? Boots had been in the nursery, but wasn't the princess supposed to be working on that? The prophecy had mostly been about how important it was to break the Code of Claw. Gregor and the Bane's death had been rather minor points compared to that, at least to Sandwich.

Eventually Gregor fell into a kind of stupor, not fully asleep but not quite awake, either. And in this state, visions of the battle he had just fought began to replay in his mind. The elation he had felt from fighting had completely dissipated. Now when he saw his sword slicing through the rats' flesh, their claws coming at him, he felt scared and weak. It was as if some other person had taken over his body for the duration of the battle. But that person had deserted him in the dungeon, leaving a kid who suddenly wanted nothing so much as to wake up in his bed in New

York City and find his mom telling him to hurry up, it was time for breakfast.

He finally went to sleep, curled up in a ball on the stone floor. Luxa wove in and out of his dreams, laughing on her bat, dancing in the arena, and then, as his dreams changed to nightmares, lying in a hospital bed where he couldn't reach her, breathing slower and slower until she stopped breathing entirely. He woke with a start, his brow beaded with sweat, in time to hear the door of his cell slam shut. Stiff and aching, Gregor crawled toward the sound. His right hand landed in a plate of something. Stew? He found a small loaf of bread. A mug of water. There were no utensils. Famished, he crouched in the dark, cramming the food into his mouth. At least Solovet didn't plan on starving him to death. No, he was her prize weapon. She wasn't trying to kill him, just punish him, humiliate him, and break him, probably. He lifted the plate and licked the remaining sauce from its surface. He could have eaten ten times as much, but it at least stopped the hunger pangs in his stomach.

That was all that had come, the food on a tray. Gregor really needed to go now. He didn't want to pee in his cell, so he went in the mug. Then he went back to his corner and curled up on the floor again.

The darkness continued to press upon him, making him feel a little crazy. He shut his eyes tight and tried to imagine he was lying on the grass in Central Park on a warm day. Basking in the sun, feeling it soak into his skin. Maybe he would get up and buy a pretzel, heavily slathered in mustard. He would take Boots for a ride on the carousel. At the children's zoo, they would feed the pig that always made her laugh until she hiccuped.

But it was no good. No good. He could not wish himself out of this dank, lifeless hole in the ground. He didn't think he could stand it very much longer. He needed light, he needed people, he needed to know what was going on! Was Luxa alive or wasn't she? That was the cruelest thing Solovet had done to him, cut him off from the world. How could she do it? How could no one notice he was gone? It had been hours now, maybe days. Didn't anyone even care where he was? Suddenly he was so upset he had to bite his lip so he didn't start screaming.

And then something happened that changed his entire perception of the world. Gregor coughed. It was just a small cough. But the instant it left his mouth, it was as if lightning had struck the room. He could see! Okay, not see exactly, because it was still dark in his cell. But he could tell with absolute certainty the proximity of the wall across from him. It was almost as if a picture of it appeared in his head. Shocked out of his despair, Gregor sat up and coughed again. There was the tray, the plate, and the mug. Somewhere in his brain he could register their shapes on the floor, as if in silhouette. But there was more. The mug gave off a faint redness that suggested heat. Why? He scooted over to the mug and wrapped his fingers around it. It was still warm from his pee.

He had finally gotten it. The thing that Ripred had been so bent on teaching him, that Gregor had been so unable to learn. Echolocation. All those hours of clicking around in that dark cave, trying to locate the rat, miserably failing, had not been a waste of time. He had radar! Just like a bat! He set the few objects he had around the room and clicked and coughed at them. It wasn't just a fluke; he hadn't gone temporarily insane. He could "see" them all, even the photograph of Luxa he'd been carrying in his pocket. Well, he couldn't actually make out the picture, only the small, thin square. But maybe that would come in time.

His preoccupation with his newfound skill kept him from going nuts. Kept him from breaking down and begging the guards to let him out. And he knew he couldn't do that. Let Solovet win. He had to leave this cell as uninfluenced by her as he had entered it, or he would just become her pawn in this whole awful war. And he would really, truly rather be dead than do that. If he gave that woman control over him, there would be nothing left inside of him.

Instead of brooding, he devoted himself to combining his sword work with his echolocation. It was even better in rager gear! Just the mild sensations he got from practicing with his sword heightened his echolocation ability. The wall was there! The plate there! The door there! The tip of his blade tapped each in turn. He couldn't wait to tell Ripred!

After a decent workout, he rested against the wall. His clothes were finally dry. He was no longer cold. His mind was electrified by the echolocation. He began to consider a plan to break out of his prison. Someone was going to have to open that door again to feed him. And when they did he would be ready. He would overpower them and fight his way back to Vikus or Ripred or Ares or someone who would take his side. He would get out of here and he would let everyone know what Solovet had done to him. He would — what was that?

Gregor flattened himself against the wall a few feet from the place where the door opened. In this position, he figured he would have a couple of seconds to attack his guards and break out. But something was confusing him. He could hear voices outside. One was deep, probably Horatio's or Marcus's. But the second was light and high and female. The person to whom it belonged was arguing with the guard, although Gregor couldn't quite catch the words. Who could it be? Not Luxa or his mom. They wouldn't be well enough. Had Dulcet tracked him to the dungeon? Or Perdita come looking for him after they had fought side by side in the Firelands?

The lock turned in the key and the door swung open. Torchlight flooded in, hurting his eyes. From outside came a shaky voice. "Gregor, it is only I. Sheath your sword."

It was Nerissa. Luxa's cousin on the royal side. Gregor did not have to ask how she had discovered he was in the dungeon, how she knew he had been poised, sword drawn, ready to attack the guard. She could see things that no one else could. Visions of events past, present, and future. She had no doubt seen him here and realized he needed help.

He knew Nerissa was his friend, but he didn't think much of putting away his sword with the guards out there. "I'm okay in here," he said, not moving.

Nerissa stepped into the cell and steadied herself on the door frame. She was as thin and fragile as ever, bent under the weight of the heavy, mismatched garments she wore to keep warm. Her long tresses had been braided into a loose plait that, by Nerissa's standards, counted as a fancy hairdo. "We have need of you in the code room."

This was the first Gregor had heard of the code room. But it had to be a step up from the dungeon. "Solovet wants me there?" he asked.

"She will. Once I have spoken to her," said Nerissa. "But you must come with me to see her first. And you must let Horatio and Marcus bind your hands if they are to risk moving you. They only do so now because I have explained the crisis that faces us. Breaking the code is our priority and it does not go well. Please trust me on this, Gregor."

Even though he did trust her through and through, it took her a while to convince him to sheath his sword and let the guards tie his hands behind his back. He hated being so vulnerable again. But if he could get out of the cell without fighting his guards it would be better. That would make him an instant fugitive and make it even tougher to move around freely. Still, he remained undecided until Nerissa said, "Luxa has been asking for you."

"She has? She's alive, then? I mean, obviously she's alive if she's asking for me, but she's awake and everything?" he burst out. The news made him so giddy he wasn't thinking straight.

"Yes, she heals. And she wishes to see you," said Nerissa.

"But I will be hard-pressed to arrange it with you in the dungeon."

That was when Gregor slid his sword into his belt and let Horatio tie the leather strap around his wrists. Then, with the guards flanking him, he followed Nerissa up through the palace. Luxa was alive! She had pulled through! He found himself grinning from ear to ear.

As they ascended from under the palace, the atmosphere in the hallways quickly sobered him up. Anxiety showed on the faces of everyone he passed. They spoke in hushed, hurried voices. From time to time, he heard wailing. He remembered the Underlander bodies piling up around him at the mouth of the cave in the Firelands. Not everyone had been as lucky as Luxa. By the time he had reached the council room, his grin was long gone.

"That's just as well," thought Gregor. He didn't plan to let Solovet see him show any emotion at all. Not anger, not fear, and certainly not happiness. As he walked in to meet her, he made his face as impassive as the stone knight's.

The council room had been transformed into a kind of war center. About a dozen bleary-eyed Underlanders were buzzing around, making notes, delivering messages, drinking mugs of tea. There were a couple of bats there as well. Piles of scrolls were strewn across the table. Platters of food covered a long table off to one side, indicating people were working here around the clock. The giant map of the Underland that Gregor had seen once before, when they had planned his trip to the jungle, hung on the wall. Groups of different colored pins were arranged here and there. It didn't take a military genius to guess those represented troops.

Ripred, who had been bathed and bandaged, had positioned himself by the buffet. By the array of empty dishes around him, he'd been having quite a feast. He was currently dipping his face into a pot of his favorite shrimp in cream sauce. Besides the rat, the only ones Gregor recognized were Solovet and Mareth, who were discussing a grouping of red-colored pins on the map.

When Nerissa, Gregor, and his guards entered, the room gradually fell silent. Solovet took one look at the newcomers and said calmly, "All excuse themselves but Mareth and Ripred." In a minute, the others had cleared out. "What is the meaning of this?" she asked.

Nerissa did not give the guards time to answer. "We have need of Gregor in the code room. I took it upon myself to have him released and now ask permission for his aid."

"And how did you know where to find him?" asked Solovet. "No, never mind. I suppose you saw him in a dream. What else does our little visionary see?"

"I saw nothing but Gregor locked in a dungeon," said Nerissa quietly.

Gregor could see by the look of shock on Mareth's face that the soldier had had no idea of his situation. And Ripred even stopped eating for a moment.

"Oh, tell me you didn't," said the rat, as the cream sauce dripped off of his muzzle.

"Only for a couple of days," said Solovet with a slight shrug. "I would have had him arrested sooner but I thought it more prudent to wait until Vikus had gone to enlist the spinners. What urgent need can you have for him in the code room, Nerissa?" She rolled a red pin between her fingertips, seemingly impatient to get back to her map.

"It is Boots. We feel she would be of more use if Gregor were there to help manage her," said Nerissa.

Solovet glanced at Gregor's face and shook her head.

"Well, you will have to do without him. I cannot risk him disobeying orders yet again and running off to who knows where," she said. "Return him to the dungeon."

"He did not run off to who knows where. He came back to battle," said Ripred. "And lucky for us he did. Really, Solovet, I don't see how this is encouraging any sort of allegiance to you."

"He's had no light, no medical care, no bed, and little food," said Nerissa.

"Oh, excellent," said Ripred. "Let's alienate the warrior altogether."

"Fine, allow him a torch and a blanket," said Solovet.

"I will take responsibility for him," said Mareth. "He will not leave Regalia."

"No, I need you here. And if he outsmarted Horatio and Marcus, there is no guarantee you can hold him," said Solovet.

"What holds him is already in Regalia, Solovet," said Ripred.

"His family was not enough to keep him from going before," said Solovet.

"Not his family. Your granddaughter. Why do you think

he was in such a rush to get back to the Firelands? Concern for me?" said Ripred.

"Luxa? What has she to do with it?" asked Solovet. For the first time she appeared interested in the conversation.

Gregor could not keep himself from speaking. "Shut up, Ripred."

"See how he protests? Oh, he's head over heels. I got my first smell of it when they were having some quarrel in the Firelands," Ripred said nonchalantly.

Gregor remembered that argument. He had blown up at Luxa for abusing Ripred and bossing everybody around. It had ended with him feeling very confused. That's when Ripred had taken a deep, noticeable sniff. So rats could smell more than fear, they could smell love as well.

"He about got himself killed in the Firelands when I just mentioned she was unwell," continued the rat. "Oh, think back about half a century, Solovet. You remember what it's like."

"He is in love with Luxa?" Solovet asked with a look of amusement. "Is this so, Gregor? Is this the reason you disobeyed my order?"

Gregor made no reply. His face burned like fire.

"If it were so, I would be far more amenable to letting you free, as I do not believe Luxa will be planning any outings anytime soon," said Solovet. "But I should like to hear it from you."

Gregor stared at the ground, thinking of what he might do to Ripred if he ever were free.

"No? Then perhaps the dungeon is the safest place for

you," said Solovet.

The guards had just laid hands on him to lead him away when Mareth burst out, "Check his pocket!"

Gregor shot Mareth a look of disbelief. This was far worse than Ripred's betrayal. With his hands tied behind his back, there was nothing Gregor could do but watch as Solovet crossed to him and plucked the photo from his shirt. She examined it closely for a moment, then laughed and held it up for Ripred to see.

"What did I tell you?" said the rat, and stuffed a clawful of shrimp into his stupid mouth.

Gregor knew then it was all there in that photo. All the proof anyone needed of his feelings for Luxa, captured in that one shot. He had been an idiot to carry it around. But how could he have anticipated this moment?

"This has simplified my job immensely." Solovet tucked the photo back in Gregor's shirt, gave it a little pat, and smiled at him. "Do not worry, your secret is safe with me." She nodded to the guards. "Unbind his hands, he is free to go."

CHAPTER

8

The second they cut through the strap at his wrists, Gregor spun on his heels and stalked out of the door. He was livid at Ripred and Mareth for revealing his feelings for Luxa to Solovet. First of all, it was a personal thing. No one's business but his own! Second, didn't they know Solovet would just use Luxa against him? Like she did everyone he cared about? Didn't they see how it would only give her more power to control him? And finally, what if Luxa found out? He had no idea how Luxa really felt about him. They had never talked about it or anything. Now someone would tell her and the idea was just so embarrassing. He was ready to find Ares and head home and —

A form brushed by him as he reached the end of the hallway, and suddenly Ripred was blocking his way. "Hold on, boy."

Gregor had his sword out of his belt so fast it was a blur. "Move. Now."

Ripred held up his paws in mock surprise. "Oh, dear. Is this where we fight to the death? I didn't expect it so soon."

"Move, Ripred!" said Gregor, and swung at the rat, who dodged his blow but still lost a few inches of whiskers on one side.

"Either I'm getting old or you're improving a good deal," said Ripred. "But I suggest you don't try that again."

Gregor lifted his sword to slice at the rat when a pair of strong arms caught his in some kind of headlock from behind. "Stop, Gregor! You do not understand what service he did you!" Mareth said.

"Get off me, man!" said Gregor, struggling to free himself. But Mareth was too strong and even though he was mad, Gregor could not have attacked him with his sword. He was actually far more hurt by Mareth turning on him than Ripred. Gregor had come to think of Mareth as a friend. Not now, though.

So he kept fighting until Mareth flipped him over and pinned him to the ground. Then Ripred climbed on top of him — Ugh! The rat had to weigh about six hundred pounds! — and exhaled shrimp breath in his face. "Just let us know when you're ready to listen."

It didn't take long for Gregor to give up since he could barely get any air in his lungs. Plus Mareth and Nerissa were looking over Ripred's shoulder with such obvious concern that it was hard not to believe they were genuinely upset by his reaction. He forced his muscles to relax, which was not easy because the rager thing seemed to be with him all the time now, bubbling to the surface at any provocation, and even though it came without effort, he could not turn it off at will. "What? What?" he growled at them.

"Gregor, we are sorry if we revealed anything of a private nature back there. But when Ripred opened that door, I followed him immediately," said Mareth. "We did not want you back in that dungeon."

"I was doing all right," said Gregor sullenly.

"After only two days. But Solovet once locked Hamnet up in that very cell for a full month because he crossed her at a war council," said Nerissa. "No light. No human contact. He was not the same when he came out."

"Vikus was fighting at the Fount. The council was completely under her control. There was no one of power to intercede for Hamnet. To suffer this at his own mother's hands . . . many of us think it contributed to his insanity at the Garden of Hesperides," said Mareth.

"And if she'd do that to Hamnet, do you think she'd be more lenient on some insubordinate Overlander?" said Ripred. "He was the apple of her eye, and she doesn't even *like* you!"

"I would have said the same as Ripred and Mareth had I been clever enough to think of it," said Nerissa. "Please, Gregor. Know that we acted on your behalf."

Gregor thought of a month in that cell. Even with his new echolocation skills, it would be unbearable. Poor Hamnet. Gregor remembered how agitated he had been in the jungle when Luxa had suggested that his self-imposed exile from Regalia had been excessive, that he could have returned at least to visit her. Hamnet had said, "No, I could never have left twice. You know how Solovet works. She would have had me leading an army again in no time." Was he thinking of that cell and how Solovet would have let him rot there until he was either completely insane or so desperate he'd do anything she said? It must have been awful for Hamnet to know in his dying moments that he had no choice but to send his son, Hazard, back to Regalia to live. Is that why he had extracted the promise from Luxa that she would never let Hazard be trained as a soldier? Gregor had always thought that Hamnet had made that request because he was so opposed to war in principle. Now he wondered if he had also said it to keep Hazard as far out of Solovet's reach as possible.

Gregor could feel the tension leaving his muscles for real now, as he began to understand his friends' motives. Still, what if Luxa found out what had happened?

"No one will utter a word of what was said in that room, you may be sure of that," said Mareth. "We will not speak and Solovet would not want it to be common knowledge."

"Okay, okay. You did me a big favor. Now let me up," said Gregor. He still spoke gruffly but he was not really angry anymore.

"Just when I was getting comfortable," said Ripred, giving a luxurious stretch that nearly crushed Gregor's ribs before he got off. "Let's get down to the code room, before that sister of yours drives the finest minds of the Underland completely nuts."

Oh, yeah. The code. He knew it was important, but . . . "But I'm going to the hospital," protested Gregor.

"Please, Gregor. Luxa sleeps, so you would not be able to truly visit her. And we have real need of your help," said Nerissa. The exertion of the last hour had set her to trembling violently. He didn't want her fainting or something.

"All right, Nerissa. I'll go there first," said Gregor.

Mareth had to return to Solovet's side, but Nerissa and Ripred accompanied Gregor to the code room. They gave him ten minutes to run into a bathroom for a quick wash and change of clothes, and then hurried him up a few flights of stairs to a chamber off of a long, narrow corridor. They walked in on quite a scene.

Although he knew this was not its purpose, the room reminded Gregor of a zoo. It was shaped like an octagon. On one wall was the door through which Gregor had entered. The one directly across from this had a carving of some sort of strange tree. A long table covered with scrolls, books, and long strips of white fabric was set up beneath the tree. The remaining six walls had arched openings of various heights that led to private rooms. Above each arch was the name of the creature that was meant to inhabit the room: Spinner, Crawler, Human, Flier, Gnawer, Nibbler. Some of the rooms were already filled with their designated guests, and this was what had given Gregor the impression of a zoo. A light green spider rested on a web, a heavily bandaged white mouse with black markings lay on a nest of blankets, a bat with creamy white fur hung upside down from a perch, and a roach peered out of an archway that was only three feet off of the ground. Every arch was equipped with a curtain that could be easily closed, but at the moment, all were open, because all of the creatures were staring fixedly at Boots.

She was standing on the back of her loyal cockroach friend, Temp, smack in the middle of the octagon, singing "The Itsy-Bitsy Spider" at the top of her lungs. The green spider, to whom the song was principally directed, seemed to be cringing. Boots was somewhat off-key, but Gregor was pretty sure it was the loudness that was making the arachnid hunch down and contract. Spiders disliked any loud noises. As she wound up the song, Boots turned to each door and gave a separate bow, saying, "Thank you! Thank you!" although no one had applauded. Gregor knew she didn't care. As long as she had an audience, Boots could go on like this for hours.

"She has been going on like this for hours," whispered Nerissa.

"Days, more like it," said Ripred in disgust. "You've got to get her to focus on the Code of Claw before the entire team bolts for home."

"Next, I will sing one for you!" announced Boots, pointing at the bat, who actually flinched.

"Boots! Hey, Boots, what's going on?" said Gregor, trying not to laugh as he crossed to her. He thought it was funny, but it probably wasn't if you'd been in the audience for days.

"Gre-go!" said Boots, and put up her arms for a hug.

"Come here, you," said Gregor, lifting her up on his hip. "How you doing, Temp?"

Temp bobbed his antennae. One was still bent from an earlier encounter with the rats. "Well, I be, well."

"I am singing to make them happy!" said Boots.

"You sure are," said Gregor. "You know what else would make them happy?"

"What?" asked Boots, her eyes widening in anticipation. Gregor realized he didn't know. He looked back at Nerissa and Ripred. "What do you want her to do?"

"Well, no one knows, do they?" said Ripred. "She's supposed to be the key to breaking this whole code wide open, but all she's done so far is terrorize the rest of us into total submission."

"I been singing," said Boots proudly.

"You certainly have," said Ripred. "Show him the ropes, would you, Nerissa?"

"I am not even meant to be here," Nerissa confided to Gregor as she led them over to the long table. "But I volunteered to help with your sister."

"So this is your special code room?" asked Gregor.

"Yes, it was built long ago. We have broken many codes here in the past and now we must unravel what we believe to be the Code of Claw," said Nerissa. "It is an unknown code that the gnawers began to use the day we freed the nibblers. So its appearance coincides with other events in 'The Prophecy of Time.' This is a sample of it." She picked up one of the strips of white fabric and showed it to Gregor. It was covered with a series of lines. Some were straight up and down, others tilted to the right or left. "It took only a short time to rule out any usual encryption methods the rats might have used. This is a new and clever code that we must break."

Gregor looked at the lines. They meant absolutely nothing. "Well, if you're expecting Boots to start translating a bunch of chicken scratch into words . . . I don't think that's going to happen, Nerissa. She's just learning to read."

"You do not need to worry about the lines. We have the messages written in letters as well," said the bat, flipping off of his perch.

"Oh, forgive me," said Nerissa. "This is Daedalus. The spinner is Reflex. The crawler is Min, and the nibbler is known as Heronian." Nerissa did not look at all well, but she kept going as she pressed the palm of her hand into her forehead. "Perhaps you met her in the Firelands?"

"No. Nice to meet you, everybody," said Gregor, and received a round of nods back.

"These are the finest code-breakers of each species," said Nerissa. "Boots is meant to represent the humans."

"And you represent the rats?" Gregor asked Ripred.

"Well, I wouldn't be anyone's first choice, but times being what they are, I'll have to do," said Ripred. "It's not really essential that a rat be here, but a rat may help. Unfortunately, I have other pressing demands as well."

"Ripred is wanted everywhere. In the war room, on the field, and in the code room. He gives much insight into how the gnawers compose their codes," said Nerissa. "But he will not break this code. That is Boots's role."

Daedalus snagged a white strip with his claw and gave it to Gregor. Above the lines on this one were a stream of regular letters. But they didn't form recognizable words. "She may ignore the lines and only concentrate on the letters."

Gregor shook his head. He hated to disappoint everybody, but he had to be honest. "Listen, as I'm sure you know, this makes no sense. And I don't know what you think my three-year-old sister can do with it, but I wouldn't set your hopes too high."

Boots took the strip of code, suddenly excited. "Oh! I know! I know!" Gregor could feel the whole room tense in anticipation, hoping for some kind of breakthrough. But once she was on the ground, Boots simply tucked one end of the strip in the back of her pants and ran. The fabric floated out behind her. "Look! I have a tail! I have a tail!"

Gregor cracked up. He couldn't help it. The whole thing was so ridiculous.

Then Ripred's nose was in Gregor's face, his lips curled back in displeasure. "You may find this amusing, but if we don't crack this code, we lose the war. Period. Nothing you or I or anyone can do out on that field can compare with the power of knowing what is going on in our enemy's brains. So, if you'd like your little sister to have the chance to continue her singing career, I suggest you help her focus!"

Gregor called Boots over, took off her tail, and settled her on his lap. He didn't know what they were doing, but he had her read the letters on the strip of fabric. She could recognize them all; sometimes a few would actually form a little word like "dog" and she would announce it with delight. But after they had read three strips, Boots had tired of the game and so had Gregor. "This helping anything?" he asked the group.

"No. Perhaps when Vikus returns, he may have some ideas," said Nerissa.

"In the meantime, we'd better proceed as if it is any code, and do our best to break it," said Ripred. "I have to get back to the war room, but I'll keep checking in." With a flick of his tail, he was gone.

"Gregor, thank you, you need not stay. I imagine they will be waking Luxa soon for a meal," said Nerissa.

"Sorry I wasn't more help," said Gregor, and made for the door before anyone could think he was of value. He had no idea how to turn all of that gibberish into coherent words, though, and he had to see Luxa.

Gregor sprinted to the hospital but was not allowed to see her until he had taken another bath in some kind of antiseptic and dressed in sterile clothes and a mask.

"Five minutes," said a doctor who led him into a secluded room. The air was filled with a cool mist that puffed out of small tubes inserted in the walls. Luxa lay on the bed in a gown. Her face, neck, and arms —the areas that had been most exposed to the ash in the Firelands — were a hot, painful red. Her breathing was still labored and he could hear her wheeze each time that she inhaled. But her eyes found his at once.

Gregor crossed to her bedside. He didn't take her hand because he was afraid he'd hurt her. But her fingers lifted and rested on his. She gave him one of her half smiles and whispered, "You stayed."

He gave a shrug like it was no big deal. And at the moment, it wasn't. He was too happy that she was alive, that he was alone with her at last, to think about what his decision to stay was costing him. He would have been completely content to stand just like that for his five minutes, but in less than one, the doctor returned and waved him to the door.

Gregor stepped outside to object but the doctor didn't give him a chance.

"Overlander, you are being called back to the code room. They said there is some emergency with your sister."

CHAPTER

9

Gregor didn't even wait to change, he just took off at a run. Underlanders did not use the word "emergency" lightly. What had happened? Had Boots fallen and hurt herself? Choked on something? If so, why hadn't she been brought directly to the hospital? Or was it some other kind of emergency? It was clear that she had worn out the patience of all of the other code-breakers. Had one of them done something? Maybe Ripred had returned and threatened her in some way and she had lost it. It was unlikely the cockroach or bat had harmed her. And the mouse had been so weak it could hardly move. But that green spider! Maybe it had trapped her in its web. Gregor still had a hard time trusting spiders. His visit to their land, when he had thought they were going to have him for dinner, had been anything but reassuring.

As he sprinted down the narrow hallway his foot slid in something. Blood. Someone had bled, leaving a trail all the way to the door. "Boots!" he cried. If they had hurt her, if they had harmed one hair on her head —

Boots flew into the hall. "Gre-go! Gre-go!" she called in distress.

He picked her up, running his hand through her curls, looking for injuries. "What's the matter? Are you okay? Did somebody hurt you?"

"No, I am okay. In here! In here!" Boots tugged on his shirt to make him enter the room. Totally confused now, Gregor stepped inside. There, crouched in the center of the stone floor, was his other sister, Lizzie.

"Oh, no," said Gregor. He had no idea how she'd gotten here or why she'd come. But he knew this was no time to ask. While she did not seem to be bleeding, either, she was hurting, because Lizzie was in the middle of one of her panic attacks. She was panting for air, shaking like a leaf, and he could see the sheen of sweat on her palms. His dad had explained this to Gregor. Everybody had a fight-or-flight response hardwired into them. When you were in danger, it triggered, pumping adrenaline through your body. This helped you either to fight off an adversary or run like crazy. Gregor guessed he must have been having a panic attack of sorts in the museum when he finally admitted what "The Prophecy of Time" had in store for him. That was pretty major. But in people like Lizzie, it didn't take much to set off the response. Sometimes she would have an attack for no apparent reason at all. She would be in a state of extreme terror, but there would be no one to fight and nothing to run from.

There was something real today. Even the thought of coming to the Underland had always been enough to give Lizzie an attack. Now she was actually here, facing off with a room full of giant scary creatures. They were doing nothing to threaten her. The mouse, bat, and spider were huddled in their rooms. The cockroach had disappeared into its alcove entirely and drawn the curtain shut. Temp had stayed, because he would never abandon Boots, but he had positioned himself under the table. Only Nerissa was near Lizzie, trying to soothe her and looking on the verge of some kind of attack herself.

Gregor swung Boots down and crossed to Lizzie. "Whose blood is that?" he asked Nerissa.

"Hermes. He flew her from the Overland. They were ambushed by gnawers and he was clawed. She is not injured, but we cannot quiet her," said Nerissa.

"Yeah, I know. She gets like this sometimes," said Gregor. He sat behind Lizzie, pulled her back into his arms, and held her. "Hey, Liz. It's okay. It's okay. Nobody here is going to hurt you."

"Oh! Gregor! You have to — come home! Now!" Lizzie got the words out.

"Why? What happened?" asked Gregor, suddenly feeling scared, too. What had happened that was so dire that Lizzie had forced herself to come to the Underland?

"Grandma — in the hospital. Dad — very sick again. I can't take — care of him!" said Lizzie.

"What? But Dad's letters keep saying everything's okay." Had this stuff just happened or had his dad been concealing things to keep Gregor from worry? "What about Mrs. Cormaci?" asked Gregor. She had always been there for them before.

"Stays with — Grandma. Really tired. You have to — come home!" said Lizzie. And with that, she threw up all over the floor.

Gregor held her while she heaved, trying to make sense of what she had said. His problems had been so overwhelming down here, he had given little thought to what was going on back home. Grandma in the hospital? His dad sick again? It must really be bad.

When Lizzie finally stopped retching, he picked her up and carried her over to the side of the room. He just sat there with her on his lap, feeling her shake. "It's okay. It's going to be okay, Liz. I'll take care of it," he said. He had no idea even where to begin.

"I brought — a bag. In my — backpack," Lizzie said.

Her backpack was sitting next to the pool of vomit. "Hey, Boots! Can you bring me Lizzie's backpack?" Gregor asked.

"I can do it," said Boots, running over to fetch him the backpack. "I can get the bag, too!" Her chubby little fingers struggled with the zipper, but she got the pack open and pulled out a folded paper lunch bag.

Gregor opened the bag up and put it to Lizzie's face. "Breathe. Nice and slow now. Nice and slow."

This helped, because people having panic attacks got too much oxygen into their systems, and breathing into a bag gave them more carbon dioxide. Gregor rubbed the tense muscles in Lizzie's back, and the combination of that and the bag seemed to calm her down a little.

"It's okay, Lizzie. You're okay," said Boots, patting her big sister's hand. Lizzie's attacks were one of the few things that upset Boots. "I am here."

Nerissa summoned a pair of Underlanders, who quickly came in, cleaned up the vomit, and left. Then all of the creatures sat still, as if they knew any movement on their part would only increase Lizzie's anxiety, while they waited to see what would happen.

And this was how Ripred found them as he swept into the room. "What's going on in here?" His nose was twitching, clearly registering the lingering throw-up smell. Then his eyes landed on Lizzie, and he became still, too, except for the tip of his tail, which twitched from side to side. An expression came over his face that Gregor had never seen before. If he had to put a name to it, Gregor would have called it tenderness. The rat's voice became positively gentle. "I didn't know we had company. But I bet I can guess who you are. You're Lizzie, aren't you?"

Lizzie lifted her face from the bag to take in the giant, scarred rat. "You're Ripred," she whispered.

"That's right. I'm glad to finally get to meet you. I wanted to thank you for all of the lovely snacks you've sent me. They're always the high point of my day," said Ripred.

Gregor could not make sense of Ripred's behavior. Why was he being so nice to Lizzie? He had never been nice to Boots.

Ripred moved in slowly. "Sometimes it helps if you talk," he said. "Do something to distract yourself."

Gregor looked at the rat in surprise. What did he know about panic attacks? Surely he had never had one himself. "My dad does math problems with her," said Gregor.

"Math is good," said Ripred. "What's eight plus seven, Lizzie?"

"Fifteen," said Lizzie.

"You're going to have to do better than that. She's like a math whiz, right, Liz?" said Gregor. It was true. The teachers at school never knew what to do with her. She could solve problems way beyond the rest of the eight-year-olds.

"Really?" asked Ripred. "What's twelve times eleven?"

"One hundred and thirty-two," said Lizzie.

"Harder," said Gregor. "She likes to cube things."

"What's six cubed?" asked Ripred.

"Two hundred and sixteen," said Lizzie.

"How about thirteen?" asked Ripred.

"Two thousand, one hundred and ninety-seven," said Lizzie without missing a beat. She did seem to be calming down a bit.

"Try thirty-seven," said a hoarse voice from behind Ripred. It was Heronian. The mouse had managed to raise herself up onto her forelegs.

Lizzie panted a moment and then blurted out, "Fifty thousand, six hundred and fifty-three."

Ripred looked at Heronian for confirmation, and the mouse gave a small nod back. Even Gregor was pretty impressed with that one.

"That's right. Apparently that's right," said Ripred. He started to pace, which was always a sign that he was working something out. "Lizzie? Do you like puzzles?" She nodded. "They can be soothing, too. Oh, I know a fun one. We can do it right here. Would you like that?"

"Okay," said Lizzie. Gregor could feel her shaking start to subside. There was nothing like a puzzle to get Lizzie's attention. He thought of the puzzle book that he had bought her on the street that time. She had volunteered to stay with their sick dad while he'd taken Boots sledding in Central Park, and he had wanted to get her a present. That big, thick puzzle book. She had loved it.

Ripred settled down in a comfortable position a few feet in front of Lizzie. "All right. Let's see. Boots, you go stand by Temp."

"Oh, a game!" said Boots, and scurried excitedly over to Temp.

"Now, Lizzie, from where you're sitting, you can see seven creatures. Two humans, one of whom is an Overlander and one of whom is an Underlander, one bat, one mouse, one cockroach, one spider, and one rat. We've just had lunch and we've each eaten our favorite food. No two of us have the same favorite food. The things eaten were fish, cheese, cake, cookies, bread, mushrooms, and shrimp in cream sauce. Now ready for the clues?" asked Ripred.

"I'm ready," said Lizzie, and clasped her hands before her. She no longer even needed the bag.

Ripred spoke quickly and distinctly. "The bat's favorite

food is either mushrooms or cake. Cookies are not the cockroach's favorite food. The mouse will eat cheese, but she didn't today. The Underlander's favorite food is either cookies or shrimp in cream sauce. The mushrooms and cookies were not eaten by mammals. The Overlander's favorite food is either cake or bread. So the question is, who ate the cheese?"

"Well, that's totally unfair," thought Gregor. No one could figure that bunch of gibberish out. But it really had settled Lizzie down.

She was staring at the floor, squeezing her hands so tightly her knuckles were white. About thirty seconds passed, then she met Ripred's eyes and gave a small triumphant grin. "You did," she said.

"Wrong," thought Gregor. Ripred's favorite food was shrimp and cream sauce.

"Hmm," said Ripred, and his tail flicked so hard it made a snapping sound. But his voice was casual. "Temp, suppose you take Boots down to the nursery and let her feed the baby mouses. Would you like that, Boots?"

"Ye-es!" said Boots. Temp pattered out from under the table and she hopped upon his back.

Ripred followed them out the door calling, "And no need to come back until I send for you!"

Gregor could hear the other creatures murmuring around the room. They seemed more relaxed and even a little excited. Min, the cockroach, poked her head out of her arch, and Daedalus kept fluttering his wings. Could it be they were just relieved to have Boots out of their hair? No, it seemed like something more had happened. But what exactly?

Just then Ripred strode back into the room. The rat was actually smiling at Lizzie. "So," he said. "So, so, so." He sat up on his haunches and then tipped his head forward in an elaborate bow. "Welcome to the Underland, Princess."

PART 2

THE
HICKING

CHAPTER

10

Ripred's implication hit Gregor like a ton of bricks. Princess! That could only mean one thing: The rat thought Lizzie was the princess in the prophecy, not Boots, and now he would want to keep her here. "No! No way, Ripred! You can't have her!" He stood up, putting Lizzie on her feet, and then pulled her by the hand toward the door. "Come on, Liz, we've got to get you home."

Ripred planted his big, ratty self in front of the door. "Well, I can't let you go now. It wouldn't be safe."

"This is true," put in Daedalus. "Hermes and your sister were ambushed at the bottom of the shaft that leads to your home. The rats surely have soldiers guarding it now."

"Then she'll go back up through Central Park," said Gregor.

"Even if we had a spare flier at the moment, that wouldn't

be advisable. There's probably a patrol posted there as well. And do you really want to drop off poor Lizzie under Central Park alone? How will she move the stone? How will she get home in the dark?" asked Ripred.

Gregor had no idea what time it was, either in the Overland or the Underland. But he couldn't just send Lizzie up to Central Park by herself no matter what time of day it was. He would have to arrange for his dad to meet her. Wait, that wouldn't work. His dad was sick again and, if they couldn't send a bat with a message up the laundry room shaft, how would they even get word to him? There was only one way to get her home. "I'm taking her myself," said Gregor.

"Just try to set one toe outside Regalia and you'll be back in that dungeon so fast you won't know what hit you," said Ripred. "And your bat, as well."

Gregor felt desperation growing inside of him. There was no way Lizzie could manage down here! He had to get her home. But everything Ripred was saying was true. "Why do you even want her? What's this 'princess' stuff? She didn't even get the puzzle right! I know you had shrimp for lunch!"

Ripred rolled his eyes at Lizzie. "You see? This is the sort of thing I've been dealing with for the past year. Enlighten him, won't you?"

"It was just a puzzle, Gregor, not what really happened," said Lizzie. "In the puzzle the rat ate the cheese."

"How did you know that? Did you just guess?" asked Gregor.

"No, it was just the only answer left. He said the mouse didn't eat the cheese. And the two animals who ate mushrooms and cookies weren't mammals, so that means the spider and the cockroach didn't eat the cheese. And cheese wasn't one of the favorite foods of the Overlander, the Underlander, or the bat. So, that only leaves the rat. See?" said Lizzie.

Even her explanation made his head spin. "No, I don't see, Liz," said Gregor. "All I see is I've got to get you home."

"Maybe she doesn't want to go," said Ripred.

"Of course she does!" said Gregor.

"Let's ask her," said Ripred. "Lizzie, if you knew that all the humans in the Underland might die if you didn't help us solve a puzzle, would you stay or go?"

"What?" asked Lizzie, immediately distressed. "Would that happen?"

"Don't tell her that!" said Gregor. "She's not even the princess! Boots is the princess!"

"And if a princess has a sister, you call them a . . . ?" asked Ripred.

"Okay! A princess!" said Gregor. "But that's just some junk the cockroaches made up. Nobody's going around calling me a prince."

"Well, if that's what's bothering you, you'll be Prince Gregor from now on," said Ripred.

"My mom and my sister and my brother, too?" broke in Lizzie, who had not yet answered Ripred's question. "Would they die, too?"

"They may even if you stay. You may, too. Then again, they may live. But if you are the princess in the prophecy and you leave us, none of us stands a chance," said Ripred.

"I think everyone in this room would back me up on that."

"IN THE NAMING IS THE CATCHING," said Nerissa suddenly. "That is what the line from 'The Prophecy of Time' must mean. We had a princess, but not the one with the right name. That was the catch. The true princess must be you, Lizzie. You are the one who will help us break the Code of Claw."

"Then I have to stay, Gregor," said Lizzie. "I can't leave and let everybody die."

"What about Dad?" asked Gregor.

"I don't know," said Lizzie. Her breathing began to get short again. "I don't know."

"I'll send money up there. And instructions. Your nice Mrs. Cormaci can hire a nurse, can't she? There are people who do that, right?" said Ripred.

"If you can get a note up there, just have Mrs. Cormaci meet Lizzie in Central Park," said Gregor.

"But I'm not going, Gregor," Lizzie said unhappily. "I have to stay." She turned to Ripred. "How will you get it to Mrs. Cormaci? The rats? The small ones who live up there?"

"Exactly. Such a relief not to have to explain myself all the time," said Ripred.

"I will write the note and have the money collected," said Nerissa. "Then, Ripred, have you need of me?"

Nerissa had turned so white her veins looked purplish-black against her skin. The strain of Lizzie's arrival must have been too much for her. Surely she would pass out at any moment.

"No," said Ripred. "Go, see to the nurse, and then rest."

"Yes," Nerissa said, making her way to the door by supporting herself against the wall. "Yes."

"Nerissa, you have been invaluable today," added Ripred, and she acknowledged this with a nod.

Boy, the rat really was in good spirits if he was complimenting Nerissa! If Ripred was happy, Gregor was not. But he knew that arguing with Lizzie at this point was no good. And Ripred had made up his mind to keep her.

A couple of Underlanders came in wheeling carts of steaming food, and Gregor realized how hungry he was. He made a gigantic roast beef sandwich smothered in mushrooms and sat back against the wall to try to figure out another plan while he washed it down with a quart of milk.

Lizzie, whose stomach was also empty, took a slice of buttered bread at Ripred's insistence. "Now come and meet the rest of the code team," said the rat, wrapping his tail around her and guiding her around the room. "I know they all must look very strange to you, but believe me, you've got more in common with them than you do with Prince Gregor over there."

"Why?" asked Lizzie, shooting a nervous look back at Gregor.

"Because you think alike," said Ripred. "Oh, by the way, you don't sing, do you?"

"Not much. I don't like music with words," said Lizzie.

An audible sigh of relief came from around the room.

"Good. Good," said Ripred. Then he leaned and whispered in Lizzie's ear so Gregor could barely hear it. "You'll have to be patient with some of them. They're very shy."

It was the perfect thing to say to Lizzie, who could be almost crippled by shyness herself. She'd always had great difficulty making friends. To be honest, she'd only ever had one friend, a weird kid named Jedidiah. He was in her grade at school and, like Lizzie, way beyond the other kids academically. He was just eight, but he could tell you how anything worked. A car, a telephone, a computer. Once, when he'd come over for a play date, he'd spent, like, an hour talking about their oven. Gregor had finally taken the pair of them out to the playground and tried to get a game of kickball going. Lizzie got cold and Jedidiah became fascinated with a traffic light. It was hopeless. Also, Jedidiah always insisted on calling Lizzie by her full name, Elizabeth, and got very upset if you called him Jed or something. Listening to the two of them having a conversation made Gregor feel like he was hanging out with a couple of Pilgrims. "What do you think, Jedidiah?" "I do not know, Elizabeth." Still, the whole family was grateful for Jedidiah. If it weren't for him, Lizzie would have no friends at all.

The fact that the other code-breakers were also shy seemed to give Lizzie courage. She gave them each a polite "hello" as they were introduced. They must have liked her, because they began to come out of their rooms. Daedalus fluttered out almost at once, but bats and humans were most comfortable with one another. Min emerged slowly. She was an old cockroach, so old in fact that she made creaking noises when she walked, and her shell had a funny grayish tint to it. Heronian struggled to her feet, dragged herself up to Lizzie, and gave her a little bow, to which Lizzie gingerly bowed back. And finally, Reflex delicately stepped out, greeted her, and scurried back to his web.

Then Ripred took her over to the tree carved on the wall. "This is the Tree of Transmission. It was created years ago to make communication easier over long distances. Humans, rats, mice, spiders, cockroaches, and bats developed it together, which was, in itself, an extraordinary achievement. It was in one of our rare times of peace, you see. We can all still use it today, though. Look at it a moment and tell me your impressions," he said.

Gregor gave the tree a hard look and this is what he saw:

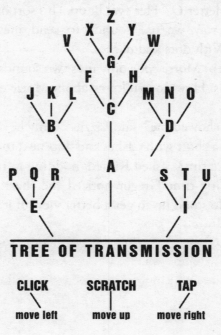

TREE OF TRANSMISSION

CLICK
move left

SCRATCH
move up

TAP
move right

"It looks like a Christmas tree decorated with the alphabet," was Gregor's first thought. But even he could see it must be related to the code.

"I think . . ." began Lizzie hesitantly.

"Go on, don't worry about being wrong," said Ripred. "Well, maybe you use these sounds . . . click, scratch, tap . . . to make letters," said Lizzie. "One click is an *E*, one scratch is an *A*, and one tap is an *I*. Right?"

"Exactly right," said Ripred. "So what if you heard one scratch and then two taps?"

Lizzie followed the tree branches with her finger as she spoke. "One scratch takes you up to *A*, the first tap takes you to the right to *D*, and the second tap takes you to the right to the letter *O*." Her eyes lit up. "It's sort of like Morse code. The way we use sounds to send messages on a telegraph. With dots and dashes."

"Yes, except Morse code only uses two sounds and we use three sounds. How do you know about Morse code?" asked Ripred.

"My dad showed me," said Lizzie. "Only he didn't have a tree; he had a chart with dashes and dots next to each letter."

"More like this?" asked Ripred, nodding to the floor.

For the first time Gregor noticed the chart carved into the floor. He stood up to get a better view of it.

A	I	H	II/	O	I///	V	II\\\
B	I\	I	/	P	\\	W	II//
C	II	J	I\\	Q	\I	X	III\
D	I/	K	I\I	R	\/	Y	III/
E	\	L	I\/	S	/\	Z	IIII
F	II\	M	I/\	T	/I		
G	III	N	I/I	U	//		

"Yes, this is like the Morse code chart," said Lizzie. "So, it's just another way of showing the Tree of Transmission."

"Right again," said Ripred. "Some find it to be a helpful learning tool. Of course, the best way to learn it is by hearing it. Scratch-scratch-click. Tap-tap-scratch. Because that's how it's transmitted."

Gregor had been there during the Morse code lesson with his dad, too. It had been somewhat interesting but hadn't stuck much in his brain. Lizzie had been fascinated by it, though, and wanted him to learn it as well so that they could send each other messages. The only thing he could ever decipher was the SOS distress signal that they used on ships and stuff to call for help. Dot-dot-dot-dash-dash-dash-dot-dot-dot. SOS. It was sent as one string with no gaps to even indicate there were three separate letters. SOS. She'd really drilled that one into him. She had played it on the bedroom wall, tapped it out with her fork at dinner, and even used a flashlight to send it with quick flashes for the dots and longer ones for the dashes. Finally Gregor had to cut her off. Lizzie would have had them practicing five hours a day. Like Gregor didn't have enough homework without her assigning him more.

"Well, if you already know how this code thing works, what's the problem?" said Gregor.

"This isn't a code, Gregor. This is just a way to send any message. Like if you picked up a phone and talked into it," said Lizzie. "And anyone could understand what you were saying."

"You've heard it before. Rat claws scratching, tapping, and clicking," said Ripred.

Gregor remembered waking up one night in a cave in the Firelands to such sounds. Ripred had told him to go back to sleep. "Like in the cave," he said.

"Like in the cave. Those messages weren't in code. The rats didn't believe there was any danger in sending them in plain English," said Ripred. "But now, with the war in full swing, everything is in code." The rat pulled one of the strips of white fabric covered in chicken scratch off the table and waved it about. "This code! The Code of Claw! The one in 'The Prophecy of Time'! And this is what we need Lizzie to help us break!"

Gregor finally understood. The clicks, scratches, and taps were not the code. They were as simple as knowing your ABCs. But the messages the rats were sending now made no sense, because they were written in code. An *A* might be a *B* or a *Q* or a *V,* depending on how the Code of Claw worked.

Lizzie took the strip of fabric and sat down on the ground with it, studying the letters. "Is it like a cryptogram? One letter stands for another letter?"

"Not exactly," said Heronian, settling down by Lizzie. "We would have broken a regular cryptogram in minutes. But there's something else involved."

"There is some trick to make it more complicated. Some sort of substitution," said Daedalus.

"Found it not, have we, found it not," said Min, creaking her way over.

"But the thing is, we haven't much time. Tick, tock, tick, tock," said Ripred, shaking his head in frustration. "Oh, now I'm hungry again." He went over and stuck a whole roast chicken in his mouth.

"Did you get the cookies I helped make?" asked Lizzie, without looking up from the code.

"No, I did not get the cookies you helped make," said Ripred, scowling at Gregor. "Where are my cookies?"

"In my backpack in the hospital probably. I brought them to the battle. Sorry, I just couldn't find the right moment to serve them," said Gregor. "You want me to get them now?"

"I do. I'd better come with you to make sure there are no more mishaps. And I'll make sure the note has gone to your father," said Ripred. He touched Lizzie lightly on the head with the tip of his tail. "Will you be all right here now?"

"What?" said Lizzie, pulling her attention from the

121

letters. "Oh, I think so."

"Good. I'll be back soon," said Ripred.

Gregor stopped at the doorway to double-check that Lizzie wasn't going to become hysterical when they left, but she was discussing some letter sequence with the others. Even Reflex had ventured out to join them. It made a cozy picture, all of them together on the floor. Freakish, but cozy.

Ripred waited until they were out of earshot before he began. His voice — in fact, the whole conversation that followed — was strangely subdued. "Listen, don't fight me on this. Let her stay. We need her to break the code to save people you have come to love."

"I love her, too. She's my sister. And she's real smart but she's not strong," said Gregor. "Not like you have to be to survive down here."

"I know," sighed Ripred. "I know. But Solovet will know she's here by now and have already given orders to prevent her from leaving while the war is on. And after the war, what then?"

"Then it's not a problem. I can take her home myself and —" Gregor came to a standstill as he remembered "The Prophecy of Time."

WHEN THE WARRIOR HAS BEEN KILLED

He would not be around to take anyone anywhere. "I've got to get Lizzie home now, somehow. And Boots and my mom, too. While I still can," Gregor muttered more to himself than to Ripred.

"You can't. No one can. But if you let her stay now, without a fight, I swear I'll get all three of them home safely after the war," said Ripred.

"No," said Gregor angrily. "What kind of deal is that? If the war's over, there's no reason to keep them here, anyway!"

"Think about it, boy. If we win the war, Solovet will call the shots. Do you really believe she plans to let any of them return?" His voice had dropped to a whisper. "She has told me otherwise. If Solovet has Boots, she has the cockroaches on her side, and if Lizzie is who I think she is . . . well, she'll be worth her weight in gold as well. No, your father will come to find them and your family will essentially be prisoners down here for the rest of their lives. Unless I help you."

This was a frightening dimension Gregor had never even considered: his whole family condemned to life down here. Once Ripred had said it, Gregor knew it was not only possible, it was likely. "How do I know I can trust you?" asked Gregor.

"I give you my word," said Ripred.

"As a rat?" asked Gregor bitterly.

"As a rager," said Ripred. "As one rager to another. I will get them home."

As Gregor was trying to decide what a rager's word was worth, if anything, the horns began to blow. Ripred cocked his head and listened to the pattern. "The rats have reached the walls to the north. The ones that surround the farmlands."

123

Gregor could be ordered out there at any moment. He might not come back. Then what?

"What do you say, Gregor the Overlander? Do we have a deal?" asked Ripred.

There was no choice but to trust him. "Yes," said Gregor.

"Good. Now go find yourself some body armor," said Ripred. "I'll see you on the field."

CHAPTER

11

Gregor's body felt weighed down by the conversation. Although he had admitted to himself while he was in the museum that he would die, he had been waging a psychological campaign against the idea ever since. Denying it, dodging it, immersing himself in the present to avoid thinking about the future or, more specifically, how he wasn't going to have much of one. There was no other way to keep functioning. But sometimes, like now, reality came right up and slapped him in the face. There was nothing to do but keep moving forward and make the moments count.

As he walked through the halls, Gregor could see his resolve reflected on many other faces. There was a war. He guessed the Regalians didn't need a prophecy to know there was a good chance they'd be dead at the end of it. And they had family and friends to worry about, too. Gregor felt a little less alone knowing that others were experiencing the same emotions he was. Less alone, but no better.

He was unsure of where he should get the body armor Ripred had mentioned, but there was a big supply room filled with nothing but weapons and stuff, so he thought that would be a good place to start. When he arrived, the armory was buzzing with people suiting up for battle. Even though it was crowded, an old Underlander woman with a tape measure was at his side in a moment.

"You have come for protection?" she asked. Gregor nodded. "I am called Miravet. I can assist you." And then she was whipping that tape measure around him so fast it was practically a blur. "You fight how? With only the sword? In the right hand?"

"That's right," said Gregor, wondering how many other options there were.

"What does your left hand do?" she asked.

"Nothing. Sometimes I tape a light here to help me see," said Gregor, indicating his forearm.

"That is all?" Miravet gave his forearm a slightly disapproving look, as if it wasn't holding up its end of the bargain somehow. Then she led him to a wall covered in breastplates hanging from hooks. "For the chest," she said, and took down a highly polished number made of silver metal and mother-of-pearl.

As Miravet was holding the breastplate up to him, a voice came from behind him. "No, Miravet, I want him entirely in black."

Gregor didn't have to turn to know Solovet was coming

up behind him. He gritted his teeth at the prospect of seeing her again.

"Why is that?" asked Miravet with a frown. Gregor found himself liking her for not immediately jumping to do whatever Solovet suggested.

"To blend with his flier and give an overall impression of darkness," said Solovet.

"The gnawers will not be impressed by an impression of darkness," Miravet said, still stubbornly holding the breastplate she had chosen.

"No, but the humans will. It implies deadliness and strength and will give them confidence to follow him," said Solovet.

"As you wish," said Miravet. She returned her breastplate to the wall and chose another of black metal and some kind of shiny ebonylike shell. "This?"

"It should do nicely," said Solovet. She stood by silently as Miravet made Gregor change to a black shirt and pants. Then she dressed him in the breastplate and other bits and pieces of armor. None of it was particularly heavy, which was good because he didn't need anything slowing him down.

As he was being fitted for a helmet, Gregor caught sight of himself in a mirror, dressed from head to toe in black. "Great. I couldn't look more like the bad guy if I tried," he thought. And here he was going in to fight the Bane, whose coat was so white it almost hurt your eyes. If he were in a movie, Gregor would definitely be the one the audience was rooting against. On the other hand . . . on the other hand . . . there was something powerful about the blackness, and part of Gregor couldn't help thinking he looked pretty cool.

But Miravet shook her head as she examined him. "You only emphasize his youth by dressing him so. He has not the hardness of countenance to wear this."

Gregor was not sure what she meant. He thought countenance had something to do with your face.

"He will," said Solovet. "Come with me, Gregor." When they had left the armory she added, "My sister is an expert in armor but not in character."

Her sister? Solovet. Miravet. The names sounded kind of the same, and it explained why Miravet was not afraid to stand up to Solovet.

"Speaking of sisters, I hear another of yours has joined us," said Solovet. "Remind me of her name?"

It was just the two of them, walking down a quiet empty hall. Gregor felt he could no longer refuse to answer her without making a really big deal of it. He didn't want to wind up back in the dungeon, especially now that he had to keep an eye on Lizzie, as well as Boots and his mother.

"Lizzie," he said.

"And you have no issues with her staying?" asked Solovet.

Sure he did. Plenty of issues. But he had made the deal with Ripred. "Not if she's the code-breaker," said Gregor gruffly.

"That remains to be seen. I myself am not convinced that it is not Boots who will be the key." They walked along in silence for a while. Then Solovet spoke up again. "Perhaps it was too harsh of me to put you in the dungeon. But you are part of our army now and, in essence, you disobeyed a direct order. In an army, one head must give direction to the rest of the body. If not, there is chaos. That is why discipline is so important. If we lose it, we lose everything."

Gregor considered this. He guessed you probably did need someone making a plan and other people who could be counted on to carry it out.

"Do you think yourself capable of following orders?" she asked.

"Maybe. Maybe not," thought Gregor. "It would depend on the circumstances." For instance, if Solovet had ordered him to secretly develop the plague as a weapon, he would never have done it. But he only said, "Seems like I'm always following Ripred's."

"Well, let us see if you can follow mine today," said Solovet.

When they reached the High Hall, Solovet's bond, Ajax, was waiting for them. Gregor knew him mostly by sight. He was a massive brute of a bat with fur the color of dried blood. Once Gregor had asked Ares what he thought of Ajax. "I do not care for him. Almost no one does. Of course, very few care for me, either." So Gregor tried to keep an open mind about Ajax.

Gregor and Solovet flew out of the palace, over the high wall that signaled the end of the city, and headed north over the farmlands. Half the people of Regalia seemed to be in the fields, working at a frantic pace. "It is our policy, when the gnawers are so close, to harvest or destroy all we can.

We do not wish to leave them any food sources," said Solovet.

The farmlands ended at another wall. This one was not quite so high as the one that bordered the back of the city, but it was at least twelve feet thick, providing a sturdy base from which to launch the army. It was packed now with heavily armed humans mounted on bats. An area in the middle of the wall was relatively empty, apparently having been reserved for the commanders.

When Ajax landed in the command center, Gregor got a clear view of the cavern beyond the wall. He had flown over it several times before, but it had always been shrouded in darkness. However, the humans had been at work here, as they had in the Firelands, peppering the cavern walls with burning torches in preparation for the battle.

In the flickering light, Gregor could see that the fighting had not yet begun. Hundreds of rats had assembled on the ground outside of the wall. They weren't milling around in their usual fashion but lined up in rows. Except for the occasional twitch of a tail or ear, they were perfectly still. Overhead, humans on bats flew in a crisscrossing pattern. Solovet's arrival brought several in to report on the number of rats, their condition, and the generals who were leading them.

Ares soon arrived carrying Ripred on his back. The rat burst out laughing when he saw Gregor. "Oh, no. Who are you supposed to be?"

"I ordered his armor myself," said Solovet with a slight smile. "Do you not approve of it?"

"He looks like he fell off of a chessboard!" said Ripred, and Gregor could see some of the nearby soldiers trying not to laugh. "Do you like that getup?" he asked, circling Gregor.

The truth was, Gregor had kind of liked it until Ripred started making fun of it. "What do I care? I don't have to look at it," he said.

"No, but the rest of us do," said Ripred. Then the rat seemed to forget all about him and got caught up in some war council with Solovet.

"How's the airlift going?" Gregor asked Ares.

"Well enough. There are still many nibblers to bring in from the Firelands," said Ares. "But the ones left behind are stronger at least."

"You doing okay?" asked Gregor.

"A bit tired. And yourself?" said Ares.

"Oh, I'm great. Solovet slapped me in the dungeon for a few days. Then my sister Lizzie showed up and Ripred decided she's the code-breaker. And apparently I look like an idiot," said Gregor.

"You look well. The black suits you," said Ares.

"Whatever," said Gregor. "Luxa's better. I got to see her for about thirty seconds."

"I was not allowed to see Aurora and Nike. But the doctors in the hospital say they mend as well," said Ares.

"Man, I didn't even get a chance to check on Howard," said Gregor, suddenly feeling guilty that his concern for Luxa had blinded him to his other friends' conditions.

"He is much improved," said Ares.

131

They stared for a while at the ranks of rats. "So, why aren't we fighting?" asked Gregor. He was a little impatient to get started.

"Solovet is still assessing the rats to see how we should engage. There are two main types of battles in the Underland. The first is a surprise attack, in which case we counterattack immediately in self-defense. The second is a challenge. Both armies assemble and we meet on the field at an appointed time. This is a challenge," said Ares.

It reminded Gregor of those movies set hundreds of years ago, where two groups of soldiers would line up across a field from one another and then one side would charge. Today's arrangement did not really seem to be to either side's advantage. The humans had more than ample time to decide how to battle the rats, but they would have to leave the security of the walls to do so. The rats could arrange a battle and possibly weaken the humans' army without having to attack the walls, but they would make themselves vulnerable to do it. There was a plus and a minus for both sides. Maybe that was why they both agreed to this kind of warfare.

Still, it seemed as if the humans had a slight edge. "I don't know. Seems like it might be smarter just to sit here," said Gregor.

"We could. But then we must live with the knowledge that an army of rats, which is likely to build, sits on the edge of Regalia," said Ares.

Yeah, that wasn't a particularly calming thought.

Gregor noticed Solovet and Ripred were looking at him

and consulting in low voices. Then Solovet crossed to him. "Gregor, Ares, we are going to position you in the second wave at the right fifth point. Ripred suggests this and, as I have never seen you fight, I must follow his recommendation."

Gregor realized this was true. Solovet never had seen him fight, with or without Ares. On his first trip to the Underland, he hadn't even had a sword. When he came back to supposedly assassinate the Bane, she had not gone on the sea voyage. Although Solovet had been planning to join in the jungle expedition to find the cure for the plague, Hamnet had refused to act as their guide if she came. When Gregor had returned from the jungle, Solovet had been confined to quarters because of her role in starting the plague. No, she had never been around when he was in battle or even in training. Well, he could show her a thing or two now. Maybe if she realized what a good fighter he was she would back off a little.

He had no idea where she had placed him in the ranks, but "second wave at the right fifth point" seemed to mean something to Ares. When the command was given to assume their places, Ares flew directly to their assigned spot on the wall. They were in the second of three rows of soldiers mounted on their bats. Gregor was annoyed to find Marcus and Horatio positioned on either side of him. "Great," he thought. "She's sending me in with bodyguards." But even the annoyance couldn't override another emotion that was building up inside of him . . . excitement. He was looking forward to the battle. Right now, his life was a depressing, confusing mess. At least when he fought he knew what he was doing and, for a while, he could forget about the rest of it.

A tense silence fell over the cavern. The air seemed to be quivering with anticipation. Then he heard Solovet quietly say, "Now."

The first wave of bats took off and the rats rose up to meet them. They had barely engaged in combat when Gregor felt Ares lifting off. There was no circling around and choosing targets this time. The bats flew in a tight formation and dove as one into the fray.

Fighting was now becoming second nature to Gregor. His rager side kicked in and he fought wherever Ares positioned him. They had less room to maneuver than they'd had in the Firelands. The ceiling was not as high and the rats were positioned in close, even ranks. This was not as big an issue for Gregor as it was for Ares. The bat's wings were so long that when he would dive, any number of rats might be in striking range. Even with his sword fully extended, Gregor did not have the reach to protect his entire wingspan. And at the moment, the rats seemed more determined to take out Ares than Gregor. In no time, Gregor had run through two rats that had been specifically targeting the bat's wings. But a third had managed to get a claw into the delicate skin near the tip and sliced a six-inch tear into it.

"You okay?" Gregor shouted to Ares.

"Yes, it can be stitched later," said Ares. "It does not much affect my flight."

"Good, let's go get the rat who did it," said Gregor.

Just as they were about to dive, an Underlander flew up and ordered them back to the wall. Gregor wanted to argue but Ares followed the command at once. He guessed this was probably a good thing, though, since he was supposed to be proving he could follow orders. Still, when they landed before Solovet, Ajax, and Ripred, Gregor couldn't help saying, "He's okay. It's just a cut."

"Dismount," said Solovet. "Signal Perdita and Mareth," she told a guard.

Gregor slid off of Ares's back, somewhat confused. If she thought Ares was hurt, then the thing to do would be to send him directly to the hospital. She didn't need Mareth and Perdita to do that.

Perdita flew in from the battle, and Mareth appeared from somewhere down the wall. He was not actually fighting, now that his leg was gone, but Gregor assumed he was acting as some kind of general or something, since he'd been working so closely with Solovet in the war room.

Although Gregor did not expect a lot of praise from Solovet, her next words were a shock. "He is woefully unprepared for battle. This is not meant as criticism; I know your time with him has been very limited. But his left side is noticeably weak. Can we not double-arm him?"

"We can," said Mareth. "I do not believe two swords are the answer. He so favors his right hand."

"A dagger, then," said Solovet. "He must at least have it to block attacks. Perdita, you will attend to that."

"Yes, Solovet," said Perdita.

"Now, I dare not risk testing him alone on the ground.

Has he a rager spin attack?" asked Solovet.

"Haven't seen it if he has," said Ripred. "He runs mainly on nerves and is still easily distracted —"

"I can spin!" objected Gregor. "When I fought the snakes in the jungle, that's how we got out of there!"

"Hmm," said Ripred. "And you were able to control it?"

"Yes. At least . . . well, at the end I was sort of dizzy," admitted Gregor. That had to be the understatement of the year. He had completely lost control, reeled into the jungle vines, and vomited. He had barely been able to climb onto Ares and it had taken quite a while for the dizziness to pass.

"Ripred?" said Solovet. "This sounds like your area."

"As if I don't have enough to do," said the rat.

"Your opinion of Ares," Solovet said to Ajax.

"Far too reckless with his wing space. Acts as if he is half his size. Lucky that tear is his only injury," said Ajax sourly.

"That's not true!" said Gregor, jumping to his bat's defense. "You should have seen him in the Firelands."

"Plenty of space in the Firelands, but that isn't usually the case," said Ripred. "And don't be so touchy. We're just trying to keep the pair of you alive."

"What style of dagger shall I give him?" asked Perdita.

Solovet stared hard at Gregor for a moment. Then she pulled the dagger from her own belt and offered him the hilt. "Take this."

It was a thing of beauty, that dagger. Not just because the hand guard seemed to be almost entirely composed of polished red jewels but because of the strong, sleek blade.

He could tell by the expressions on the others' faces that something unprecedented was happening.

"I can't take that. It's yours," said Gregor. But he wanted it. If he had to have a dagger, he wanted the one right in front of him.

"I rarely battle now. I would not have it grow rusty from disuse," said Solovet.

"Take it. Add a little color to your ensemble," said Ripred.

"Thanks." Gregor's fingers closed around the hilt and he could not help hitting the dagger blade into the blade of his sword. There was a satisfying ring of metal on metal. When he examined the blades he saw neither had been nicked. It was a first-class dagger, maybe even as strong as his sword. He couldn't help liking Solovet just a little for giving him this weapon. The feeling was short-lived.

"So, should we go back in now?" Gregor asked, tucking the dagger in his belt on his right hip to have easy access to it. He was dying to try it out.

"You two? No," said Solovet, as if the very idea was preposterous. "I am sending you both back to training."

CHAPTER 12

At first Gregor thought Solovet was joking. But she was not the sort of person who kidded him. If she said training, she meant training. He tried to control his temper, but he had left the battle only minutes ago. His rager side was still hot. And Solovet's order, obviously meant to humiliate him, stung. "That's crazy! You need me out there!" he burst out.

Solovet raised her eyebrows. "We have been fighting the gnawers for centuries. I think we will muddle through without a barely trained boy."

"Well, that's news to me," said Gregor. "You've been sending me on your most dangerous missions since I landed in this place."

"But not because I expected you to astonish us with your fighting," said Solovet.

138

"I can fight! Ask Ripred! He put me on the front line in the Firelands!" retorted Gregor.

"Well, someone had to keep an eye on you. I thought sandwiched between Perdita and me you might actually come out of the whole thing alive." Ripred shrugged. "But don't think it was an easy job."

"What? That is such a lie!" said Gregor. To suggest he had been on the front line for his own protection was outrageous. He yanked the helmet off his head and was about to throw it in Ripred's face when, out of the corner of his eye, he saw Perdita give an almost imperceptible shake to her head. Gregor didn't know why — maybe it was because he respected Perdita so much — but he managed to redirect the helmet so it ended up wedged under his arm. He noticed how closely everyone was watching him and knew he had to get himself under control. He took a deep breath and crammed the anger back down inside of him. "All right. When's the training session?"

"You will be sent for," said Solovet. Gregor gave a short nod and climbed on Ares's back. As the bat took off for the city, he heard her give a laugh and say, "Now who is alienating him?"

To which Ripred chuckled, "He rises to the bait so easily."

Gregor knew then that at least part of pulling him from the battle and criticizing him had been a test. To see if he could keep his head and take orders. And he had all but failed.

"I should have just shut up," said Gregor. But they had

been tearing down the one thing he thought he was any good at.

"It is hard, when they provoke you so," said Ares glumly. "It took me quite a while to learn to, as you say, just shut up."

They reported back to the hospital so that Ares could get his wing sewn up. While Gregor hadn't received any new wounds, he'd popped the stitches on the cut on his calf and the area was slightly inflamed. He was sent to soak in some bitter-smelling medicinal bath and stitched up again. They gave him fresh clothes and he put on his sword belt but left off the armor. Then he and Ares were both free to go.

"I must sleep," said Ares. "The many trips to the Firelands have worn me down."

So Gregor was left to himself. He knew he probably should check in on his sisters. Luxa might be awake, and he was still due at least four of his five-minute visit. But suddenly he felt overwhelmed by everything, and the only person he wanted to see was his mom.

The doctors gave him permission to enter her room but warned him not to upset her. His mom was lying down, slightly propped up by pillows, but her eyes were open. Gregor could tell just by looking at her that the fever had passed but that she was still very tired. He pulled a chair up next to her bed and took her hand.

"Hey, Mom," he said.

"Hey. I was wondering when I was going to see you again," she said.

"Sorry. Lot of stuff going on," said Gregor. He couldn't

begin to tell her about it. Wouldn't know where to start. Besides, he was not supposed to upset her. So he just rested his head on the edge of her bed and didn't even try to explain. Her hand stroked his hair and the knot of bad feelings — anger, fear, humiliation, desperation — began to unravel. He wanted to stay there forever, letting her soothe him, pretending he was just a kid and his mom could make everything okay.

"I only hear bits and pieces. I know a war started. I see them carrying the wounded past my room sometimes. You going to tell me about it?" she asked.

Gregor shook his head without lifting it.

"And I can't make you anymore. I know that," said his mom. She gave the back of his neck a squeeze. "Just tell me this. The family doing okay?"

Grandma in the hospital. His dad in relapse. Mom right here, too weak to sit up. Lizzie in the code room. Boots caring for sick and orphaned mouse pups. Gregor marked for death. All of them trapped in one way or another.

He lifted his head. "Everybody's hanging in there, Mom," he said.

"Okay. Okay. I just have to trust you now, Gregor. To do what's right for us," she said. "I love you, baby."

"I love you, too," said Gregor. "Now you should get some sleep." He kissed her on the forehead and left before he broke down and told her everything.

And then he needed to talk to someone badly, someone he didn't have to pretend with. He went straight to Luxa's room and badgered the nearby doctors until they agreed to let him in for another short visit. They made him wash his hands in disinfectant, but he did not have to wear the mask this time.

Luxa looked remarkably better, given that only about six hours had passed since he'd seen her last. She was still wheezing slightly as she breathed the misty air, but she was sitting up, leaning against a stack of pillows. There was a tray on her lap with broth, pudding, and what looked like mashed sweet potatoes. She was rearranging the potatoes into a tower with her fork, just like his sisters did at home. Her face brightened when she saw him and he could feel some of the heaviness of the day fall away.

"Mmm, what's for lunch? That looks really good," he said.

Luxa frowned at her tray. "It makes good buildings. My throat is still too sore to eat anything I actually like."

"Everybody likes pudding," said Gregor. He scooped up a spoonful and held it up to her mouth. She ate it, swallowing painfully.

"Ouch," she said. Her eyes widened as they lit on the dagger at his belt. "What did you do to get that? Kill Solovet?"

"No, she gave it to me," said Gregor.

"Oh, I hate you. She never even allows me to hold it," said Luxa.

Gregor pulled the dagger from his belt and handed it to her. "Knock yourself out."

Luxa turned the dagger over in her hands, admiring it. "What are you, her favorite now?"

"Oh, yeah. She dressed me up in this totally stupid black armor and then threw me out of battle until I learn to fight," said Gregor.

"You are back in training? I would not take that too personally. She does it all the time," said Luxa.

"Really?" said Gregor.

"Of course. No one is ever good enough for her. She would give Ripred pointers if she thought he would not eat her," said Luxa.

That made Gregor feel a lot better. Maybe going back into training was no big deal. Besides, if he were fighting, he wouldn't be here with Luxa now. "How long do you have to stay in the hospital?"

"I should be out now," said Luxa grouchily. "They let Howard out. He is even treating people."

"You were sicker," said Gregor.

"I do not suppose it matters. They will not let me do anything, in or out. Now that I am back, Solovet will have me watched around the clock," said Luxa. "I am surprised you do not have bodyguards."

"I did. For a while," said Gregor.

"How did you get rid of them?" asked Luxa.

Gregor felt himself blush. That wasn't a question he was ready to answer. He could hardly just blurt out, "Oh, because Solovet knows I'm in love with you now." So he did his best to come up with something else. "Uh . . . I guess with my sisters and mom down here and all . . . You really should eat some more."

Luxa choked down a couple more spoonfuls of pudding.

"Mareth says your sister Lizzie plans to stay, too."

"Yeah. Ripred thinks she's the code-breaker. They've got her in some room with a tree on the wall," said Gregor.

"The Tree of Transmission. Henry and I had to learn that. It was awful. Our teacher was a nibbler who was about a thousand years old. He'd make us send messages for hours." Luxa began to laugh. "Then one day Henry wrote, 'Help me, I am dying of boredom,' and the nibbler refused to teach us anymore."

Gregor laughed, too, but behind it was the discomfort he always felt whenever Henry was mentioned. Henry's closeness to Luxa and Ares. Henry's betrayal. Henry's body smashing apart on the rocks.

"That seems like a whole other lifetime," said Luxa quietly.

"Things change fast down here," said Gregor.

"Yes," said Luxa, twirling her fork in her potatoes. "Look at you and me."

That was it. That was his opening to tell her how he felt. Make it official. He might not get another chance. Who knew how much longer he'd even be alive? Another day? Another week? But Gregor couldn't seem to speak. In the silence that followed he could hear the precious seconds running out.

Tick, tick, tick, tick, tick, tick, tick, tick, tick, tick, tick, tick, tick, tick, tick. . . .

Then someone was at the door. "Overlander, you are summoned to the arena for training," said a voice.

"Okay," said Gregor.

"Do not forget your dagger," said Luxa, handing him the weapon.

He could hear the disappointment in her voice as he stuck the dagger in his belt. She knew they only had a matter of hours, too. How could he face an army of rats and not have the courage to say something so simple and obvious?

Suddenly he felt his hand reaching into his pocket and pulling out the photo of them dancing. The one that had convinced Solovet he was crazy about Luxa. He placed it on her tray. "This is the reason I don't have bodyguards," he said, and promptly headed for the door, too afraid to see her reaction.

But as he rounded the corner, he caught her smile.

CHAPTER
13

An Underlander met Gregor at the end of the hallway with his armor. While he dressed, someone roused Ares and the two of them went to the arena.

"Have a good nap?" asked Gregor.

"All twenty minutes of it," said Ares tiredly.

"Maybe we'll get some time after training," said Gregor. He knew he should probably try to get some sleep, too. It was so hard to keep track of night and day down here, without the help of the sun.

When they flew into the arena, they found it was jam-packed with mice. It had become a kind of refugee camp for those who had survived the ordeal of being driven from their homes and sentenced to death by the Bane in the Firelands. A thick layer of straw had been strewn on the moss-covered ground. Stations for food, washing, and medical treatment were along the walls. There was an area set aside for the mice to relieve themselves. The place reeked of disinfectant but it was not enough to overcome the smells of waste and sickness and too many bodies in too small of a space.

While they were circling around, a bat flew in carrying a half dozen mouse pups and a small boy with a head of curly black hair. "Hey, there's Hazard. Let's go say hello," said Gregor.

The bat with Hazard landed in an area by the wall. Gregor had barely touched down in front of him when they were swarmed by a group of frantic, squeaking mice. Ares stretched out his wings, forming a protective barrier between the crowd and the bat carrying the mouse babies.

"What is it? What's going on?" Gregor shouted to Hazard.

"The babies. We are trying to reunite them with their parents," said Hazard. "But it is a difficult task."

Gregor bet it was. There were hundreds and hundreds of mouse pups in the nursery. Their parents could be anywhere — lying dead in Hades Hall, in the Regalian hospital, still waiting to be airlifted from the Firelands — but they might be here in this mob, desperate to know if their babies had survived.

"Hey, quiet! Quiet!" shouted Gregor, standing on Ares's back and holding his arms in the air. The mice settled down a little. "No, you've got to be really quiet. And back up before someone gets hurt!" By this time, a few people had run over to help them. They made the mice move back to give the bats some breathing space. "How did you plan to do this, Hazard?"

"We are starting a list. I am to bring the babies, six at a time, and call out their names to see if their parents are here to take them," said Hazard.

"They're sending you to do this?" Gregor asked. They must've really been shorthanded if they had given the job to a seven-year-old.

"I am the best one. Because I can speak to the babies," said Hazard. But his lime-green eyes were full of doubt. "They can tell me their names. But you are louder than I, Gregor. Will you call them out?"

"Of course. Who's that?" Gregor asked, pointing to a small gray-and-white-speckled pup.

"This is Scalene," said Hazard, handing him the pup. "She is all alone."

Gregor lifted the shivering pup up over his head. "Okay, this pup is named Scalene," he called. "Anybody know who she belongs to?"

There was an immediate cry. "To me! To me!" The crowd opened up as a mouse ran forward. "She is my baby!" At her mother's voice, Scalene began to wriggle to get out of Gregor's hands, whimpering and squeaking.

Ares dipped his nose to the ground and the pup ran straight down his neck and bolted between its mother's forelegs. She nuzzled it quickly, but then looked pleadingly at Hazard. "There are two more. Euclidian and Root. Do you have them?"

"Not on this flier. But there are hundreds in the nursery. They may well be there," said Hazard.

The mouse nodded and led her lone baby away.

Gregor helped pass out the rest of the pups. Two pairs of siblings were instantly claimed. When the final pup's name was called, no one answered.

"His name's Newton." Gregor held the squirming black mouse high above his head and tried to raise his voice so it filled the whole arena. "Newton!" But there was still no reply.

"I believe he is from the jungle colony," said a voice.

Gregor had a bad feeling about that. Luxa had told him the mice they had seen gassed to death at the volcano had been from the jungle colony.

"Any of us will take him," said a mouse near the front.

"I can only give him to his parents now," said Hazard. "And they may still be in the Firelands."

The mice did not protest. No one wanted to further complicate the situation.

"I'll take him back to the nursery and start bringing the others," said Hazard.

"Okay, listen up! Hazard's going to be bringing in more pups. But you have to leave this space open and not rush up when he lands. All right?" said Gregor. There was a general murmur of agreement from the crowd.

Two of the Underlanders volunteered to take over Gregor's job and assist Hazard when he returned. "They await you, Overlander. At the south tunnel," someone told him.

When Ares lifted into the air, Gregor could see that none of the mice had moved. They would wait there in agonized silence as long as there was any chance their children might show up. He felt that awful helplessness that had consumed him as he'd watched the mice dying in the pit. This was just an extension of it. And at that moment, Gregor knew exactly why he was going to kill the Bane.

"Let's go train," he said, now anxious for any advantage the dagger might be able to give him.

"Yes," said Ares. "Ajax had a point. I must learn to use my wings better."

When Gregor slid off of Ares's back next to Perdita, she began to launch into a spiel about how they had all been called out of battle for further training, but Gregor cut her off.

"No, you guys are right. It would be better if I had a dagger. So how do I use it?" he asked.

Perdita clapped him on the shoulder in approval and went right into his training. They concentrated mainly on defense positions, although she did show him a couple of basic attacks. "You would have to be almost in physical contact with the gnawer to kill it," said Perdita. Gregor could see that because the dagger blade was so much shorter than his sword, this would be true. He was rarely in such close proximity to the rats.

The lesson went well. It was much easier to fight with two weapons. He remembered how having the torch in his left hand in the jungle during his spin attack had probably made the difference between life and death.

"Good, Gregor. Excellent. Now let us try you out on your flier," said Perdita.

Ares had been overhead, working with Ajax on

minimizing his wingspan on different moves. He must have done well, too, because Ajax grudgingly told Perdita, "At least he is able to take instruction."

Gregor could feel the difference in Ares's flight maneuvers. They were sharper, more abrupt. Perdita and Ajax ran them through a series of drills and then Ripred showed up and they got some real practice. They dove down at him pretending they were in actual battle. At first, Gregor held back, but Ripred kept snarling at him to fight. And while Gregor knew Ripred wouldn't try to kill them, the rat had no trouble leaving a scratch or small puncture wound anytime he got through their defenses. By the end of the lesson, Gregor and Ares were pretty bloody, and even Ripred had a couple of cuts where Gregor had tagged him.

"Better," said the rat as he waved them in. "But you have a tendency to forget that dagger's in your hand and compensate with the sword."

"Yeah, I could feel myself doing it," said Gregor.

"And, Ares, when you're down and decide to open those wings, do it! Bam! You can break necks with those things if you use them," said Ripred.

"So I have been telling him," said Ajax.

"I will keep working on this," said Ares.

A messenger bat arrived with an order for Ares to join the next airlift team.

"He's pretty tired," said Gregor.

"So are we all," said the bat.

"I can do it," said Ares.

"What about training?" asked Gregor.

"He's done for now. Let's see your spin," said Ripred.

After Ares took off, Gregor tried to show Ripred his spin attack. It was hard to do without the real threat of death before him. His feet felt awkward and he got dizzy almost immediately. "I was better in the jungle," he told Ripred.

"Well, you stink now," said the rat. "Let's start with the dizziness. You've got to learn how to spot."

Ripred showed him how to pick a spot somewhere and find it with his eyes each time he turned. "I do it with sound, by echolocation but, of course, that's out."

"Oh. Yeah. Maybe not," said Gregor.

"Can I assume by that smug look on your face that you've finally had a breakthrough?" asked Ripred.

"Kind of. In the dungeon," said Gregor. "I mean, something happened."

"I'll take him from here," Ripred told Perdita.

Before he knew it, Gregor was under the palace in their old practice space, fighting off Ripred's attacks in complete darkness. Except it wasn't darkness anymore, because he could do that thing, that echolocation thing, and somehow "see" things around him. If he clicked or coughed or even spoke in a certain direction, he could register detailed shapes and heat and movement.

"We should have thrown you into the dungeon months ago," said Ripred.

"It's weird. It's like having a whole new sense," said Gregor.

"Yes. Let's try that spin attack now. Pick a distinctive

spot on the wall and keep coming back to it," the rat instructed. "Wait, use me to start."

Gregor tried. He could find Ripred with echolocation on the first few spins but then he started to get confused and dizzy. It was too many new things —spinning and spotting and seeing with his ears — for his brain to compute all at once. Finally he tripped and his feet went out from under him.

"All right, all right. That's enough for today," said Ripred.

"No, it's not. I haven't got it," said Gregor.

"We'll get it next time," Ripred said.

"There might not be a next time!" said Gregor. "Or next time might be in a cave full of rats!"

"You're too tired. It's counterproductive," said Ripred. Gregor began to object but the rat cut him off. "Gregor! You've made excellent progress today. But it's time to stop!"

What a reversal this was from their old lessons, when it was Gregor who was always trying to cut out and Ripred driving him on. "Will you keep working with me?"

"After you've eaten and slept. Let's go check up on Lizzie. You can rest in her room there," said Ripred.

"Yeah, let's see if they've cracked that code yet," said Gregor. He was starting to get concerned about how long it was taking. "So, we'll really lose the war if they don't break it?"

"If Sandwich is to be believed," said Ripred. "And even if the prophecy were not a factor, I would say yes. We need that intelligence rather badly. Come on."

You could sense the frustration as soon as you entered the

code room. The floor was ankle deep in those long white strips of fabric marked with encrypted messages. The team was gathered around Lizzie as she hurriedly wrote down some letters on a strip with a bright pink marker that must have been in her backpack. "So then it would be T . . . H . . . E . . . Q . . . oh, no . . . another H. That's not it."

The team gave a collective huff of disappointment.

"So, how are we doing? Any luck with the Prime Factorial Ciphers?" asked Ripred.

"No luck," said Daedalus. "Heronian thought to try a two-letter inversion, but that just failed as well."

"It is so maddening. There must be some key. Some simple key. Otherwise, the majority of gnawers could not keep it in their heads," said Heronian. "Something they could not forget."

"How's our new player doing?" asked Ripred, curling his tail around Lizzie's shoulders.

For the first time, the mood lightened. "Only once, must you show her, only once," said Min approvingly.

"She thinks in unusual ways," said Daedalus, dipping his nose down to touch Lizzie on the head.

"And she does not sing," added Reflex, which made them all laugh.

But despite the praise, Lizzie did not look happy. "I haven't been much help really," said Lizzie. "I haven't broken the code or helped anyone else do it, like the prophecy I read says."

"You read the prophecy?" asked Gregor. He couldn't believe Lizzie was accepting the news of his death so calmly.

"I had Nerissa make her a copy," said Ripred.

Lizzie handed it to Gregor. "Doesn't she have pretty writing?" she said.

Gregor looked at the prophecy. The lines about his death had been rewritten to read:

WHEN THE MONSTER'S BLOOD IS SPILLED
AND THE WARRIOR'S ROLE FULFILLED

"Very pretty," said Gregor, glad they knew enough to try to protect her.

A fresh cart of food was being rolled into the room. "Okay, you'd better break before you're all useless. Let's clear this mess away. We'll eat. And for the next half hour no one is to utter the words, 'What if we tried . . . ?'" said Ripred.

Gregor and Lizzie gathered up the lengths of white fabric and piled them into the rat room according to Ripred's instructions so that he could make a more comfortable nest than the one the humans had provided. Food was spread out on the floor, both raw and cooked, and everyone sat down to eat. Ripred, who seemed determined to keep the team's mind off of the code for a while, told funny stories and even had Min laughing. Gregor, who had never seen Ripred try to be likable and charming, was surprised to see he could be both. If you didn't know better, you would think Ripred had a genuine fondness for this oddball crew. But Gregor knew his main objective was getting the code broken. And if the rat

155

thought a few laughs would move him closer to that end, he'd be funny. He'd tell jokes. He'd slip on a banana peel if one were handy.

Gregor ate a huge grilled fish, seven slices of buttered bread, some greens, and most of a cake. Then five minutes later he felt hungry again and finished the cake with a big mug of milk. It had been weeks since he'd had regular meals and he needed to catch up. He looked over at Lizzie, who was picking at some stew. "Eat up, Liz, it's good."

"I know. It is. I am," she said, and took a small spoonful.

"Now I told you everything's arranged with your father, right? He's got round-the-clock nurses. He'll be fine," said Ripred.

"I know. I was just . . . I was thinking about my mom. I know it would upset her to know I was here, but I haven't seen her in months," said Lizzie. Her eyes were bright with tears. "Maybe I could just look at her when she's sleeping."

"That would do no harm," said Heronian.

"And it would ease the child's mind," said Daedalus.

Gregor wasn't so sure about that. His mom's condition might only worry Lizzie more. And if his mom woke up and saw her third kid down here, she'd probably become hysterical, wear herself out, and get even sicker. Still, Lizzie hadn't seen her in ages.

"Just for a minute," said Lizzie.

"Your call," Ripred said to Gregor.

"Thanks," said Gregor. The rat spent ninety-nine point nine percent of the time bossing him around. But here, when he actually could use a little advice, hey, it was suddenly all up to Gregor. "Okay, Liz, I'll walk you down, and if she's asleep, you can go in. If you eat your stew."

Lizzie wolfed down the stew while Gregor prepared himself for what lay ahead. His mom had been healthy and strong when she'd left the Underland. Now she was bedridden, way too thin, and had scars from the plague. He was pretty sure he could count on another panic attack from his sister.

The palace was a new and, therefore, potentially frightening place to Lizzie. She held tightly to Gregor's hand as he guided her down the many flights of stairs to the hospital level. It didn't help that things were so grim now, the people so stressed and sad, the air so heavy with medicines and disinfectants and the smoke from the extra torches that burned everywhere these days.

Gregor had Lizzie wait at the end of the hospital corridor that led to his mom's room. He was half hoping she was awake and he could just say a quick hello and take Lizzie back upstairs. Maybe he could even try and wake her, although that didn't seem quite fair. But when he reached his mom's room, he encountered an entirely different problem. Eight badly wounded mice lay on mats on the floor and his mom was nowhere to be seen.

"They must have moved her to a smaller room," was his first thought, and then it hit him. "Oh, no," he said. "I want to see a doctor!" he shouted, running into the hall. "I need a doctor here!"

He shot down the corridor past Lizzie, ignoring her questions, and grabbed the first doctor he met by the shoulders. She was a small woman with dark rings of fatigue under her eyes. "Where is she? Where's my mother?"

"Oh, the Overlander!" said the woman.

Gregor could see alarm in her eyes. Then he realized he had pinned her up against the wall. But he didn't let go. *"Where is she?"*

"Gregor! Gregor, release her! She had no hand in it!" Howard appeared from somewhere and pulled him off of the doctor.

"In what?" demanded Gregor.

"Solovet sent a team of guards in without warning. They had orders to take your mother to the Fount," said Howard. "There was nothing we could do."

"But why? Why? I'm staying. She knows I'm staying!" said Gregor.

"It can only be further insurance," said Howard. "You are but a short flight from your home."

A short flight? A million miles was more like it. Across the universe to the end of time and back again. Gregor didn't feel he could possibly be any farther from his home.

"I'm going after her," said Gregor. "I'm getting Ares and I'm — man!" He just remembered Ares had been sent on the airlift. "Where can I get another bat?"

"You cannot. You must know that," said Howard. "Gregor, the Fount may be safer for her at any rate. It is not under attack, the hospital not so crowded."

Lizzie was tugging at his hand. "What did they do with her? Where is she?"

Gregor pulled her in for a hug. "It's okay. It's okay," he

said, forcing himself to be calm for her sake. "They just moved her to another hospital."

"Up to the Fount. That is my home. . . . Is this Lizzie?" asked Howard.

"I was — going to — see her," said Lizzie.

"Here comes that panic attack," thought Gregor.

"My mother lives at the Fount. She works in the hospital, as I do. I am sure she will take very good care of her," said Howard.

"I'm going to go talk to Solovet," said Gregor. "Where is she?"

"I believe she is overseeing the battlefield," said Howard.

"You go back to the code room, okay, Liz?" said Gregor.

"I don't — know the way!" said Lizzie.

"I could take you," said Howard gently. He was the oldest of five kids. Gregor remembered how great he was with Boots and Hazard.

"Please. Take her back. And I'll go see about Mom," said Gregor.

Getting to the battlefield was no easy matter. Even finding a way out of the palace took some doing. Usually he came and went on a bat. The lowest doors and windows were two hundred feet in the air. The guards at the platform that lowered to the ground flatly refused to give him a ride. Finally he found an unsuspecting young bat in High Hall who agreed to carry him to the arena for "training." Going to the arena would at least get Gregor outside of the palace, but it was in the opposite direction he needed to go. So, once the bat had flown off, he ran back across the city. The streets were congested with wagons pulling food and supplies to the palace. He dodged people and questions and kept moving past the palace until he reached the northernmost part of the wall that surrounded the city.

He was in luck. A door had been opened to allow the farmers to bring in the harvested crops. At least he did not have to find some way over the wall. But he knew the guards would recognize him — as an Overlander and, therefore, as the warrior — and they'd have strict orders to keep him in the city. Rather than risk being turned back and reported, he stowed away behind some baskets in a wagon heading back out to the fields. This would at least get him partway to the battlefield.

As the wagon rolled away from the city, he worked out what he would say to Solovet. He would tell her, in no uncertain terms, that either she would bring his mother back or he would not fight for her. Period. He knew he could end up in the dungeon. But eventually she would need him to fight the Bane. And she'd want him better trained and willing to follow orders. Wouldn't she? Or would she just see the whole thing as another challenge to her authority and make an example of him? Maybe he'd get better results if he approached it from another angle and told her Lizzie couldn't work without her mom nearby.

The wagon came to a stop several miles from the city. The fields were well lit with a system of gaslights, so he still had to take care not to be seen. Gregor slipped out the back and found himself waist deep in some kind of wheatlike plants. He ducked down and continued to move through the field until it simply ran out. The Underlanders were harvesting their way toward the city. He had reached the end of the crops and nothing but stubble lay between him and the wall from which the war was being waged. He decided to run for it. Who was going to stop him out here, anyway? A couple of farmers?

Gregor did hear some shouts as he sprinted across the barren fields, but no one was actively pursuing him. He guessed they figured he'd be stopped by the wall and, since he didn't have a flier, pretty much stuck there. That was okay. If he made it to the wall he'd make it to Solovet. He did see a bat fly over him, probably to report his presence, and for a moment he was distracted watching it, wondering if guards would be sent to carry him back.

That's when he tripped. He thought he had just caught his foot on some stubble, but when his hands hit the ground he could see the thin layer of earth cracking beneath him and the rock floor giving way under that. "It's another earthquake!" he thought.

But as the three-foot claw broke through the field and slammed within inches of his arm, he knew this was no earthquake.

CHAPTER

14

Gregor jerked his arm back and instinctively rolled away from the claw. He was on his back, about to spring up, when the earth at his feet burst open and a massive paw shot into the air. He yanked his legs in and scuttled backward like a crab, as the paw, with its five ivory-white claws, descended, leaving a deep furrow in the ground.

For a second, it crossed Gregor's mind that the thing was attached to the Bane. That the white rat had grown so disproportionately large that it now had these deadly, shovel-like paws. But this was no rat paw. Even the Bane couldn't grow claws a yard long. So what was it?

As Gregor twisted over onto his feet, hoping to make a run for it, the area before him erupted in a fountain of dirt. He caught just a glimpse of a bizarre, pink flower about the size of a manhole cover before it was on his face. "It's one of those killer plants! Like in the jungle!" he thought. The fleshy tentacles brushing over his lips and eyes made his skin crawl. "Eugh!" he cried as he jumped up and stumbled back. His hands gripped the hilts of his weapons, but he stopped just before he drew them. He was not under attack.

For the first time he got a good look at the creatures coming out of the ground. They definitely weren't plants. Or rats, either, although he was pretty sure they came from the rodent family. They had large bodies covered with dark, bristly fur and long, powerful tails. Each had four paws equipped with five killer claws. The back paws were noticeably smaller and weaker looking than the front ones, though. Coming out of the place where one would expect a nose was a large rose-colored blossom rimmed with waving tentacles.

Strange as they were, the animals seemed somehow familiar. But why? And then Gregor remembered.

It had been a warm summer day when he was about seven. His family was down at the family farm in Virginia. Gregor's dad had been teaching him how to play Ping-Pong in the basement. He'd been chasing down a ball that had landed under an old armchair, and when he'd stood up, there it was. Trapped in the window well where it must have fallen. Unhappily crawling along the gravel. A star-nosed mole. Of course you could measure its weight in ounces instead of hundreds of pounds, but otherwise it was remarkably like the creatures surrounding Gregor now. He had loved the mole, so they had watched it for a while. His dad had explained how it usually stayed underground, how those front feet were amazing at digging and, even though it couldn't see well, that bizarre nose was so sensitive to touch it could basically feel what something was. They had finally gotten a shovel from the shed, gently scooped it out, and set it free. But Gregor had been left with a warm feeling about the funny little creature.

"Wow, check it out," said Gregor, and gave a laugh. "I think I met a friend of yours back home."

But what were moles doing in the Underland? No one had ever mentioned them to him before. Surely he would have heard of them when the plague was running rampant because they were mammals — they would have been affected along with the rest of the warmbloods. Could it be that no one knew they existed down here? That they'd been living far deeper in the earth than the rest of the Underlanders and had only just surfaced? He wanted to communicate with them, but they just seemed to make a quiet wheezing sound. Did they know English?

Four moles had tunneled out into the field by this point. They were sort of snuffling around him, touching his sneakers and his body with their tentacles. They seemed to be trying to figure him out. Had they ever even met a human? Certainly not an Overlander. That was a big distinction down here. Everybody he met knew he was not from Regalia. There was his skin for one thing, and his smell for another.

Gregor opened his hands and held them out to the moles. As their noses gently caressed him he felt a stab of concern. It didn't matter if they were harmless or if they had dug into this field by accident. They were tunneling in behind the humans' line of defense. If Solovet knew they were here, she'd probably treat them harshly. Gregor didn't like to think how harshly. He knew he had to do something fast.

"Hey!" he said. "Hey, you moles! You've got to get out of here!" He began to gesture to the tunnel openings. "Go on now! Shoo! Go on back to wherever you came from!"

Gregor had the moles' attention now. They had stopped nosing around him and had their heads directed toward him. But none of them were leaving. Gregor spoke more urgently. "Listen, man, you got to go. You understand what I'm saying? There's a war on. They won't want you here." He attempted to push the nearest one toward a hole. It was like trying to move a bus.

While they didn't leave, the moles were beginning to stir in an agitated fashion. Gregor had the feeling that they did understand at least part of what he was saying.

A scout on a bat flew overhead close enough for Gregor to see the look of shock on her face. The bat made a beeline for the wall where Solovet was overseeing the battle. Gregor knew it was just a matter of minutes before soldiers would be diving down at these poor animals.

"Get out!" he shouted at the moles. "Get out before you get hurt! They don't want you here! This land belongs to the humans! The humans!"

Those last words were barely out of his mouth when the moles went nuts. The wheezing sounds they were making became loud and angry and they began to snarl at him.

"What? What did I say?" said Gregor, whipping out his

blades. He did not want to fight with the moles —he had been trying to protect them! — but it didn't look like he was going to have any choice.

Vikus's words from the prophecy room ran through his head. "Remember that even in war there is a time for restraint. A time to hold back your sword." This seemed to be one of those times. Gregor didn't know what had caused the moles to attack, but he was sure there was some kind of misunderstanding. He didn't want to kill them. He just wanted them to leave. He made every effort to keep them at bay without wounding them.

The moles had transformed from mild and confused creatures into rabid beasts. They could move a lot faster than Gregor would have guessed. Immediately he was encircled and had to fend off swipes from those fearsome claws from four sides. There was nothing to do but start spinning. He tried to remember about using the echolocation to spot, but it was still too new to depend on. He would have to count on his eyes. So he chose a wagon in the distance, burned its image into his brain, and tried to lock on it for a second each time he rotated around. It was hard, though, because his eyes had plenty of other stuff to pay attention to.

Four moles times ten front claws equaled the equivalent of forty blades coming at him. "These things need their nails trimmed," he thought. But he quickly learned that wasn't going to happen. Whenever he hit one of the claws with the full power of his sword, he met with solid resistance. There was a clang, almost of metal on metal. He could block their attacks, but he could not cut through the claws. "What are those made of?" he actually said aloud. Then he remembered that to reach the field the moles had had to dig through solid rock. Maybe a lot of it. Their claws must be made of very hard material. After that he just concentrated on blocking and hoped that his sword would hold up.

He spun for another minute before he realized this would not be enough. He couldn't just stay on the defensive; they would wear him out fast and then one of them would slice him in half. On the next round, he managed to clip a few tentacles off one of those pink noses. The mole gave such a wail of pain that Gregor almost stopped to make sure it was all right. That's when a claw caught his left side, ripping open his shirt and cutting through his sword belt. It dropped around his feet and he lost a step kicking it free. Another claw made contact, leaving a deep gash on his left hip. Boy, Solovet had been right about his left side being vulnerable! And the moles had sensed it right away. The pain gave him an extra rush of adrenaline and he forgot about spotting, forgot about the moves Perdita had taught him with the dagger, forgot that he had actually liked the moles, forgot about everything except staying alive.

The pink flowers! The waving tentacles! Those were his targets now. Then the occasional small shiny black eye or soft underside of a lifted paw as he whirled around. For a guy who couldn't dance much, he was pretty amazing. His feet were moving in some intricate pattern of steps that he was sure he could never replicate in a calmer moment. He could smell the blood, the moles', his own, before he saw it.

But then it began to fill the air, splattering his face, and somewhere in his brain he knew he wasn't fighting alone anymore. Soldiers on bats had descended, driving their blades into the moles' backs and faces, killing them. Gregor slowed to a shaky standstill in time to see the last one beheaded with a single blow from Solovet's sword. Then she was shouting orders in a voice so furious he could not make sense of what she was saying. He caught words like Overlander . . . hospital . . . breach . . . diggers. Diggers. Diggers!

Gregor was dizzy. Sick. Someone hiked him up onto a bat and he cried out. The wound on his left hip was excruciating. In minutes he was back in the hospital, stretched out on an operating table. A bitter taste filled his mouth. Then nothing.

The pain in his hip woke him later. It was not so sharp now, more of a hot throbbing. He opened his eyes groggily. Before they had operated, they must have drugged him with that fast-acting stuff Howard said they reserved for emergency surgery. Vikus's face floated into focus beside his bed. Gregor felt better just knowing the old man was back in Regalia. He was the only one who might be able to shield him from Solovet. Keep him out of the dungeon, anyway.

"Who?" was all Gregor could get out. But Vikus understood him.

"They are known as diggers. We had thought them all to be long dead," said Vikus. "But some must have remained in the Underland, living in secrecy. Those four in the field cannot be the entire population. Others are out there. And they have allied themselves with the Bane."

"Why?" asked Gregor.

"This land, the land upon which Regalia is built, belonged to them many years ago," said Vikus wearily. "When Sandwich arrived, he wanted it. The diggers would not leave. So he began a war."

"He won," said Gregor. Even in his foggy state, he could feel the injustice of it all. It was a nice chunk of real estate, Regalia. Rivers. Springs. Relatively easy to defend. How long had it been the diggers' home before Sandwich had descended from the Overland and laid claim to it?

"He won. First there was battle, and when that threatened to fail, he poisoned the diggers' water supply. This was not a tactic they had any knowledge of. Only a few were thought to have escaped, none to have survived," said Vikus.

"Killers. You," said Gregor. That was the name Hazard had said the other creatures in the Underland used for the humans, but not to their faces. "That's why."

"Yes, that is why we are known as killers," Vikus said. "Why so many still hate and fear us. Why the diggers still want us dead."

"Didn't attack me," Gregor said. "Not at first." Not until he'd said they were on the humans' land.

"They must have realized you are not one of us," said Vikus. "At least, they gave you the benefit of the doubt."

Gregor closed his eyes and let the information swim around inside him. So Sandwich, the founder of Regalia, the eerily accurate visionary who had created this new world

169

far below the surface of the earth, was first and foremost a butcher. And yet, they all still struggled to understand those fancy words he had carved in the prophecy room. How they lived and died by them. The prophecies were held in such reverence that Gregor had never even thought to question whether their author had been a good or bad person. But now he knew. He'd been risking everything under the direction of a man who had set out to slaughter an entire species to get his hands on a good piece of property. And Gregor carried his sword.

"Not good," Gregor said.

"It is horrendous. It is a shame that we have never lived down," said Vikus.

"What now?" asked Gregor.

"Now we pay for it," said Vikus. "For it is only a matter of time before the remaining diggers will tunnel into the palace. And then the Bane will follow."

CHAPTER
15

Gregor knew he should rally at the words. Despite his wound, he should struggle to pull himself together, prepare to fight. At this very moment, the moles could be tunneling into the arena where the mouse refugees were recovering, or the nursery, or the very hospital room in which he lay. Behind them would come an army of rats to kill everyone inside the palace. He must be ready. So why wasn't he even trying to move?

He could blame the drug or the wound or sheer exhaustion, but an entirely new obstacle immobilized Gregor. Ever since he had been in the Underland, he had fought with the knowledge that he had been in the right. To keep the ants from destroying the plague cure, to stop the snakes in the jungle from killing himself and his friends, to free the mice from the rats. But he didn't feel right about what had just happened with the moles. Okay, a few hours ago he hadn't known who they were or what had happened to them. When he'd begun his spin attack, it was in self-defense. But now they were all dead. And if Vikus's story was accurate, the moles were the ones who had been in the right. Regalia was their land. The humans were invaders who had not even won in a fair fight. To make matters worse, the moles hadn't attacked Gregor at first. They had given him a chance to at least say where he stood. And he had stood with the humans. It was a terrible feeling, to be on the wrong side of what was right. Not with the rats — he still felt that after what he had witnessed in the Firelands he was right to try to protect the mice — but with the moles. . . . Of course, who knew what stories the rats might be able to produce to justify their own vicious behavior? The rats and the humans had been fighting so long; the list of atrocities on both sides was appalling. Gregor had felt above that somehow, until he had killed the moles.

When a nurse came in with pain medicine, Gregor couldn't swallow it fast enough. It was the ache in his heart that he most wanted to block out.

But the oblivion provided by the drugs could last only so long. The next time he awoke, the floor of his room was covered with bandaged humans and bats on pallets. Even with his unique status as the warrior, Gregor was encouraged to move elsewhere in the palace if he could manage it. He was glad to get out of the hospital, where the moaning and blood were more than he could presently handle. Besides, he wanted to get back to the code room to see if they'd made any progress. He could tell by the number of wounded that things had been heating up. If they didn't break that code soon, they were all going to end up dead.

Using the walls for support, Gregor made his way down the halls toward the code room. Lizzie would certainly be there and, hopefully, Boots as well. He was grateful now that his mother had been moved to the Fount. She was just one less family member he needed to get out of Regalia.

His progress was slow. Every niche of the palace seemed packed with people. Not all of them were wounded soldiers. Whole families were camped out wherever they could find a spot. By bits of conversation he heard as he limped along, he found out that the rats had fought their way into the fields through the tunnels the diggers made. They were at the very walls of the city now. The people who lived in Regalia had all been ordered into the palace for their own protection. The Bane was even closer than Gregor had thought.

When he entered the code room, he found a small crowd eating a meal on the floor. Lizzie and Boots ran up and threw their arms around him.

"Hi, you! Hi, you, you, you!" said Boots. There was an apprehensive quality he had never heard before in her voice.

"You're staying, right? You're staying here now?" asked Lizzie, gripping his wrist tightly as if she was afraid he'd vanish on the spot.

"Sure, if you guys have got room for one more," said Gregor.

Then Luxa appeared in the arch to the rat room. She looked much better. Her skin had lost that hot red tone, and while she coughed occasionally, she seemed to breathe normally. Her violet eyes were tired but clear.

It was the first time he had seen her since he'd given her the picture. He'd thought he would feel uncomfortable, but all he felt was glad to be near her.

"You living here, too?" Gregor asked.

"I gave over my quarters to the injured. Ripred has been so kind as to offer Hazard and me the use of the rat room," Luxa said with a wry smile.

Aurora and Nike had moved into the code room as well and were sharing the bat quarters with Daedalus. And Temp was there, ever watchful of Boots.

"We are all here with the understanding that we must stay silently in our rooms or leave when the code team is working," said Luxa. "Ripred has made that very clear. But now we dine. Are you hungry?"

Gregor was. He sat down on the floor with the others and ate about a gallon of beef stew. Lately, he'd felt like some kind of predator, like a lion or something, that gorged itself and then didn't eat for a few days. The war had not been conducive to the three-meals-a-day schedule he'd been raised on.

Ares straggled in at some point. Gregor's hand locked on his bat's claw in their bond gesture, but they exchanged only a few words. Ares bolted down a couple of fish and went directly to sleep in the bat room.

Then Ripred came in and ordered everyone to bed for six

hours of rest. The rat paid little attention to Gregor except to say, "We may need you on the field soon."

Luxa rose and reached down to help him to his feet. But once he was up, he didn't release her hands. In fact, he held on tighter.

"To bed!" said Ripred, bumping him in his sore hip with his nose.

"We will talk tomorrow," Luxa said.

The human room was spacious enough for two decent-sized beds. It also had a closet with a toilet and a basin with a faucet that provided cool water. Gregor found himself trying to approximate the bedtime routine they had at home. He and his sisters brushed their teeth, although they had to use their fingers. He made sure Boots peed one more time so she wouldn't wet the bed. Then he tucked his sisters in together.

"Tell a story about me," said Boots. She loved to hear about herself. He had a pretty big repertoire of Boots stories worked up. But he couldn't bring himself to tell some happy tale about Boots on the carousel, Boots at Halloween, Boots and the birthday cake. Everything was so awful. Reliving good memories required an emotional strength he lacked right now. What if he started crying or something? He'd scare her to death.

"Not tonight, Boots," said Gregor. "Tonight everyone has to go straight to sleep." He kissed them both on the foreheads.

"I'm glad you're here," Lizzie whispered.

"Me, too," said Gregor. He climbed into the second bed

and shifted around to find the least uncomfortable position for his hip. It hurt, though. And he had eaten too much. And he was more worried than sleepy. He lay there for more than an hour before the sound of his sisters' breathing lulled him into a sort of doze.

"Gregor. Gregor," he heard his mom's voice calling his name, and sat straight up before he remembered his hip. His hand pressed on the wound, as if that would stop the throbbing, and he looked around. No, of course his mom wasn't here. And even if she were, her voice wouldn't sound like it had in his dream. Calm, and in control, and like a mother. Oh, how wonderful it would be to have a parent who was in charge again, who could protect him, who could tell him what to do. He knew his parents loved him and were doing their best. But the closest thing his family had to a parent at the moment was Gregor. He glanced over to check on his sisters and saw that Lizzie's half of the bed was empty. Now where could she be at this hour? Probably working on that code. Gregor was just about to go find her and make her get some sleep when he heard a voice.

"Better now?" It was Ripred.

Gregor had shut the curtains to the human room at bedtime but left about an inch open so the torchlight from the main room could shine in. He didn't want his sisters waking up in total darkness. Now he shifted around on his bed until he was able to see Ripred through the crack. The rat was curled up on his side on the floor. Huddled in the curve of his body was Lizzie.

"Yes. I feel better next to you. You're so warm," said his sister.

"Slow, deep breaths," said Ripred, and Gregor knew Lizzie must have been having another panic attack. But why hadn't she come to him? Why had she gone to Ripred? "Want to try a few more math problems?" the rat asked.

"No," said Lizzie. "Just want to sit here."

Gregor didn't know what was stranger: to see Lizzie, who jumped at her own shadow, snuggled up against a giant rat, or to see the untouchable Ripred, who seemed to loathe almost everyone, who always slept alone even when other rats were available, comforting his little sister.

"How did she die? The one who was like me?" Lizzie asked.

What was she talking about now? How did who die? When had Ripred known someone like Lizzie before?

"Silksharp. At the Garden of Hesperides," said Ripred.

"I know about that. Gregor told me. The dike broke and there was a big flood. So she drowned?" asked Lizzie.

"I tried to get there." Ripred shook his head. "Too late."

"And your wife? And the other pups?" asked Lizzie.

"Lost them all. All gone. No chance to even say goodbye." There was a long pause, then the rat continued. "I went off alone for months. I wanted to die. I tried to. But it takes a lot to kill me."

Gregor's fingers dug into his blanket as he tried to incorporate what he had just heard into his idea of Ripred. Wife? Ripred had had a mate. Pups? He had been someone's dad. One of his pups, Silksharp, had been like Lizzie. And

177

he had lost all of them when Hamnet had broken that dike. But Hamnet had been one of the few people who Ripred didn't loathe. When he had shown up in the jungle, why hadn't Ripred ripped his throat out? Because he knew Hamnet had not intended to break the dike? Because he had seen him trying to save the victims from the flood? Or did he simply think Hamnet had suffered enough?

"So you came back," said Lizzie.

"I couldn't stand it. The thought that they had died and nothing was to come of it," said Ripred.

Through the curtain, Gregor could see that Ripred's head had sunk down onto his front paws. His eyes were closed. Lizzie's hand reached up and she stroked his ears. "And that's when?" she said softly.

"Yes. That's when I decided it all had to change," Ripred whispered.

Lizzie wrapped her arms around Ripred's neck and pressed her head against his. In a few minutes, they had both fallen asleep.

CHAPTER
16

Too much. Too much to deal with. Too many things to make sense of. When Gregor arose the next morning, his mind was in such a fog he couldn't even decide what to have for breakfast. Boots just piled things onto his plate and he ate them, not even tasting the food.

Ripred ordered the room cleared except for the code team. Temp took Boots to the nursery, where they seemed to have a regular job. Aurora and Nike went to assist Hazard with reuniting the nibbler families. Ares headed off to check if he was still needed for the airlift. Gregor and Luxa were lingering in the hall when Ripred brushed by. "You two. Meet me at the city wall in a half hour. You may as well see what we're up against."

When he was gone, Luxa looked at Gregor. "Why do you suppose he gave us a half hour?"

"I don't know," said Gregor. Then he thought about the conversation he had overheard the night before. About how Ripred had lost everyone he loved with "No chance to even say good-bye." Was the half hour a gift so that Gregor and Luxa would have that chance? If it was, Gregor didn't want to waste it. He wanted to be alone with her, to really talk to her. But where could they go? The whole palace was overflowing with people. Then he had an inspiration. The museum! Maybe, just maybe, it had been put off-limits. "Come on, I want to show you something."

She looked at him quizzically but didn't object when he took her hand and led her through the halls. They had to go single file for most of it—the place was so packed—but they never lost hold of each other. He was right. Not only was the museum restricted but the entire hallway to it had been cordoned off. They stepped over the rope and slipped into the room.

Once inside, Gregor wasn't sure what to do.

"What did you wish to show me?" asked Luxa.

He hadn't really had anything in mind to show her. He had just wanted to go somewhere where they could have some privacy. Where they could talk without everyone hearing every word they said. But now that they were in the museum, that seemed like an embarrassing thing to say. "Uh, it was just . . ." Gregor's eyes landed on the stack of photos from Hazard's birthday party. "These pictures," he said. "I thought you might like to see them."

He piled some coats and an old piece of canvas on the floor and they sat, leaning back against the shelves, looking through the pictures. That is, Luxa looked at the pictures. Gregor mostly looked at her. Watching the different emotions slide over her face. Pleasure at how festive the arena looked, all decorated for the party. Laughter at a photo of Boots in her princess costume feeding Temp a bite of cake. Sorrow at the shot of Hazard with his arms wrapped tightly around Thalia, the little bat who had died when the volcano erupted in the Firelands.

"I think this will help Hazard," said Luxa. "He fears that he will forget the faces of those he loved. His mother's image is already hard for him to recall. He thinks he can remember Hamnet, because he looked so much like me, and Frill is still clear."

"Yeah, it'd be hard to forget Frill," said Gregor, as the image of the striking giant lizard came clearly to his mind.

"But he worries he will lose Thalia," said Luxa. "May I give this to him?"

"Of course," said Gregor. "Take some for both of you."

Luxa went through the photos, selecting a stack, but then she frowned. "There are no others of us together. We should each have one."

She was right. He had given her the photo of them dancing and now wished he had another copy. Something to carry in his pocket until . . . well, until it was beyond mattering. "Maybe there's still some film in the camera," he said. There was. And since it was an instant camera, they could have the pictures right away. So he held the camera in front of them and they burned through the rest of the roll. For a few minutes, the world outside the museum seemed to go away, and they were just two twelve-year-olds goofing around like they were in a photo booth, making faces, laughing. But when Gregor said, "Okay, last picture," something happened. They moved closer together, her temple resting against his cheek, and their expressions lost their silliness. "Last picture," thought Gregor, as the image slowly developed. "Last picture ever." They had both managed to smile, but their expressions were tinged with sadness as well. This is who they really were. Not two carefree kids whose next big decision would be whether to get ice cream or see a movie, but two people who knew a war lay outside the door, waiting to tear them apart. "I'll take this one," said Gregor. "You keep the one of us dancing." When the war ended, that's what he wanted her to remember, that one time they had been that happy.

"I think our half hour must be nearly run out," said Luxa in a low voice.

"Yeah," said Gregor. Ripred would be waiting for them on the wall. "Luxa, if I don't get a chance to see you again like this . . . it's just you should know . . . that I . . ." It wasn't just a matter of being afraid to say the words anymore, it was a matter of how painful they were. Knowing there was no future in them. He couldn't continue.

"I know," said Luxa. "So do I."

What happened next would probably have taken months, even years to work up to if time hadn't been so short, if the war had not sped things up and given them a sense that whatever living they were to do must be done now or not at all.

Their faces were so close together that he barely had to turn his head when they kissed. Something not unlike the rager sensation, but warmer, more tingly, traveled through his body. Their lips parted and he could see her face registering the feeling as well.

There was a scuffling in the hall and Miravet came in with her arms full of his armor. "There you are. I have been hunting for you all over the palace. I have orders to prepare you for battle," said the old woman. She waved Gregor to his feet and began to dress him at once. "Luxa, it would do you no harm to be fitted as well."

"Solovet doesn't want her to fight," said Gregor.

"It will matter very little what Solovet wants if those diggers claw their way into the palace. Every man, woman, and child of us will be fighting," said Miravet. "Better she be suited up beforehand."

"Yes. I must go to the wall first," said Luxa.

"Then you come see me, my dear," Miravet said firmly, but she reached out and patted Luxa's cheek. How different from Solovet, who never seemed to show Luxa any real affection.

When he was dressed in his black armor, Gregor and Luxa made their way to the High Hall. Ares was waiting for them, and it was only a brief flight to the wall of the city. Gregor suspected they were a little late, but Ripred didn't make an issue of it. He was too busy surveying the action below him with Solovet.

"Do you want us to go in now?" Gregor asked.

"Not yet, Gregor. But stay close at hand," said Solovet.

She caught sight of Luxa. "You are not to be here now. I need you in the war room."

"Ripred ordered me out," said Luxa.

"Ripred was wrong and he sees that now," the rat said.

"I would prefer to stay," insisted Luxa.

"No. Vikus is about to begin negotiations for an alliance with the spinners and the crawlers. We both think your presence would be valuable. Ajax will take you," said Solovet.

"All right, then," said Luxa. She gave Gregor one last look as the bat flew off, and he seemed unable to tear his eyes from her retreating form.

Ripred's tail jabbed him in the side, bringing him back to attention. "Solovet pointed out that she is rather a distraction to a certain member of our army," he said. "And who needs that?"

Gregor didn't say anything. Secretly, he was glad that they'd sent her back. She *was* a distraction. Even now he was wondering what she was doing. He struggled to focus on the scene before him.

The battle was in progress. It was similar to the one a few days ago, in that the rats seemed to be positioned in some sort of formation on the field below. But in that earlier encounter, they had never come within twenty yards of the command center. Now they were fighting right up to the base of the city wall. It was about thirty feet tall, too high for a rat to leap onto. But some were attempting to climb it. The surface was covered in big slabs of polished stone, but between the slabs was a network of thin seams. Using these, the more agile rats were able to get a foothold.

Ripred's head hung over the side of the wall as he watched one particularly game rat make it about halfway up before a human on a bat swept up and ran it through with a sword. The rat fell to the ground, having climbed its last wall, but this didn't satisfy Ripred. "Now that she has discovered that route, they will all know it can be used." As if to prove his point, a second rat scurried directly up the wall using the same path as the first. It got a few yards higher before a soldier took it out.

"Yes, it is time, then," said Solovet as she gave a signal.

"Time for what?" Gregor asked Ares.

"Time to pour," said Ares grimly.

Then Gregor remembered the children's song that had really been a gruesome prophecy. They had discovered its true nature only a few weeks ago in the Firelands. It had foretold the rats' attempt to completely wipe out the mice. And then it had this stanza:

> NOW THE GUESTS ARE AT OUR DOOR
> GREET THEM AS WE HAVE BEFORE.
> SOME WILL SLICE AND SOME WILL POUR.
> FATHER, MOTHER, SISTER, BROTHER,
> OFF THEY GO, I DO NOT KNOW
> IF WE WILL SEE ANOTHER.

For centuries the Underlanders had thought the words were just harmless nonsense and somehow referred to a tea party where cake was sliced and tea was poured. Now everyone knew better. The rats were the "guests" at the door. They were already being sliced open with swords. And so, as Ares said, it was time to pour.

The cauldrons must have been ready to go at a moment's notice. They were made of thick, black iron and had arched metal handles like baskets. Bats flew them up onto the wall, and teams of humans, wearing protective gloves and goggles, tipped them forward, releasing gallons of boiling oil onto the rats below. Horrible shrieks filled the air and the entire enemy line fell back, leaving a half-dozen scalded rats writhing at the base of the wall.

"Shall we torch them?" a soldier asked Solovet.

"Just two, I think," she replied. "I do not want the smoke to interfere with our sight lines."

Burning torches were immediately dropped on the two least fortunate rats, and they became fireballs. They ran in frantic circles then and rolled to put the flames out, but it was useless. Their coats were already soaked in oil. The smell of burnt fur, then burnt flesh, filled the air. Then the rats fell unconscious, probably from shock. But their bodies still lay burning at the foot of the wall.

It was one of the worst things Gregor had witnessed in the Underland. Not as bad as the mice being suffocated in the pit, or maybe that terrifying moment when mites had eaten Howard's bat, Pandora, down to a skeleton in seconds. But this was right up there. He swallowed hard to keep his breakfast down and looked around at the others.

Ripred's face was expressionless. All he said was, "That should discourage them for a while."

Solovet made a sound of agreement but her attention was back on the battle. There was no sense of either triumph or revulsion along the wall in general. The Regalians had seen it a hundred times. Gregor had the feeling they all viewed the act as unpleasant but necessary. The rats had fallen back from the wall. It had had the desired effect.

Gregor clenched his hands on his weapons' hilts to steady their shaking. Maybe he was just green. Maybe after a while this was everyday stuff. Maybe all was fair in love and war. He thought back to the diggers and how Sandwich had poisoned them and stolen their land. That wasn't fair. Even in war there should be lines you didn't cross. And for Gregor, pouring boiling oil on your enemy and setting them on fire fell into that category. He knew they had burned up rats in the Firelands, but it had felt like a desperate act to save themselves and the mice, not a cold and calculated strategy. Could it be that he was the only one who found what they had just done to those rats repellent?

It turned out he wasn't. There was someone else present on whom the event had had a significant effect. Someone else who was not hardened yet. Someone else who still found war new. Gregor didn't know where he had been lurking, perhaps in a nearby tunnel, but the torching of the rats brought him bounding into the thick of the battle. He reared back on his haunches and gave an earsplitting roar. The Bane.

"Ah, so there's my little charge at last," said Ripred.

There were audible gasps even from the veterans on the wall. The Bane had grown several feet since Gregor had last seen him up close a few months ago. He had to be eleven or twelve feet long by now and he dwarfed the largest rats on the field. His iridescent white coat gleamed in the torchlight, throwing off bits of pink and blue.

"Pearlpelt," thought Gregor. Less than a year ago he had been a sweet baby rat shivering in his arms. Of course, everyone had been a baby once. Not everyone grew up and tried to wipe out another species, no matter how difficult their lot had been. Looking at the monstrous creature, Gregor couldn't help thinking about how he had been supposed to kill the Bane when he had first discovered him. Back in the rat's maze as he nuzzled his mother's dead body. If Gregor had done it, would the mice still be alive? The rats kept down? The war avoided?

"It would still have been immoral," said Ares in a low voice, as if he had been reading Gregor's mind. "We would have committed the same crime the Bane did when he murdered the mouse pups in the pit."

"The prophecy said he would be evil," said Gregor.

"But did we not decide that sparing his life was the actual fulfillment of the prophecy? That you had made the right choice?" asked Ares.

It was true. Gregor placed himself back in the maze. Even knowing what he knew now, he could not have cut the baby's throat. The Bane had been completely innocent then.

And as for fulfilling the prophecies . . . now that Gregor knew what Sandwich had done to the diggers, he had to wonder what sort of guidance the man had been giving him all along. He was increasingly conflicted about the prophecies as time went on.

"That's what we decided," Gregor said. There wasn't time to get into it now.

He could see a wide circle opening up around the Bane. Even the other rats scattered to avoid the erratic paws and tail.

"He is even larger than I was led to believe," said Solovet.

"I hear he's been gorging himself on dead nibblers in the Firelands. Feed him and he will grow," said Ripred.

"Can he fight?" Ares asked.

"They say he can. But we haven't seen much of him. The rats have been keeping him somewhat under wraps," Ripred said.

"He can't beat you," said Gregor. He had seen the Bane attack Ripred and come out on the bad end of it.

"Maybe, maybe not. That was a couple hundred pounds ago. Surely they've trained him since then. And there's his sheer mass to consider. And, of course, I couldn't get near him under the circumstances, unless I fought through every rat on the field," said Ripred. "So the question isn't if he can beat me, it's if he can beat you."

They were all staring at Gregor now. "Is it time to find out?" he asked. It was.

As Gregor adjusted his armor, Ripred emitted a stream of advice on fighting a creature with a significant size advantage. The Bane would clearly best him in any strength move. Gregor must rely on speed and agility if he was to stand a chance. Remember, too, that the Bane would have a much longer reach than the rats he had previously fought, so they must allow for extra time to move toward and away from their target. And there were some other things, but Gregor stopped hearing them because he was so focused on the Bane.

A few particularly courageous teams were taking dives at him, but he was swatting them out of the air like flies. As Gregor mounted Ares's back, he saw the Bane's claws connect with a bat's wing and shred it like tissue paper. The bat and its rider plummeted straight down and were mobbed by a pack of smaller rats.

"Ares," Gregor began.

"I know. I will watch my wings," said Ares.

Most of the human army was airborne now, but almost no one was fighting. The Bane's arrival seemed to have thrown everyone into confusion. The rats were jubilant, their opponents daunted. And everyone was waiting for Gregor to fly out and take on the Bane.

Then the Bane spotted him. He leaped into a spot directly in the center of the field and waited, tail flicking, ears flattened back against his head, drool dripping off of his fangs. "Warrior. Warrior," he hissed. "Come and get me."

Gregor knew that in a matter of minutes he could be dead. "Ripred?" he asked. "My family?"

"I gave you my word," said the rat.

Gregor squeezed his eyes shut for a moment, calling up the image of the stone knight to give himself strength.

"Okay, then," said Gregor to Ares. "Ready when you are." He could feel Ares's chest rise and fall, as he took one last deep breath, and then they launched into the air. A hush fell over the field as Ares flew out and made a wide circle around the Bane, who crouched, never taking his eyes off of them. Gregor opened himself, inviting his rager side to take over. The Bane's points of weakness began to come to him in a series of quick flashes. Eyes, neck, liver, an artery pulsing beneath the foreleg, the key spot between two ribs that led right to the heart. They were on their second circle, almost directly behind the Bane, when Ares dove. The Bane, who had had his head tilted back to watch them, sprang into the air and twisted around to meet them. Ares veered off to one side but the Bane's front paw swiped after them. In a move they had only just practiced in their last training session, the bat snapped his wings closed and rolled. Gregor swung, sheering off three of the Bane's claws, and then flattened onto Ares's back as he whisked them out of range.

The humans shouted words of encouragement, but the hit had only needled the Bane. He began to track them now, turning to follow their path, making it harder to find an opening. They didn't need one, though, because suddenly the Bane attacked. He snagged the edge of Ares's wing and swung them in toward his teeth. But before he pulled them into his mouth, the Bane had to get them past his nose. Gregor's sword sliced through one nostril, causing the Bane to jerk his head back and roar. Ares took that opportunity to rip his wing free and the fight began in earnest. It was hard to break down the moments, they came so thick and fast. They stayed almost entirely in the Bane's range, with Ares twisting and diving and flipping as Gregor took on the claws and fangs. Forget about power, the Bane was fast. Maybe not quite as fast as Gregor, but pretty close, so Gregor couldn't let down his guard for a second. What seemed to throw the rat the most were assaults on his face, so Ares began to direct them right into his eyes repeatedly. If they got in close enough, Gregor could use the dagger to attack as well as defend, and he had just ripped open a foot-long gash over the Bane's eye when it happened. The rat dropped onto his forelegs and whipped his tail over his head, catching Gregor on the left side of his back. The unexpected blow knocked him off of Ares and sent him headfirst toward the ground. The pain was initially paralyzing. Gregor was unable to inhale, let alone twist into some convenient position for Ares to retrieve him. Ares barely made it under him at all. He could literally hear his bat's claws scrape the ground as his chest slammed onto Ares's neck, forcing the last remaining air out of his lungs. Fortunately, the Bane was taking a moment to recover from his last wound. Blood was pouring down over his face, staining the pure-white fur crimson. With both his nose and eye damaged, the Bane was becoming disoriented.

Something bad had happened to Gregor's back. He could tell when he placed his hand where the last blow had landed. The area wasn't covered by metal armor but by a thick leather panel. When Gregor pressed on it, he had difficulty locating his two lower ribs. No, they were there, but wedged a couple of inches too far into his body. No wonder he couldn't get any oxygen. But he was just going to have to make do without it. "Tail," Gregor gasped in Ares's ear. It was all he could get out but Ares understood. The bat dove straight down over the Bane's head. As the tail came reflexively up in defense, Gregor mustered every ounce of strength he could and swung. His blow cut the tail cleanly in two, leaving just a two-foot stump behind. A fountain of blood spurted from the wound, soaking Gregor as he collapsed on Ares's neck.

The Bane could not immediately register his loss. He circled around to find his tail again and again and finally, when he saw the severed part lying on the ground, pawed at it for a full thirty seconds as if he could bring it back to life. Seeing he could not, the Bane tilted back his head and gave a wail unlike any sound Gregor had ever heard a rat make.

That's when Gregor realized what he had done. He had wanted to take out the tail because it was such a powerful weapon. But it was so much more than that to the Bane. Gregor flashed back to the time he had watched the rat nearly have a nervous breakdown under Regalia. To calm himself, the Bane had first sucked, then gnawed on his tail until it was a bloody mess. It was his comfort, his security blanket, the thing he reached for when he could not cope. And, man, was he ever not coping well without it!

The Bane went completely insane, whirling around in a circle, snapping at anything in his path. Then he caught sight of Ares, who had turned and was heading for Regalia as fast as his damaged wing would allow. It made sense, since Gregor was clearly unable to continue fighting. But rather than retreat as well, the Bane bolted after them. The rat ran at a breakneck pace toward the wall and, with one astonishing leap, landed on the top. His huge body knocked a dozen or so humans to the ground as he came in. The others vaulted onto bats and fled, as the Bane ran back and forth along the wall, screaming unintelligible words.

Ares, who had cleared the wall only seconds before his pursuer, turned back to face the scene. As the Bane continued his rant, paws and noses began to poke up over the edge of the wall. In less than a minute, the front line of the army had joined the Bane, and more heads were appearing.

A beautiful silvery-coated rat climbed right up onto the Bane's back. Gregor knew her. Twirltongue. The rat that was so persuasive she had almost convinced him to betray Ripred. He'd always suspected she had great power over the Bane. Anyone could see he was a complete mess, that he could never organize something like the mass murder of the mice, or even this war, on his own. But seeing Twirltongue riding the Bane's back, talking in his ear, confirmed Gregor's worst fears. If the Bane couldn't think coherently, Twirltongue would do it for him.

"Take the city! Leave no one alive!" bellowed the Bane.

And on his command, the rats poured into Regalia.

CHAPTER
17

Gregor inched forward on his stomach so his head hung over Ares's shoulder. Screams filled the air as the rats swarmed through the streets of the city, killing any humans they could find. The majority of the population had already reached the safety of the palace. But there were still hundreds of people en route, on foot, and in carts, as the army of rats swept down upon them. Some drew swords, but they were not prepared to defend themselves against such a vicious assault, and Gregor watched several people literally ripped apart.

"My fault. I didn't finish him off," said Gregor. He struggled to raise himself.

"It was not possible," Ares said. "Lie still!"

The Regalian army's priority changed from fighting to rescuing, as they attempted to carry the victims to safety.

Ares dove down and plucked a pair of children from a wagon just as their mother had her throat torn open. He brought them to the balcony of the High Hall and set them gently down. They huddled together shaking and weeping, until someone came and took them inside. The entire hall was filled with bats delivering people and then jetting off again.

"Gregor, I must leave you," said Ares. "There are others I can save."

"Yes. Go. I'm okay," Gregor said, sliding off of Ares and onto his hands and knees. His bat hesitated. "Go. I'll get help."

But as Ares flew off, Gregor knew help would be hard to come by. The High Hall was in turmoil. The air was full of beating wings and the floor was quickly filling with bleeding humans. Gregor was in too much pain to call out over the din or even signal his distress. And there were so many people in dire need of attention. The best he could do was drag himself over to the side of the balcony and prop himself up against a large stone urn. In this way, he could at least avoid being trampled.

That was it. That was all he had. Something was really wrong. The pain in his back was excruciating. Maybe the Bane had killed him with that tail move, damaged one of his vital organs or something, and he was just waiting to die. It was the lower ribs on the left half of his back. The side he was weak at defending. What was on your left side, anyway? The only thing he could think of was his heart, but the injury seemed down too far for that.

Gregor tried to breathe as shallowly as possible. Any

movement of his ribs made it worse. He wanted to moan, but even that seemed too difficult. There was plenty of moaning around him, anyway. Moaning and crying and screaming. He wished everybody would be quiet, just for a moment. Then maybe he wouldn't hurt so badly. If he could just have a moment of peace.

The longer he sat there the more convinced Gregor was that Sandwich's prophecy — at least the part about him and the Bane — was being fulfilled.

WHEN THE MONSTER'S BLOOD IS SPILLED
WHEN THE WARRIOR HAS BEEN KILLED

He was dying. And probably the Bane was, too. Gregor had seen the blood gushing out of his tail. Even a creature as big as the Bane had only so much blood. Did the rats have a way of stopping it? Or, like Gregor, was the big, white rat curled up somewhere, watching the final seconds of his life run out?

Tick, tick, tick, tick, tick, tick, tick, tick, tick, tick, tick, tick, tick, tick, tick. . . .

Gregor could just see over the edge of the low wall that rimmed the balcony. The rats were everywhere now. Climbing over the rooftops, shredding the contents of the homes, devouring the bodies of the dead. The human army had regrouped and was back on the attack, but it was nearly impossible to target the rats in Regalia. There were too many doors and windows for them to duck into to hide, to leap out of unexpectedly. With the ornate carvings on every building, there was no structure they couldn't scale, except the palace.

Far across the city somewhere was the arena filled with the nibbler refugees. Gregor vaguely wondered how they were making out. There were giant stone doors that could be closed between the city and the arena, but what about the tunnels that led into the arena from the other side? There was no way to know.

Things slowly quieted down. The light dimmed somewhat. "It's evening," thought Gregor through a haze of pain. "Soon it will be night." Then he remembered there was no day or night down here. Maybe he was losing his sight. Things did look kind of fuzzy. Yes, he was pretty sure he couldn't see right, and that was probably the first sign that he was about to —

"Gregor!" He heard the alarm in Howard's voice. Then it took on a more soothing tone. "Gregor, it is Howard. Can you understand me?" Howard's face swam into focus. "You are injured? What is wrong?"

"Back." Gregor's lips moved to form the word, but no sound came out. Howard must have been used to reading lips, though, because his hands slid around Gregor's body. His fingers found the indentation at once. As they probed his ribs, electric flashes of light filled Gregor's eyes. "No!" This time he was audible.

"Gregor, I know this must hurt you very much, but I think I can help. You must sit up," Howard said.

The idea was almost comical. Gregor couldn't move, let alone sit up.

198

"Doctor! The Overlander has need of a doctor!" Howard called.

A woman hurried up, felt Gregor's injury, and then they were moving him out from the urn. Now he could moan all right, at least he was making some dreadful sound. He wanted to beg them to stop, to just go away and leave him alone, but that wasn't happening. The woman stood behind him, holding him so that he sat upright by supporting him under his arms. It forced his back to straighten out. She was giving some kind of instructions. Howard knelt in front of him, gripped his hands, and squeezed them hard. "Breathe, Gregor. Take very deep breaths."

"No way!" thought Gregor, whose strategy was breathing as little as possible. "No way!" And he ignored the suggestion.

"Breathe, Gregor! Do it!" shouted Howard. "Inhale!"

Clearly Howard was not going away. Clearly they were going to keep torturing him until he did what they wanted. So Gregor forced himself to take a deep breath and nearly blacked out. Something that smelled sharp and tangy was under his nose. Gregor could feel his eyes and nasal passages stinging.

"Breathe!" he heard Howard command. And so it went on. Again and again. Taking breaths, being brought back to consciousness, only to be forced to try again. Finally when he really thought he couldn't bear it for one more instant, he took a gigantic breath, and suddenly the ribs on his left side popped back into place. The air rushed out of his body in a cry of relief. He could fill his lungs; he could speak again. His back ached, but the blinding pain had lifted.

"Better?" Howard asked, leaning back on his heels.

"Yeah," said Gregor, giving a little laugh. "Yeah."

They eased him out of his armor and cut off his shirt, which was too bloody and torn to be saved anyway. Howard found the new photograph of Gregor and Luxa and slipped it in Gregor's back pants pocket without comment. The doctor swiftly examined the rest of him, prodding him here and there. Compared to what he'd just been through, it was like being tickled. "I can find no immediate sign of internal damage," said the doctor. "Give him pain medicine, wrap the ribs, and get him to a bed." Then she was gone before Gregor could thank her.

Howard gave him a dose of medicine that was designed to kill pain but not make him sleep. Then he began to wrap Gregor's ribs in strips of spider silk.

"Where's Ares?" Gregor asked as Howard wound the bandage around him.

"I believe he is still searching for those in need of rescue," said Howard. "Although I caught a glimpse of his wing. No one can believe he is flying on it."

"He's stubborn," said Gregor.

"Like you. I hear you severed the Bane's tail after you were hit," said Howard.

"Oh, yeah," said Gregor. It was true. He had made that last cut even after his ribs had been knocked out of whack. "I guess I had a lot of adrenaline pumping through me. What else is going on?"

"Well, we have found you now. Many stories of your fate have been circulating. The fliers have been evacuating the city. Most of the humans are thought to be retrieved or dead by now. The nibblers are barricaded in the arena, but don't be surprised if they decide to airlift them back to the palace. The arena is difficult to defend," said Howard. "The palace is our only remaining stronghold."

"What about the diggers?" asked Gregor.

"No sign of them," said Howard.

"But Vikus said there were more," Gregor said.

"It is likely. We do not know for sure. But tunneling into the palace will take far more effort than reaching our crops. Sandwich had it built on a particularly deep shelf of stone," said Howard.

"But they could still do it," Gregor said.

"If that is their aim, they will do it," said Howard, tying off his bandage. "There. Do you think you can walk now?"

Howard helped him to his feet. Gregor felt sore but it was his eyes that were bothering him. "I still can't see right."

"It is not your eyes. Look out at Regalia," said Howard.

Gregor stared out into the city and realized the problem. Of the thousands of torches that usually kept it aglow, only a handful remained. Once, shortly after he had arrived in the Underland, Gregor had asked Vikus why the humans didn't throw the city into darkness when there was to be an attack. The old man had said, "We need our eyes to fight, they do not." How would the humans fight now?

They watched in silence as, one by one, the remaining lights went out. The last torch arced like a shooting star from the top of a tall building before it was snuffed out on the ground.

Just as the city fell into total darkness, the scratching began.

CHAPTER
18

It started simply, with just one claw on one stone surface. Then another and another joined it until the scratching rang through Regalia, blocking out any other sound.

"I've heard that before." Gregor had to raise his voice for Howard to hear him. "Or something pretty near like it."

"In the Underland?" asked Howard.

"No, in my apartment back home. Ripred sent a bunch of small rats up to scratch on our walls and scare us into coming for the plague meeting," said Gregor.

"And did it scare you?" asked Howard.

Gregor remembered how they had all fled the apartment, trying to escape the claws that were threatening to break through the plaster. "You bet."

"Then I am less ashamed to admit it scares me as well," said Howard. "It is only to affect our minds. The rats

203

cannot possibly scratch their way into the palace."

"Well, it works," said Gregor. He needed to get away from the creepy sound, before it really did a number on his nerves. "Can you get me back to the code room? I could lie down there."

Now that his ribs were back in place, Gregor could walk okay. "But do not try any strenuous movements for a while," Howard warned him. "The bones can shift out of place again. If they do and I am not there to help you, you know now how to remedy this. Here, carry these smelling salts with you." He pressed a small container about the size of a matchbox into Gregor's hand.

"Great," thought Gregor. "Not only do I have to breathe until I black out, I have to revive myself." But with all of the dead and severely wounded lying in the High Hall that seemed a little whiny. The floor was sticky with blood. Many of the injured had not been attended to yet. "You stay here, Howard. I can get to the code room on my own," he said.

"I will stop by later to check on your condition," said Howard.

"Whenever you get a chance. Really, I'm okay," said Gregor. He began to work his way slowly through the crowded halls toward the code room. "Excuse me. Excuse me. Can I get by, please?"

A path opened when people saw who was asking. Many of the Underlanders reached out to touch him or allowed themselves a smile. Some seemed amazed to see him at all. "You live!" cried out one old man. "We heard the

Bane had killed you!" Gregor began to worry what rumors may have gotten back to his sisters and tried to move faster.

When he got back to the code room, he found Lizzie weeping on Ripred's shoulder while the rest of the code team hunched in their rooms. Boots was patting Lizzie's hair, but she looked on the verge of tears herself. It was like a dress rehearsal of what would happen when he really was killed. Gregor wished he could have avoided seeing it.

"There, what did I tell you? He left the battle alive," said Ripred, nudging Lizzie's chin so her head turned to see Gregor. "He's just fine."

"Gregor!" said Lizzie. "I thought you were dead!"

"No, just kind of bruised up," said Gregor, rubbing his hand over his bandage.

"Gre-go!" Boots ran over, stood on her tiptoes, and planted three kisses on the bottom edge of his wrappings. "All better?" she asked.

"All better. Thanks, Boots," said Gregor.

"You might have sent word of your whereabouts," said Ripred reproachfully. "We lost track of you after you retreated. That was hours ago."

Gregor had the feeling the rat would really like to bite his head off, but he didn't dare do anything else to upset Lizzie. "Oh, my ribs were messed up. Couldn't do much until Howard and a doctor found me and popped them back into place."

"Like Aurora's wing." Luxa had appeared in the arch of the rat room. Her face was very pale but she wasn't crying.

"Yeah, a lot like when Aurora dislocated her wing in the jungle," said Gregor. "Now she's as good as new, and so am I." Temp nudged Gregor in the leg. The cockroach had a clean shirt in his mouth. "Thanks, Temp." Gregor tried hard not to wince as he put it on. Clearly he had to downplay his injury as much as possible. "So what's been going on here? Any luck with the code?"

But apparently this was the wrong thing to say because it only set Lizzie off on a fresh round of sobs.

"No, we have not had any luck on the code, because your poor sister has been so worried about you," said Ripred. "It has cost us precious hours."

"It's not his fault. I'm no good at it. I'm no good at all. If the rats come I won't even be able to help fight. I'm worthless," Lizzie choked out.

"Don't be ridiculous. You can't throw a rock without hitting thirty warriors down here, but code-breakers are as rare as trees," said Ripred.

"I'm not the code-breaker. I want to be, but I'm not. Maybe it's Boots after all," said Lizzie.

"Well, stranger things have happened, but I'm still betting on you," said Ripred. "Now climb on and we'll work together."

"You're staying?" asked Lizzie.

"Yes, I'm staying until we crack this thing," Ripred said. "Solovet may wage her war without me."

Still sniffling, Lizzie scooted up onto Ripred's back. She lay on her stomach with her elbows on his head and peered down at a strip of cloth on the floor. "Maybe if we reversed the Copernicus Cipher," she said, wiping her nose on her sleeve.

"Let's give it a try," said Ripred. The rest of the code team gathered around and silence fell on the room. That is, except for the scratching. It was very faint here, so far from the outer walls of the palace, but Gregor could still hear it.

Luxa came to his side and whispered, "Should you be resting?" He nodded and let her lead him into the human room. He gratefully sank onto the bed, positioning himself on his right side to avoid any pressure on his bruised ribs and the wound on his hip. She sat next to him, holding his hand. "One or the other of us always seems to be recuperating."

"Only way we get to see each other," said Gregor.

"True enough," said Luxa. "They say you and Ares fought the Bane magnificently."

"Who says? Not Ripred?" asked Gregor.

"Well, not Ripred. But he did admit you did better than he had hoped. And then he took all of the credit for it," said Luxa.

They both laughed, and there was Ripred's nose poking over the end of the bed. "Some of us are trying to work, if you don't mind. I don't really have to explain how imperative breaking this code is, do I?"

"No, we are sorry," said Luxa.

"Why don't you two do something useful?" said Ripred.

"Like what?" Gregor asked.

"Like running some more of the code by Boots, just in case she happens to recognize it as something other than a tail. It will at least keep her out of everyone's hair," said Ripred. "Report anything of interest, just in case she is the princess."

"I know. 'WHAT SHE SAW, IT IS THE FLAW OF THE CODE OF CLAW,'" said Luxa.

"Whatever that means," Gregor mumbled to Luxa after Ripred had left.

Boots and Temp were sent in, along with about fifty yards of white strips covered in code. "Where do they get this stuff, anyway?" Gregor asked. "I mean, who writes it down?"

"The rats send the code through rock seams that carry sounds well," said Luxa. "This is a tap." She hit the stone wall once with her fingernail. "A click." She made two very quick, softer hits. "And a scratch." She scraped her nail briefly on the wall. "A short pause indicates the break between letters and a longer pause, the break between words. I cannot really replicate it at full speed. Can you, Temp?"

"Like this, it sounds, like this," said Temp. He placed his foot on the floor and began to drill out a series of taps, clicks, and scratches that were so rapid that Gregor's ears could never have sorted them out. Especially those taps and clicks. Of course, when his dad had played a Morse code message for them on the computer, even a really slow one, that had seemed unintelligible, too.

"We have many spies positioned at strategic points to record the messages. It is not difficult to intercept, as the rats make no effort to conceal it when it is encoded. Then the messages are written down by humans and flown to the code room," said Luxa.

No one had been bothering to translate the chicken-scratch code into regular alphabet letters — probably all of the code team could read it like that, anyway — so Luxa quickly drew up the Tree of Transmission as a guide. She may not have enjoyed learning this stuff in class, but she didn't even have to go out in the main room to copy the tree. She could remember the whole thing by heart.

"I guess that old mouse must have been a pretty good teacher," said Gregor.

"I suppose so," Luxa said. "The tree is not difficult for me to recall."

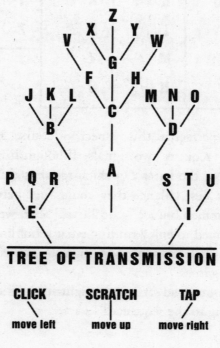

"It is constructed so that many of the letters most commonly used are represented with fewer beats. The letters *E, A,* and *I* for instance, require only one signal. *T* and *R* require only two," said Luxa. "Here, this is easiest to see on the chart." She drew a grid like the one carved into the code room floor.

A |	H ||/	O |//	V ||\\
B |\	I /	P \\	W ||//
C ||	J |\\	Q \|	X |||\
D |/	K |\|	R \/	Y |||/
E \	L |\/	S /\	Z ||||
F ||\	M |/\	T /|	
G |||	N |/|	U //	

"It is not perfect in this respect, of course. Because the letter *B* only requires two signals, although it is much less common than the letter *O*, which requires three. But the tree was the best balance they could find between speed and ease of remembrance," said Luxa. "Shall we begin?"

Boots seemed to enjoy finding what set of lines matched which alphabet letter a lot more than she had enjoyed their earlier code games.

"Okay, Boots, find straight-straight-straight-left," Gregor said, pointing to the sequence | | |\.

Boots traced along the tree with her chubby finger. "Straight . . . straight . . . straight . . . left . . . makes *X*. It makes *X*, Gre-go!"

"Good job!" said Gregor, and wrote an *X* above the corresponding lines with one of Lizzie's markers. And so they went on, transcribing the code in low voices, letter after letter, for about an hour. By that time, Gregor had pretty much learned the tree himself. At least learned it well enough to send Luxa this message:

```
II/  \  I\/  \\. I/\  \.
/. I  I/\.  I/  III/  /  I/I  III.
I//  II\.  I\  I//  \/  \  I/  I//  I/I.
```

She laughed, wadded up the strip of fabric, and tossed it back at him. But as they went on with their task, Gregor wondered if it had been a mistake. She had thought it was funny at first, but now she looked kind of sad. For one thing, it was Henry's joke. So there was all that baggage. For another, any references to dying right now weren't exactly humorous. People had thought the Bane had killed him until he'd walked in. He wished he hadn't sent it but it was too late now.

Boots lost interest in the tree so they made up some other games with the letters on the strips, trying to find words, reading them backward, using their own strategies to try and break the Code of Claw. Luxa and Temp took over the lesson more and more until Gregor was really just observing. Simple, direct thoughts were all his brain could muster. He wanted to go to sleep. He wanted more pain medicine. He wanted to go home. He wanted to go home. He wanted to go home. By the time Ripred called for everybody to take five, Gregor was practically in a trance. He didn't want to join the others for tea and cake, but he was afraid Lizzie would get upset if he didn't, so he dragged himself out of bed.

The code team was too discouraged for chitchat. They ate in silence, occasionally twitching or murmuring something indistinct.

Hazard came in unhappily and sat next to Luxa, leaning his head on her shoulder. "What is wrong?" she asked him.

"They will not let me continue matching the nibbler pups with their parents. They say it is too dangerous. That all of the nibblers must be brought to the palace now," said Hazard.

"They will be safer here," said Luxa.

"Yes, now that the diggers can be heard tunneling toward the arena," said Hazard.

Ripred jerked his head up from his cake. "Can they?" He bounded over to the door. "Am I to get all of my updates from seven-year-old boys?" he bellowed. "Tell Solovet I am not being kept informed!"

"It's not the rats scratching?" Gregor asked.

"Oh, no, Gregor. This sounds completely different," said Hazard.

Ripred turned back to the group, murmuring, "At least they are not digging for the palace. Although why not worries me."

"You think they have another plan to enter it?" asked Luxa.

"I think if they don't, they're working on one," said Ripred. "But as they have never succeeded before, it will have to be quite a plan. In the meantime, they know we'll wear ourselves out bringing in the nibblers."

"Dulcet says I will be needed later," Hazard said. "That I should rest. But I am not sleepy. Can I help in here?"

"Why not?" asked Ripred. "Perhaps some new blood will refresh our minds."

"What are you doing?" asked Hazard.

No one seemed to have the energy to answer. Finally Lizzie, who hated it when people ignored her questions, spoke up. "I'll show you." She took the nearest strip of fabric and an aqua-blue marker from her backpack and sat next to Hazard. "This is a message sent by one rat to another. Those little lines stand for these letters." She quickly wrote the correct alphabet letters above the lines.

"Like the chart on the floor?" asked Hazard.

"Uh-huh," said Lizzie. "Only even when we turn it into letters we still can't read the message because it's in code. A really hard code."

"Does each letter stand for another letter?" Hazard asked.

"Yes, but there's some extra trick on top of that. Like maybe you're supposed to throw out every third letter or something, and then it will make sense," said Lizzie.

"Can the letter *A* ever be a letter *A*?" asked Hazard.

"We don't think so. See, basically, this is like a cryptogram, and a letter is never itself. There's another kind of puzzle that's called an anagram, where you just take the letters and mix them around to form another word. Like the word 'nap' could be the word 'pan' and the 'a' doesn't have to move, or the word 'cat' could be the word 'act'—"

"Or the name 'Gregor' could be the name 'Gorger,'" said Gregor, giving Lizzie a poke in the side.

"That's what I said when Gregor told me about the Underland. That he and Gorger really had the same name," said Lizzie.

Man, that seemed forever ago! When he'd told his family the story of his first trip. "Yeah, Hazard, I'm talking about meeting giant spiders and throwing myself off a cliff, and all Lizzie can say is that this nasty old rat king named Gorger and I've got the same name. Because the letters matched. Oh, she saw that right off," said Gregor. He took a deep drink of his tea and was vaguely wondering if he should eat more cake when Heronian spoke up.

"She saw that right off?" the mouse asked slowly. "She saw that right off?"

"Sure did," said Gregor. "Well, you know how she can mess around with words." He didn't see what the big deal was. Noticing that "Gregor" had the same letters as "Gorger" couldn't hold a candle to doing that crazy who-ate-the-cheese-for-lunch puzzle.

But this new information produced a strange reaction in the room. One by one, the members of the code team raised their heads and stared at Lizzie, who was twisting the aqua marker around and around in her hands.

"I saw that right off. I did," Lizzie said to herself. "That's what I saw."

"What she saw, it is the flaw in the Code of Claw," said Daedalus. "Think about exactly what it was that you saw, Lizzie."

Lizzie's eyes shifted to the code tree and began to dart around the letters. "An anagram. I saw an anagram. Where some letters can be themselves." Her mouth dropped open slightly and her breath came out in short pants.

Gregor had seen several panic attacks begin like this and was tempted to intervene. But everyone else was frozen, not daring to interrupt whatever was going on in her head. So he waited, too.

"An anagram — of Gregor's — name," said Lizzie.

"In the naming is the catching," Reflex said in a quivering voice.

"Maybe — that line — wasn't about my — name at all!" Lizzie suddenly dropped her marker and snatched up the piece of code she had been showing to Hazard. She read it, her lips moving silently over the letters. When she looked up, her next words were barely audible. "Gre — gor. Gor — ger. I think — I know — how to break — the code!"

PART 3

THE
WARRIOR

CHAPTER
19

Lizzie flipped over the strip of fabric and wrote the alphabet on the blank side as the words tumbled out of her mouth. "Okay, okay, what if it's like an anagram, and there are letters that don't change. Then all you would need is one key word and a really simple code and the rats could still keep it in their heads."

"And you think it's 'Gregor'?" asked Ripred.

"It's the word I saw," said Lizzie.

"It would be a good choice. You could remember it by 'Gregor' or 'Gorger,'" said Heronian.

"It is even easier," said Reflex. "The words only require four letters: *G-O-R-E*. 'Gore.' One needs only to remember the word *gore*."

"Yes," said Lizzie. "Yes. So the *G, O, R,* and *E* stay the same." She wrote these letters above themselves on the alphabet.

E G   O R
ABCDEFGHIJKLMNOPQRSTUVWXYZ

"And now we use a cipher so simple that no one could forget it," said Daedalus.

"Single shift, be the simplest, single shift," said Min.

Lizzie nodded and began to fill in the letters.

"*A* is represented by *B, B* is *C, C* is *D, D* would be *F* because the *E* remains unchanged. . . ." Heronian said, although Lizzie was way ahead of her. Her aqua marker speedily filled in the remaining letters.

BCDEFGHIJKLMNOPQRSTUVWXYZA
ABCDEFGHIJKLMNOPQRSTUVWXYZ

"Try it! Go on, try it!" said Ripred, thrusting an unbroken strip of code before Lizzie.

Lizzie's hands were trembling as she lifted the strip and began to read. "Diggers — arrive — at — camp —near — Regalia. Tunnel — under way."

For a moment, they all just sat there, stunned at their success.

"That's old. We need the latest transmissions." Ripred ran to the door. "Fresh code! Fresh code!" he called. He bounded back to Lizzie, scooped her up with his nose, and tossed her in the air. He spun halfway around and caught her so she landed on his back. "A letter can be itself!"

Lizzie was laughing as she flung her arms around his neck.

"A letter can be itself! A letter can be itself!"

And suddenly the whole code team burst into some kind of brainiac celebration. Reflex began to shoot lines of silk around the room like they were streamers. Daedalus was scooping up heaps of code with his wings and flinging them in the air. Heronian leaped back and forth over Ripred and Lizzie. And even old Min had geared up into some creaky old cockroach dance.

Boots was in heaven, running here and there, spinning in the streamers of silk, and boogying on Temp's back. "A letter can be yourself! A letter can be yourself!" she crowed.

"Yes, a letter can be yourself, you clueless little thing," said Ripred. But he was happy. Joyful even.

Hazard wrapped his arms tightly around Luxa. "So everything will be all right? Now that they've broken the code?"

"It will be better at least, Hazard," Luxa said, hugging him back. But when she looked at Gregor, he could tell she was thinking of the rest of the prophecy. Of his death.

"Everything's going to be just fine, Hazard," said Gregor. The last thing he wanted to do was crush this moment of victory with his own troubles. "Good job, Liz!" he said, high-fiving his sister.

"It was all of us," said Lizzie. "And Hazard, too. He's the one who made me think about the anagrams."

"Can I go tell the nibblers the code is broken? I am sure it will lighten their hearts," Hazard said.

"No!" said Ripred, suddenly serious. "No one outside of this room must know we have broken the code. I will

221

personally inform Solovet. The rest of you must swear to secrecy."

All the code team nodded in agreement, so Gregor nodded, too, although he thought Hazard was right and that the news might give everybody a big psychological boost.

A young woman brought in a basket filled with tightly rolled bundles of code. The code team gathered around it, eager to decipher the latest messages. Despite the general excitement, Gregor began to think about that nap again. But Ripred had other work for him. He enlisted Gregor, Luxa, Hazard, Boots, and Temp to decode the piles of accumulated messages, just in case there had been anything of value in them. Luxa suggested they work back in the bedroom, so Gregor was able to lie down again, anyway. They had to do two passes on each strip of code, one to write it as the alphabet, the second to decrypt it with the Code of Claw. Most of the messages were old news — updates on the battle to free the nibblers, the alliance with the diggers, the Bane's location — but some yielded important information in terms of which species had sided or not sided with the Bane. The cockroaches had not, the spiders were trying to remain neutral (so Reflex's presence here must be a secret), and it was too dangerous to try to approach the ants. Gregor found it difficult to believe the ants would join either the humans or the rats. They had made it very clear they wanted both species dead. Probably nothing pleased them more than a big old war between the two.

Try as he might, Gregor could not keep his eyes open. At one point Luxa whispered, "Sleep, we will manage this."

So Gregor just let himself drift off. When he awoke, everything was quiet. Luxa, Hazard, and Boots were asleep on the bed across from him. Temp snored gently on the floor. Ripred must have sent everyone to bed. Gregor tried to go back to sleep, but his back and hip hurt. He was hungry again, too. He made his way to his feet in stages and went into the code room. Lizzie and Ripred were asleep on the floor, as they'd been the other night. Ripred opened one bleary eye, took him in, and then let the lid slowly slide shut. Gregor went over to the food cart and rooted around for a snack. He found a tureen half-filled with lukewarm beef stew and finished it off. His stomach felt better, anyway.

Gregor wished Howard would come by with some more medicine. But when he thought of the wounded, and his shoes sticking to the bloody floor of the High Hall, he knew Howard hadn't had a second to do it. He could send a message to the hospital, but again, they were so busy just keeping people alive he felt like a wimp bugging them. He wondered about his mom up at the Fount. Was she getting the care she needed? Or was the hospital there as overwhelmed as the one in Regalia? And what about his dad and grandma? Boy, he hoped his dad wasn't having any ideas about coming down here to rescue them all. Maybe his relapse was bad enough to keep him in bed. It was an awful thing to wish on his dad but it was better than having him drop straight down into the jaws of the rats.

He poured a mug of cold tea and gave up on the idea of returning to bed. He wasn't really tired now, anyway. Might as well make himself useful. The area on the stone grid was covered with the latest messages all neatly transcribed in Lizzie's aqua marker. But there were still bunches of the old code spilling over baskets. Gregor grabbed a handful of strips and settled himself down to work. It was mostly the same-old same-old stuff about troop movements that had occurred weeks ago. And then out of nowhere came this message:

// III\ I\\ // I/ / // I\\ \I.
II\ I\\ \ II\.
I\\ \\. \I I\\ //.

He wrote it as the alphabet:

UXJUDIUJQ. FJEF. JP. QJU

And then applied the Code of Claw using Lizzie's system. The words stabbed him in the heart.

Twitchtip. Memories of the rat swam before his eyes. Her nose buried in the moss of the arena because the smell of humans made her ill. The desperate look on her face as she spun around in the whirlpool. Her claws digging into his life jacket, as she choked out, "Don't — let — go!" And he hadn't let go. He had risked his life to save an outcast rat when no one else would bother to try. And then they were friends, despite the rat/human thing. Twitchtip

224

was the first one who knew he was a rager. She had given Boots food. She had dragged herself through the rats' maze to help Gregor find the Bane, then forced him and Ares to leave her to die. But she hadn't died. Not right away. The rats had kept her alive in a pit and probably tortured and starved her while they tried to extract information out of her about Gregor. And finally, only recently, she'd left the world. As alone as ever.

The tears splashing down on the words surprised him because he hadn't cried in such a long time. Not for his mom or Ares or the mice or Thalia or Luxa, or even for himself when he knew about the prophecy. It was just that it had all been so awful, Twitchtip's life. Banished to the Dead Land because of her remarkable sense of smell, living alone in that harsh world before she finally, desperately, had teamed up with Ripred. Bleeding to death in the maze but not fast enough, not soon enough to escape falling into the hands of the rats who hated her for being a scent seer and then hated her even more for helping Gregor.

"All right. All right now." Ripred was looking over his shoulder at the message.

"It's not all right!" Gregor's voice was harsh, but low, because he didn't want to wake everyone to see him like this. "I should have gone back for her."

"We thought she was dead," said Ripred.

"But we didn't know. And they had her all this time. And we never even found out for sure," said Gregor. He thought of his dad, wasting away for years in that rat pit. Had she died in the same one they'd found his father in?

"Even if we'd known, there's almost no chance we could have gotten her out," said Ripred. "It isn't likely they —"

"Just shut up, Ripred! I mean, what do you care? You never even liked her! You treated her like trash. You only made that deal with her to help yourself, so I could kill the Bane for you. Don't act now like — like she mattered to you!" said Gregor. He hadn't kept his voice down. Practically everyone was awake now. Frightened by his outburst. Afraid the rats had broken into the palace. "Just shut up!"

Gregor stormed into the rat room and yanked the curtain closed behind him. He sank down on the bed and wept. He knew it wasn't just about Twitchtip, it was about all of the dreadful things that had happened and the ones that awaited him in the coming hours. A hand, Lizzie's he thought, tentatively edged around the curtain. "Leave me alone!" The weeping sent new shock waves of pain through his ribs, but it was a long time before he'd cried himself out. Then he just lay on the bed watching the soft flicker of light from an oil lamp on the wall. It was quiet outside again. Everyone must have gone back to sleep.

Footsteps entered the code room. "Where is Gregor?" asked Howard in an exhausted voice.

"In there," Luxa replied. She had not gone back to bed, then. She was waiting for him. "We had word of Twitchtip's death. They had her imprisoned in a pit until recently. He is greatly upset."

There was a moment of silence while Howard absorbed the news. "So should we all be. Only Gregor's grief should not be mixed with shame, as should ours," said Howard.

He had not attempted to save Twitchtip from the whirlpool at first but had taken excellent care of her afterward. "She did us all a great service and what poor treatment we gave her in return."

Howard opened the curtain to the rat room and came in. "I am sorry," he said. Gregor didn't reply. "Come. Sit up. You must have need of this." Howard helped him to a sitting position, administered a dose of painkiller, and gave him the rest of the bottle for later. He painted a new coat of medicine on Gregor's hip and calf stitches, and applied fresh bandages. Finally he examined his back. "Quite a bruise, but the bones are holding in place," he said as he wrapped the ribs again. Then he sat on the bed, elbows on his knees, digging the palms of his hands into his forehead, trying to find the right words. "Gregor, of all those Twitchtip knew in her life, I am sure she would wish you the least amount of grief," said Howard.

"You helped her, too. After the whirlpool. In the maze," said Gregor.

"Because you were right," said Howard. "You were the only one of us who looked past her fur and teeth and claws and saw who she really was. If we are ever to have peace, that will be the first step. The alternative is this." Howard waved a hand vaguely, somehow suggesting their current situation. "Slaughtering one another. Walling ourselves in with our dead. So pointless. All of it." He gingerly touched his eyes, bloodshot and swollen from fatigue. "You must rest your back if it is to heal."

"You need some rest, too, Howard," said Gregor.

"No. If you could see the hospital . . ." Howard looked down at his hands. They were shaking badly. "Only I begin to fear I will do more harm than good."

"Just for a few hours. Lie down. I promise I'll wake you," said Gregor.

Howard looked at him as if he couldn't quite process the words. "A few hours?"

"You *are* going to hurt somebody. Lie down." He stood up and pushed Howard back on the bed.

"Two hours. No more," said Howard.

In the time it took Gregor to pull the blanket up, Howard was asleep. Gregor came out into the code room. Everyone was up again, back at work. Boots came over and put her arms up. He couldn't lift her, with his back and all, so he sat down and pulled her onto his lap.

"Ow," said Boots. She pressed her hand to her nose. "Ow." This was the sign she had used for Twitchtip, to indicate the rat's hurt nose, when she was still too little to say her name. "She died."

"Yeah," said Gregor, thinking it had been better before Boots had understood about dying.

"You put her here," Boots said, patting his chest over his heart. Well, not exactly — she got the wrong side. But he knew she meant his heart.

"I'll put her there," Gregor confirmed. He caught Luxa's sad gaze. She had had her own connection with Twitchtip. They had protected each other in the maze for as long as they could.

Gregor set Boots back on her feet and went over to help

Luxa with the strips of code. "I truly believed her dead, Gregor," she whispered.

"I know," said Gregor. "I guess I must have, too. But I didn't deal with it. I had, like, this fantasy that she'd escaped. She was safe back in the Dead Land or something."

"She is safe now," Luxa said wanly.

"That's how it works down here," Gregor said. Nothing was really safe until it was dead. He looked at Ripred, thought about the rat's family, and wished he hadn't yelled at him. If anyone knew about being tortured in a pit it was Ripred, who had been left by the Bane to die in the Firelands, his teeth overgrowing until they'd locked in a grotesque fashion. Ripred had treated Twitchtip like he treated almost everybody else. Not great. But Ripred hadn't killed her and if she had lived, Gregor felt sure he would have made good on his promise to let her join his band of rats. Not that it mattered now.

A basket of new code rolls came in and Ripred put everybody, even those who had been translating the old stuff, on them. They had been working only a few minutes when Min began to click in distress. "Bad news, here be, bad news!" The cockroach was too agitated to read the message outright, so Luxa hurried to help her. She could translate the chicken scratch into letters and then break the code on sight now.

"When — diggers — reach — arena — launch — attack —" she read.

"What? Where?" asked Ripred, jumping to her side.

Luxa held up the strip of fabric so they could both see it.

"By the river," he read aloud.

"By the river," Luxa repeated. "No one can attack by the river. They would be torn to shreds in the rapids."

"Not anymore. Have you seen it lately? Since the earthquake?" said Gregor.

"No," said Luxa. She had been too ill to notice anything on their flight back from the Firelands.

"It's very low. They would have to swim down several hundred yards from the north beach, but they could do it," said Ripred.

"You have been in the war room. What defense have we in place at the docks?" asked Luxa.

"Nothing," said Ripred. "Nothing at all."

CHAPTER

20

Ripred began to pace. "All right. First priority. We split up the code team. If the rats should enter the palace, we can't have you all sitting in one bunch. I want Min, Reflex, and Luxa in the war room. Lizzie, Daedalus, and Heronian stay here. Shred every bit of evidence that we've broken the code. Gregor, Hazard, Boots, and Temp go to the prophecy room. Nerissa is there with a key. Lock yourselves in and don't open it until you've been told to."

"Why? I should be getting on my armor," said Gregor.

"You think you're in any condition for battle? Attack me," Ripred ordered.

Gregor's back screamed as he reached for his weapons. He managed to pull them from the belt but ended up dropping his dagger on the floor.

"You can't fight like that. Even if you could, we'd never

waste you in ordinary combat now. We need you to fight the Bane. But don't worry. I don't expect he'll be swimming down the river," said Ripred. "They've got him hidden in a cave more likely, with a team of spinners to keep his tail bandaged."

"I thought the spinners were neutral," Luxa said, eyeing Reflex.

"Neutral meaning they help both sides so when the war ends they've aided the victor," said Ripred. "They're helping you, aren't they? Now move out!"

Gregor retrieved his dagger and took a step toward the door. "No, wait. I want Lizzie with me."

"Really? You want Lizzie in the prophecy room with nothing to do but . . . read prophecies all day?" said Ripred pointedly.

Gregor knew what he meant. Ripred had taken great care to keep Lizzie from knowing about the real "Prophecy of Time" and what it predicted for Gregor. Everybody had. If she came to the prophecy room, she'd read the truth.

"I'll be okay in here, Gregor. Ripred's right. We have to split up," said Lizzie.

"If danger approaches, I will find a way to fly her to safety," Daedalus said. "I know of a window not far from here."

"All right," said Gregor. Maybe that was better, anyway. Maybe Daedalus could even find a way to fly her home. "How long will this take?"

"No telling. Better grab some blankets and one of those carts," said Ripred, nodding to a group of fresh food carts that had recently been wheeled in.

Lizzie piled a stack of blankets on Temp's back and Boots climbed on to ride. Gregor tried to push a cart, but he ended up having to let Hazard do it.

"I will come see you as soon as I can," said Luxa, giving Gregor's arm a farewell touch.

The group split up, according to Ripred's instructions, and Gregor led the way to the prophecy room. It was very slow going, especially with the cart. Gregor considered abandoning it, but he had no idea what they were in for.

Nerissa was waiting for them. She drew them into the prophecy room, closed the door, and locked it at once. The key disappeared in the pocket of her skirt. She'd made no provisions for eating or sleeping, but there was a stack of new torches by the wall.

"Why did Ripred want us in here?" Gregor asked her.

"It is one of the few rooms in the palace with a door. It will offer some protection," said Nerissa.

"Some," agreed Gregor. But not much. The door was made of thick wood. It would take time, but the rats could eventually claw through it. He estimated that diggers could take it out in less than a minute. At least there would be some warning. He wondered if that mattered much, though. If Gregor didn't heal up pretty quickly, who would defend them? Nerissa had probably never even held a sword. Hazard and Boots were little kids. Temp could fight and would fight if the going got rough. But he'd be no match for rat soldiers.

Gregor decided to put all of his energy into getting better.

Howard said he needed to rest, so he would rest. They fashioned the blankets into beds along the walls, and Gregor lay down. If he didn't move, the painkiller Howard had given him made him comfortable enough. He willed himself to ignore what was happening outside the door, and dozed off.

Hours passed and then became days. Temp amused Boots and Hazard. The three of them chattered away in Crawler while Gregor ate, took painkillers, and slept. No one came by to give them any word. Occasionally they would hear footsteps running down the hallway and voices shouting indistinct words. But nothing else. As Gregor's back improved, he became more and more anxious about what was transpiring in the palace. Had the rats attacked? Were the humans prepared? Why had no one updated them? He suggested that they open the door and just call out for information, but Nerissa adamantly refused.

"This is not your battle, Gregor," she said. "This is your time to wait."

Waiting, it turned out, was a lot tougher on Gregor than fighting. Nerissa tried to distract him by showing him different prophecies, telling him their histories. He learned a lot about Regalia's past, but not much about its present. "Come on, Nerissa, what's one little peek going to hurt?" he begged.

"Look at this poem, Gregor," said Nerissa. "It is by far my favorite. When all seems lost, I comfort myself with its words."

Gregor sighed and turned his eyes to a short poem on

the wall in the corner where Nerissa usually curled up.

> *On soft feet, by none detected,*
> *Dealing death, by most rejected,*
> *Killed by claw, since resurrected,*
> *Marked by X, two lines connected.*
> *Finally, they intersected,*
> *Two lines met, one unexpected.*

"That comforts you? Why?" asked Gregor. To him it was just more junk from Sandwich, whom he now had a very low opinion of.

"Read you the title?" asked Nerissa.

Gregor noticed the title for the first time. Above the poem were written the words:

THE PEACEMAKER

"Perfect. The Peacemaker," thought Gregor. What did Sandwich, the digger killer, know about making peace? "So you think a peacemaker's coming? When?" asked Gregor.

"No one knows. Perhaps tomorrow. Perhaps in a thousand years. But the peacemaker will come. Just as the warrior did," said Nerissa.

Something tugged at the back of Gregor's brain. The peacemaker. He'd heard it before. When? It came to him. A long time ago, when he had just arrived in Regalia for the second time, he'd been walking around the palace at night and overheard Solovet and Vikus arguing over whether or

235

not he was to be trained. Solovet had wanted him armed immediately, of course. "And the prophecy calls Gregor 'the warrior,' after all. Not the 'peacemaker,'" she had said.

"Well, it's not me, Nerissa. And I won't be around when whoever it is shows up. But I hope they do," said Gregor. "Now can we open that door?"

Nerissa shook her head. He couldn't wrestle the key away from her. Well, he probably could but he didn't want to. Maybe when Nerissa fell asleep he could slip the key from her pocket and just look out for a second. He had to find out what was going on. Besides, the room could really stand some fresh air. They'd been using an empty pot by the door for a toilet and the place smelled like a sewer.

While Gregor waited for Nerissa to sleep, he tried using his swords again. He was still sore, and there wasn't much room, but he could swing his blades. He figured he might be able to fight at about seventy-five percent, if it came to it, and that only made him feel more secure about his plan. Even if a couple of big old rats were sitting right outside the door waiting to pounce, he could take them.

By the time Nerissa had finally drifted off, Boots, Hazard, and Temp were asleep, too. This was just as well, because Gregor didn't really feel great about stealing the key. "Borrowing the key," he corrected himself. "And then I'll put it back before anyone knows it was gone." He crossed to Nerissa and carefully pulled the key out of her pocket. As quietly as he could, Gregor walked to the door and slid it in the keyhole. He was just about to turn it when he heard shouting. There were footsteps, scuffling, and a human cry. Then a tremendous blow hit the door, causing it to reverberate. Scraping, and then another blow followed by a rat claw that punctured the wood directly in front of Gregor's face. He automatically stepped back and pulled his blades. More shouts and footsteps. A gruesome gurgling sound from the rat. Blood seeping under the door. Silence.

Gregor turned and saw the others awake and looking at him in fear. He reached down, withdrew the key, and returned it to Nerissa without a word. She was nice enough not to say, "I told you so."

The seconds ticked by. So rats were definitely in the palace. Possibly right outside the door. There was a small opening, about the size of a peephole, left by the rat claw, but as there was no light in the hall, Gregor could see nothing. His anxiety grew with every passing minute. Rats were in the palace. They had found him. Had they found Lizzie? Luxa? What was going on? When would someone contact them? He could fight now. He should be fighting. But what if he left and the prophecy room was attacked again? That door wouldn't hold long. Who would protect Boots and Hazard and Temp and Nerissa?

Gregor's head jerked up as the claws scraped the door. He took careful aim and drove his sword right through the peephole.

"Well, at least you're useful again," he heard Ripred from behind the door. "Open up in there! The palace is secure!"

Nerissa unlocked the door to reveal Ripred, who was bloodstained but not visibly wounded.

Questions began pouring out of Gregor's mouth but Ripred cut him off. "Many are dead, but everyone of significance to you still breathes. We were able to defend the city thanks to your sister's breaking the Code of Claw. The rats have been driven away, but they will regroup and rally around the Bane. We need you in the war room now, boy." He turned to Nerissa. "I will send instructions for the rest of you later. Until then, sit tight."

Gregor followed Ripred through the halls where kids his age were loading dead humans, rats, and mice on stretchers and removing them. Sometimes it took six of them to carry a body. "They're too young to be doing that," he thought. Then he remembered what he and Luxa had been doing lately, and it seemed like a pretty tame job. Of course, he was different. He'd left any vestiges of childhood behind months ago. Hadn't he?

The war room was crowded with people and creatures, but Gregor's attention immediately went to Luxa. She must have been in battle. Although her clothes were clean she wore a fresh bandage on her forehead. Her cough was back, too.

"You shouldn't have fought," said Gregor, tucking in a stray edge of her bandage.

"This is my home," said Luxa. "How fares your back?"

"Good to go," said Gregor.

"Excellent," said Solovet. "We shall be leaving to pursue the gnawers shortly."

"I will send for Aurora," said Luxa.

"No, Luxa. You are unfit. And we need you here," said Solovet.

"You cannot ask me to stay behind," said Luxa. "Not after what has been done to Regalia."

"But stay you must," say Solovet.

Luxa cocked her head slightly. "Must I?" Gregor could feel a battle of wills coming on and felt guilty because he was on Solovet's side. He didn't want Luxa going after the rats for a number of reasons. She wasn't well; he wanted her somewhere safe; and, mostly, he didn't want her to see him die.

Ripred stepped between Luxa and Solovet. "Listen, Your Highness, it's Regalia we're thinking of. We're going out to finish this thing. But when it's over, your people will be desperate for guidance. Rats overran the council room and almost none survived save your grandparents, who are acknowledged to be powerful, but no longer trustworthy. It will be you the Regalians expect to lead them."

"He speaks the truth, Luxa," said Solovet. "With the demise of the council, power will shift to you."

"I am not yet of age," said Luxa. "You know I cannot officially lead."

"It doesn't matter. Not in times like these. Not after the courage and brains you've demonstrated recently. Trust me, it will be you. If they followed you into this war they will follow you out of it. Now can you see how you are too dear to risk in battle?" asked Ripred.

He didn't sound like he was flattering her, just laying it out on the table, equal to equal.

Luxa stared at Ripred, considering his question. Then

she dropped her eyes to the ground. "Yes, I do see. I will remain here."

Ripred and Solovet exchanged a pleased look and were turning back to the business of war when Gregor saw the ghost of a smile playing on the corners of Luxa's mouth. "She's lying," he said. Disbelief, hurt, and then rage washed in rapid succession over Luxa's face at his words.

"Why do you say this?" asked Solovet.

"Because I know her. If you want her to stay . . ." Gregor had to swallow hard before he could get the next words out. "Lock her in the dungeon."

CHAPTER
21

Solovet studied Luxa a moment and then gestured to a pair of guards. "Do so. Confine her flier, as well."

Gregor forced himself to watch as they seized her and carried her, screaming, down the hall. She was beating at the guards but her words were for Gregor, full of hatred at his disloyalty. The things she said cut right through him. That she should never have trusted him. That he was as bad as Henry had been. And while it was not included in her rant, Gregor felt sure that he had lost all of the affection she had ever felt for him. His feelings, on the other hand, had only intensified when he betrayed her. So he watched until the guards turned the corner at the end of the hall, taking her out of his life forever. Even the sight of Luxa despising him was precious to him now.

When she was gone, his hand fumbled in his back pocket

to make sure he still had the photograph they'd taken in the museum. It was there. He didn't pull it out. But later, in some tunnel or cave, while the others slept, he would spend some time with it. Tell the picture of Luxa what he would never have the chance to explain to her in person.

"It was a wise move, Gregor. She will always hate you for it, but with time, she will understand its necessity," said Solovet briskly. She went back to study the map on the wall.

Somehow having Solovet's approval didn't make Gregor feel any better. He disliked her so much. And she thought things like turning the plague into a weapon and setting rats on fire were wise moves. He would much rather have had her condemn him.

Vikus came up and patted his arm. Gregor hadn't even known the old man was in the room. "She will not always hate you. If she still cares for Henry, who put her life in jeopardy, will she not care for you who tried to save it?"

"I doubt she sees it that way," said Gregor. "It's done. Let's not talk about it."

"We shall depart from the river in one hour. Gregor, you must go to the armory to prepare," Solovet said.

One hour? Was that all that was left? "I'll dress on the trip. I want to be with my sisters," said Gregor.

"They will be accompanying us," said Solovet. "Lizzie still may have use as a code-breaker. Boots will rally the crawlers. Rest assured, I shall keep them at a good distance from the battle."

There was no arguing with Solovet. And her reasons for taking his sisters were valid. Still . . .

"They'll be safe," Ripred said. "Count on it. One rager to another."

When Gregor went to the armory, food had been brought for him. After he ate, Miravet sent him to a nearby bathroom to bathe. Everything had a feeling of finality to it. Last hot meal, last bath, last set of clothes. As he was dressing, Howard came in to treat his wounds. "You look a lot better," said Gregor.

"Because I slept for two straight days," said Howard.

"Oh, man! I was supposed to wake you. Sorry, Ripred sent me down to the prophecy room and I totally forgot," said Gregor.

"Do not trouble yourself. I am practically the only coherent person in the hospital. There should be at least one," said Howard. "Your wounds are much improved." He removed the stitches from Gregor's calf, although he left the ones on his hip, and put on fresh bandages. Then he refilled Gregor's bottle of painkiller. "Well, then," said Howard, rising. "I must get back."

"Last time I'll see Howard," Gregor thought. He stood up and hugged him good-bye. "You'll keep an eye on Luxa, right?"

"As if she were my own sister," Howard said. "Fly you high, Gregor."

"Fly you high," said Gregor. He wished he could have said more. About how grateful he was to Howard for all he'd done, about how if he'd had a big brother, he would have wanted him to be just like Howard. Someone who was kind and brave and not afraid to say he cared about things

243

or to admit he'd been wrong. But now Luxa would have Howard for a brother, and that was more important.

Gregor's armor had been retrieved from the balcony, cleaned, and repaired. Miravet had made some adjustments to make it fit more comfortably over his injuries. When he was suited up, a little girl hurried in with the pink backpack Gregor had taken on his last trip to the Firelands. He had tossed it somewhere in the hospital, forgetting about it in his worry for Luxa. It contained the flashlight York had returned to him, batteries, duct tape, water bottles, Lizzie's cookies, and the travel chessboard. "Howard bid me bring you this," said the little girl. "He thought you might need it."

"Tell him 'thanks.' It will be a big help," said Gregor. The girl gave him a shy smile and ran off.

When Gregor arrived at the dock on the river, he found a solemn ritual going on. The Underlanders were doing funeral rites for the dead. Each human, bat, or mouse body was placed on a small raft of some kind of woven plant fiber. A torch was inserted in a holder at their shoulder. A woman softly chanted some words Gregor couldn't catch. Then the raft was set in the river and released. Although it was not as fierce as it had been before the earthquake, the current was still strong enough to quickly carry the rafts away. As far as he could see down the river tunnel, torches reflected off of the water.

So this was how they buried their dead. Sent them on a lit raft down the river to the Waterway, the giant sea, where they would be swallowed up by the waves. It made sense.

There was little earth to bury them in. Gregor had seen what he would call soil only in the jungle and in the farmlands. Stones might work, but it would have to be somewhere outside of the city. You could burn the corpses, if there were only a couple, but hundreds? The air would be thick with smoke. There were no strong winds here, like there were in the Firelands, to blow it away.

The six kids he had seen earlier hauled in a stretcher with a dead rat. It was dumped into the river with no ceremony.

Ares landed on the dock next to him. "Lot of dead," said Gregor.

"Yes," said Ares. "Hundreds have made this journey already."

"How did you fight the rats?" Gregor asked. He wanted to know what had happened while he was in the prophecy room.

"When word came of the invasion, the gnawers were just entering the water from the tunnel north of here. We waited until they were swimming and attacked from the air. It was very difficult for them to swim and defend themselves, but they had great numbers. Many were destroyed but some made it into the palace. A group raided the hospital, killing the patients. Others swarmed through the halls, fighting where they met resistance. Eventually they were driven back out to river, and those who could swam for safety," said Ares.

"No Bane?" asked Gregor.

"No Bane. He has retreated toward his own land. The others will find him and regroup their army," said Ares.

It took Gregor a moment to recognize the mouse they placed on the next raft. He looked smaller, more vulnerable, dead. "Is that Cartesian?"

"He died defending the nursery," said Ares. "But the pups are safe."

Gregor felt sadness well up in him. He hadn't known the mouse well, but they had traveled together. Witnessed the nibblers dying at the volcano. Played hide-and-seek with Boots and the mouse pups. He went over and patted the mouse's soft fur before they lowered his body into the water. Ripred had said, "Everyone of significance to you still breathes." By that he must have meant Gregor's family and Luxa. But there were many others who Gregor cared about. Who knew if they were alive or dead?

The rest of the traveling party arrived. Lizzie, Hazard, and Boots were blindfolded and being carried by guards. "No point in giving them nightmares," said Ripred. Gregor thought of the grisly halls and was glad of the precaution.

Ares was best suited to carrying Ripred, so Gregor, his sisters, and Temp joined Vikus on his big gray bat, Euripedes. Solovet was beside them on her bat, Ajax.

"Greetings, Pincess," Gregor heard Boots say behind him. He turned around and saw her peeking at Nike from under her blindfold.

"Greetings, Pincess," said Nike, lifting her black-and-white-striped wings.

"We are both Pincesses," Boots said with a laugh.

Gregor pulled the blindfold down over her eyes. "Stay in there, you." He turned to Nike. "Good to see you. You coming with us?"

"I am carrying some of the code team," said Nike. Reflex and Heronian climbed on her back. "Daedalus and Min remain here."

"Isn't their job done now?" asked Gregor.

"There's still plenty of information to decipher," Ripred said. "And the code could unexpectedly change."

As they lifted off, Gregor realized there were so many friends he hadn't said good-bye to. Mareth, Dulcet, Nerissa, Aurora — well, forget Aurora, she was locked in the dungeon with Luxa, and probably cursing him, too. Maybe it was just as well. Even that one good-bye with Howard had drained him. And there were still more painful ones in the hours ahead. He thought his friends would understand.

They flew down the tunnel and out over the Waterway. It twinkled with the flames of the torches on the rafts of the dead. About fifty soldiers on fliers joined them, and there were several mice traveling as well. "Are the mice coming to fight?" Gregor asked Vikus.

"Not these. They have a special purpose. The rats are still receiving information from their spies in the area. We have chosen four lines of communication to sabotage. We will disable a rat who transmits the code, replace it with a nibbler, and feed false information to the rats," said Vikus. Gregor saw a group of soldiers and a nibbler peel off and disappear into the dark. "There goes the first team now."

"What sort of information will you give the rats?" Gregor asked.

"Lies. We will tell them that our losses are higher than

expected, that no force can be assembled to follow them, that you have died due to injuries inflicted by the Bane," said Vikus. "Since the rats do not know we have broken the Code of Claw, they will take these things as truth."

"That's why Ripred wanted to keep it a secret," said Gregor.

"It is the most powerful weapon we have. The difference between losing and winning the war," said Vikus. "The rats will believe they are safe for the moment. But soon we will attack them on the Plain of Tartarus, where they now gather."

"A surprise attack," said Gregor.

"When they are asleep, with no plan for counterattack," said Vikus. "It is our best hope. Regalia still teeters on the brink of destruction. The diggers have created paths to our arena and possibly elsewhere. We destroyed the ones we could find but who knows how many exist? If the Bane lives and the rats attack again, I do not think we can hold the city."

By the time they broke for a rest at the mouth of a tunnel, their party was somewhat diminished. All of the nibbler code transmitters and their guards had left them. The soldiers had stopped at a landing a few miles back. Solovet had not been on the ground more than five minutes when she announced she was going off, too.

"Where?" asked Gregor.

"The spinners are still conflicted about whom they choose to side with. They require my personal guarantee of their safety when the war ends," said Solovet.

"I will rejoin you in two days' time on the Plain of Tartarus. If you battle before then, do not forget that your weakness is your left side."

And then she took off on Ajax with Gregor's old bodyguards, Horatio and Marcus, flanking her on their bats. It was just like her to up and go with nothing more than a combat tip.

It turned out they were making camp for a while. Ripred and Vikus had their heads together, poring over maps. Lizzie, Reflex, and Heronian were busy decoding messages that came in on bats. Nike, Ares, and the two remaining guards and their bats took turns patrolling the area. Boots, Temp, and Hazard were playing one of their games in Crawler.

Gregor was left to his own devices. He went deeper into the tunnel and practiced with his sword and dagger. His back was still sore, but he didn't think he would even notice it in battle. It felt good to use his muscles. When he was warmed up, he added in his echolocation, running through the tunnel in darkness and then striking points on the walls and ceiling. It was very freeing not to be constantly worried about his batteries running out.

After about a half hour he was good and loose. He decided to try to get Ripred to spar with him for a while. Maybe he could use a break from those maps. But when Gregor reached the mouth of the tunnel, no one was doing anything. All of the activity had stopped.

"What's going on?" asked Gregor.

"We just intercepted a message. The rats know of Solovet's

trip to the spinners. They mean to ambush and kill her," said Ripred.

"How do they know?" Gregor asked. "Did they spot us?"

"No. One of the spinners must have leaked the information. Perhaps a lowly soldier, perhaps the queen herself. Their loyalties are very divided," said Vikus. He looked calm, but his skin had a strange gray cast.

"We'll go after her. Ares and me. We can overtake them. We've got, like, fifty soldiers with us and —" Gregor began.

"No, boy. We can't," said Ripred.

"But she's got next to zero backup. You're just letting her fly to her death?" said Gregor.

"Yes. We are. We must," said Vikus, as if trying to convince himself.

"Okay, I don't know what's going on. I mean, I don't even like Solovet, but I'm not going to just sit here and let her die!" said Gregor.

"You have to, Gregor!" Lizzie said. "Don't you see? If we rescue her they'll know we've broken the code."

"What?" asked Gregor.

"The only way we could have read the message is if we had broken the code. If they find that out, there will be no surprise attack, because they will instantly change their rendezvous point. All of the lies we are planting will be suspect. And they will issue a new code immediately that may take weeks to break," said Ripred.

"But you found out about the rats attacking from the river and you acted on that," said Gregor.

"That was simple to explain. They were so close; we had

only to send some scouts up the river and pretend to discover them. This is entirely different," said Ripred.

"She would not want us to try to save her," Vikus said hoarsely. "Not at this price."

"But . . . maybe we could . . . maybe we could make it look like we were just going after her, anyway," Gregor suggested. "That wouldn't be suspicious."

"Wouldn't it? If she had wanted to travel with an army she would have traveled with an army. One showing up at the eleventh hour will point directly to the breaking of the Code of Claw," said Ripred.

Gregor was still not quite ready to accept this. "There must be something we can do."

"There is," Ripred said. "We can sit here and wait."

CHAPTER

22

So Gregor sat and waited as the seconds went by. Not with the urgent ticks he had heard so often since the war began, but with slow deliberate ones that had long silences between them.

The code team continued decrypting messages. They couldn't afford to be idle no matter what the circumstances. Boots, who didn't really know what was going on, fell asleep on a pile of blankets. Temp and Hazard resumed their discussion in whispers. But Gregor, Ripred, and Vikus seemed suspended in time as they waited for word of the ambush.

"Maybe they missed them," thought Gregor. "Or there was a fight and Solovet, Marcus, and Horatio were able to hold their own and escape." Why not? They were on bats and were excellent soldiers. But whenever Gregor sneaked a glance at Vikus's ashen face, he felt that this would not be the case. He wished he hadn't said that thing about not liking Solovet. He didn't, though. How could he after her involvement with the plague and her throwing him in the dungeon, and Ripred's warning that she would never let his family go? In a way if she died it would probably be easier for Ripred to get his family home. Of course, if what they had said about Luxa being in power after the war was true, Gregor was sure she would send his family home, no matter what her grandmother said. Wouldn't she? He was glad he still had Ripred's promise as a backup.

Solovet. No, he could not pretend he liked her. Still, there had been moments along the way when she had treated him decently enough. When he'd landed in Regalia she'd been the first person to reach out and touch him, taking his hands in a gesture of welcome that had felt genuine. She had protected him by insisting he be trained, and now he knew that if she hadn't he would be dead. And she'd given him her own dagger. He fingered the hilt guiltily, thinking of how she was under attack without it. At least he had tried to go after her, despite his feelings for her. He hoped whoever broke the news to Luxa would mention that. Maybe she wouldn't hate him quite so much.

After a couple of hours, Heronian said quietly, "We have received word. All three humans and their fliers were killed in the ambush."

Ripred ran a paw over the diagonal scar on his face. "Well, I have this to remember her by."

So Solovet had given Ripred that scar. When? During a

war between the humans and the rats? During a sparring match they'd had for fun? Gregor thought about how Solovet had left all kinds of scars, on rats, on her family, on the Underlanders' frail attempts at peace.

Ripred turned to Vikus. "That's the way she always said she wanted to go."

"Fighting." Vikus's lips formed the word but no sound came out.

"Yes, fighting. Not on some sickbed but with her sword in her hand," said Ripred.

Gregor tried to think of something consoling to say to Vikus, but he was never good at this stuff. Howard was, Luxa was, but all of the words he came up with seemed trite and empty. It was even more difficult because while he knew Vikus must have loved Solovet — they'd probably been married for, like, forty years or something — he also knew they had fought a lot. Their ideas on how to handle problems were totally different: Solovet calling for force, Vikus for working things out. When he discovered his wife's role in the plague, Vikus had been crushed. But he must have loved her, because he was utterly stricken now.

Hazard came over and kneeled next to Vikus, slipping his hand into his grandfather's. Vikus gave it a squeeze but didn't say anything.

"Sorry about your grandma, Hazard," Gregor said. He could manage that. "You okay?"

"Yes. In truth, I do not know how to feel. Solovet rarely spoke to me. I don't think she cared for me. Perhaps it was because she and my father hated each other so much," said Hazard with his usual frankness.

The words were simple and without malice, but their effect on Vikus was immediate and devastating. Solovet and Hamnet. All of the awful family history between his wife and his son — the tragedy at the Garden of Hesperides, Hamnet's mad flight from Regalia, the anger that passed between them in the jungle, losing Hamnet not once but twice.

Vikus made a strange sound in his throat. His hand went toward his cheek, then fell to his side. "Vikus? You all right there?" Ripred asked. Vikus tried to answer but the words that came out of his mouth were thick and garbled. "Doctor!" Ripred called at once. "Get a doctor in here!"

Ripred continued to talk to Vikus, pushing his nose right up into his face, urging him to stay calm. In less than a minute a doctor had flown in, taken one look at Vikus, dumped something down his throat, and had him loaded onto a bat.

Hazard hung on the doctor's sleeve. "What's wrong with my grandfather?"

"He is having an attack. We must get him back to Regalia," said the doctor.

"Is he going to be okay?" asked Gregor. His voice sounded almost as young as Hazard's. Half of Vikus's face had gone slack and Gregor realized he couldn't move it. It was scary to see him like that. Gregor didn't want Vikus to leave him. He didn't want to lose the one Underlander whom he knew had always had his best interest at heart.

"We will do all we can," said the doctor, and the bat took off.

"A stroke," said Ripred. "I'm surprised it didn't happen sooner. This last year has been murder on him."

"Was it what I said? About my father?" Hazard asked worriedly.

"Goodness, no. It would have happened with or with-out your words. Now you go back and, I don't know, see if you can't help with the code, okay?" said Ripred. Hazard obeyed. When he was out of earshot, Ripred whispered to Gregor, "Probably not the best time to have brought up all that business with Hamnet. But he would have been thinking about it, anyway."

"People recover from strokes, though. Right?" Gregor asked.

"Some do. With time," said Ripred. He didn't seem to want to continue the conversation.

The cave seemed very vacant without Solovet and Vikus. "Now what?" said Gregor.

"Now I need a human who can command. Mareth's back in Regalia. . . ." said Ripred. He sent for Perdita. When she arrived, he got right to the point. "Solovet's dead. Vikus is disabled. You just became the acting head of your army."

Perdita looked shocked and then conflicted. "There are others with more seniority."

"I don't want them. I want you," said Ripred. "I need someone we can all trust."

Ripred began to go over the battle plan with Perdita,

leaving Gregor to deal with the double tragedy on his own. First Solovet, then Vikus. Although Vikus might recover. If he didn't . . . Gregor's thoughts turned to Luxa again. He slipped the photo of them in the museum from his pocket and tried to think of happier times, but it was no good. He kept visualizing her face at the moment he had told them to lock her in the dungeon. He couldn't stand that being the last thing between them. He got a strip of code and asked Lizzie for a marker. She was writing with a quill and ink. "The markers all dried out," she said. She dug a red one out of her backpack. "You might get a few more letters out of this one. If you get the tip wet."

Gregor spat in the cap of the marker, closed it, and let it sit a minute. He would have to make his note short. He thought about writing it in the Code of Claw, but if the rats intercepted it, they would know it was broken. He settled on using the marks from the Tree of Transmission. That would make it seem a little more private somehow. After a couple of minutes he opened the marker and tested it. The results were faint but legible. He wrote:

"Go ahead," he thought. "Write it. You'll be dead before she even reads it. And anyway, it's true."

The last few words were too hard to read. Gregor nicked his index finger on his sword and wrote over them with a thin, smeary line of blood. There.

It wasn't much of a letter. He felt stingy using just thirteen words. But even if he'd had boxes of markers, what more would he have said? Maybe explained better why one of them had to live. So both of them could. So one of them

257

would remember the other as they went through life. That it wasn't going to be him, so it had to be her. And he had to be able to think of her growing up and doing things and someday being happy if he was going to be brave enough for his last moments with the Bane.

Luxa was smart. She'd figure out what he meant. He hoped.

Gregor rolled up the message and gave it to Lizzie to deliver to Luxa in Regalia.

"Why don't you give it to her yourself?" asked Lizzie.

"Because she's really mad at me right now," said Gregor. "She'll read it, though, if she thinks it's from you. Besides, you'll probably go back before I do." Lizzie agreed to take it. Gregor wondered if Lizzie would hate him, too, when she found out he'd been lying to her all along about the prophecy.

Gregor announced he was going to practice some more and went back into the tunnel. Then he just lay down on the stone floor with his head propped against a rock. He didn't feel like sword fighting, so he turned off his flashlight and clicked. His echolocation ability was improving by leaps and bounds. He could see so much — the jagged edges of the ceiling, individual pebbles on the floor, even small details in the rough surface of the walls. He experimented using different sounds — coughing, humming, whistling. In a quiet moment, he realized that even the sound of his own breathing could send images back to him. He felt comforted, because that meant as long as he was alive he would be able to see.

His heart rate slowed and he dozed, slipping in and out of sleep, alternating between dreams and images of the tunnel. Fear crept into his dreams. He was lying helplessly on his back, when a rat appeared over him, then another, then he was surrounded by their faces. Gregor shook his head to awaken only to find he hadn't truly been asleep. The rats were still looming over him, and they were real.

Without even attempting to rise, Gregor yanked his sword from his belt and sliced the air over his body to protect it. The rats fell back, giving him a chance to spring to his feet. By this time his dagger was out and he was about to start killing, when the voice reached his brain: "Stop, Overlander!"

Gregor hesitated. He knew the rat's voice. It was higher-pitched than Ripred's rough growl. Female. But not Twirltongue's silver tones that had so easily led him astray. Twitchtip? No, she was dead. And this voice didn't belong on his voyage across the Waterway, or in the impossible twists and turns of the rat's maze. It came with memories of jungle heat and sweat and the smell of sweet deadly blossoms. He clicked and tried to focus in on the speaker. "Lapblood?"

"Yes, it's me. Put away your sword. We're not here to fight you," said Lapblood.

Gregor clicked again. The small pack of rats was hanging back, none of them in attack position. He slowly slid his blades back in his belt. Rat or no rat, he didn't think Lapblood would lie to him. Not after what they had been through together. Besides, if the rats had been after his blood, they'd have taken him on the ground. "What are you doing here?"

"We've come to join with Ripred against the Bane," said Lapblood. "I'm supposed to meet him now for our battle orders."

"For real? How many of you are there?" said Gregor. Echolocation was great, but he wanted to use his eyes again. He snapped on his flashlight, causing the rats to squint in the sudden brightness. "Sorry." He pointed the beam to the floor.

"There are a dozen of us here in the tunnel. But hundreds wait in the caves below," said Lapblood.

"Hundreds?" Gregor said. He knew Ripred had a small band of rats loyal to him in the Dead Land, but where had hundreds come from?

"Did you think every rat wanted the Bane for their leader?" asked Lapblood. "That we would willingly live under his rule?"

"Pretty much," admitted Gregor. "I mean, except for Ripred, we haven't seen a whole lot of resistance from you guys."

"Well, you're wrong," retorted Lapblood. "Many of us have no use for that bloodthirsty, twisted creature or the connivance of those who guide him."

"That's good to hear," said Gregor. He noticed two smaller rats crouched at Lapblood's side. They were too big to be called pups, but they weren't fully grown, either. "Are they . . . ?" He didn't want to say the names in case he was wrong. "Who are they?"

"Flyfur and Sixclaw. My children," said Lapblood.

The children she had gone to the jungle to save by finding the cure to the plague. Mange's children, too, then, although he had never lived to see them again. He'd been ensnared and eaten by giant carnivorous plants. But his pups had lived. Gregor peered closely at them. They stared back, scared but tough. "You look a lot like your dad," he said, and was surprised by the emotion in his voice, by how moved and glad he was that they'd survived.

"And your mother?" asked Lapblood.

It seemed like an eternity since anyone had asked him that. People avoided the topic of his mother's health in general, as if bringing it up was just a painful reminder of her sickness. But Lapblood knew better. "She's okay, I think. I mean, she was real sick from the plague, but she got better. Only last time I saw her she had pneumonia and they evacuated her to the Fount. It turned out to be a good thing, because the hospital at Regalia was so packed, but I haven't had any news of her since. Ripred says he'll get her home for me. After the war. Since I can't. Ripred says he will." Gregor realized he was babbling and pulled himself together. "Thanks for asking."

Gregor had a sudden impulse to touch Lapblood, to place his hand on her head and feel that silky fur again. But he knew that would seem weird, if not downright threatening, to the other rats. So he just headed up the tunnel. "Come on. Ripred's up here."

Lapblood followed him while the rest of the rats remained deep in the tunnel. This was just as well. Gregor was afraid the arrival of even one rat might start a panic attack in Lizzie. But she took her cue from Ripred, and he was pleased to see Lapblood.

"Good. You made it. How many do we have?" he asked her right off.

"At least seven hundred. Perhaps as many as a thousand," said Lapblood.

Ripred raised his eyebrows, a bit impressed. "That many? You've been busy."

"Where do you want us?" asked Lapblood. Ripred quickly gave her a time, position, and instructions. She nodded, turned to Gregor, and said, "Thank you for what you did in the jungle."

Gregor had saved her life, but Lapblood had saved Boots. "You, too."

Lapblood touched her muzzle to his wrist, then she was gone.

"Just another good-bye," thought Gregor. Another last time. But it was nothing compared to the ones he would have to face in the next couple of days.

Ripred ordered them all to bed. Gregor's slumber was deep and dreamless. He was awakened by Ripred's nose nudging his shoulder. Gregor rubbed his eyes and looked around. No one else was up. "Over here," the rat whispered, and Gregor followed him to the far end of the cave. "This is the day," Ripred said.

"The day I die," Gregor thought. But he only said, "So soon?"

"Yes. We have to move fast. But there's something I want

to say to you in private," said Ripred. "It's regarding a certain line in 'The Prophecy of Time.'"

The warrior's death. "Here it comes," thought Gregor. He braced himself for the good-bye, but the rat's next words were something entirely unexpected.

"The thing is . . ." said Ripred. He glanced around to make sure everyone else was still sleeping. "The thing is, I don't believe in Sandwich's prophecies."

CHAPTER

23

Gregor was floored. "What? But you . . . always do what they say."

"No, I don't. If I really believed in them, would I have run after the Bane and tried to kill him myself? It would have been pointless. I pretend like I believe in them, even try to convince myself I do for short periods, because everybody else down here does. So if you want to make them do something, it has to fit the prophecies, you see?" said the rat.

"Not really," said Gregor. What was Ripred saying?

"Look, there are hundreds of prophecies predicting all kinds of things. If you wait around long enough, numerous events that resemble each and every one of them are bound to come up. Take that plague. We've had loads of plagues down here. Might have been interpreted to fit any of them," said Ripred.

"But you're always trying to interpret them," Gregor said. "*I have to*. If I don't come up with some reasonable interpretation of them first, someone else comes up with a foolish one," said Ripred. "And then it's a whole lot of extra work changing everyone's minds."

"What about in the jungle? After the ants destroyed the starshade and we had all given up," Gregor protested.

"I really thought Neveeve might have been right about the starshade being the cure. When it was gone, you were all ready to start digging your graves. The idea that we might have misinterpreted the prophecy was the only way to get you moving. I jumped on it. And we kept thinking. And we found the cure. The alternative was to let everyone sit there boo-hooing until they died," said Ripred.

Gregor frowned. "What about the warrior stuff? And me leaping?"

"Maybe you only leaped because that prophecy suggested that was the thing to do," said Ripred. "Maybe that children's song about killing the mice really only was a children's song. Maybe Sandwich was a madman who locked himself up and wrote crazy poems on the wall. And maybe — you're not going to die."

Not going to die? The words hit Gregor like a truck. Could it be possible? No, everyone knew he was going to die. He would prove it to Ripred. Gregor tried hard to think of one incident that could not be contested. "But . . . how about Nerissa? When she was a little girl, she told Hamnet he would be in the jungle with a hisser and a kid ten years later."

"I admit that one's hard to explain. Unless Hamnet sought out a hisser because of her suggestion and then didn't say no when Hazard's mother appeared in his life. Or it could be a strange coincidence. They do happen. Anyway, Nerissa is not Sandwich, and it's him we're talking about," said Ripred. "'The Prophecy of Time.' Look how easily we bent it to replace Boots with Lizzie. What does it really call for? A war? We have those all the time. A code? Every new war has a new code. The death of a warrior? Well, if we can swap princesses so easily, why not warriors? Thousands will be dead at the end of this mess. But I'm not convinced you will be. One rager to another, I think you can beat the Bane. I think you're better than he is. And I don't think any mumbo jumbo of Sandwich's can change that. Unless you let it. So you fight, Gregor the Overlander. And don't you let your guard down for a second because you think anything's inevitable!"

Gregor's head was spinning with this new way of thinking. That they were really fulfilling Sandwich's prophecies on their own. Basing decisions on what his words said. He gave an incredulous laugh. "I thought you were going to tell me good-bye."

"No such luck," snorted Ripred. "But keep this under your hat. If everyone finds out what I really believe, I'll lose what little credibility I have. Come on, let's wake up the others. It's going to be a long day."

Gregor went over and blew raspberries on Boots's stomach, so she woke up giggling. "Stop! I need more sleeping!" she said, and pretended to go back to sleep three times to get more wake-up raspberries. As Gregor hauled her over to eat breakfast, Boots poked him in the chest. "You seem like you again," she said.

"I seem like me again?" Gregor asked. Then he knew what she meant. He hadn't really teased Boots in a while. Hardly ever smiled even. But Ripred's words had given him something he'd abandoned since he'd first read "The Prophecy of Time." Hope. That he might live. That Sandwich was wrong.

He wondered if the rat was lying to make him fight his best. But he didn't think so. Ripred's not believing in the prophecies explained certain things. Not just why he had tried to kill the Bane himself but how easily he had tossed out Boots for Lizzie, and how he had always been so sarcastic about Nerissa's ability to see the future. Probably didn't want her coming up with a whole new room of prophecies to control people. Not that Ripred didn't use the prophecies to his advantage. He had manipulated Gregor repeatedly with them. Even used the warrior's death to get Gregor to let Lizzie stay. But the rat was always doing whatever it took to get his way.

Gregor realized something else, too. He didn't want to believe in the prophecies, either. Not just because they forecast his death but because he loathed Sandwich. Ever since he had learned about how he had murdered the diggers for the land that was now Regalia, Gregor had wanted to distance himself from the man. To discredit him. To reject his guidance. Now Ripred had given him a way. "It's just me and the Bane. And I'm fighting him because he killed all of those innocent mice and people, and I have to stop him. Not because Sandwich says so but because I say so. And Ripred's right. I'm better than the Bane. And I can do it," he thought.

So Gregor was able to get through the moment he had dreaded above all others: saying good-bye to his sisters. He fixed up the pink backpack, refilling the water bottles and putting fresh batteries in his one remaining flashlight, and gave it to them to keep.

"Won't you need the flashlight in battle?" Lizzie asked with concern.

"I cracked that echolocation thing," Gregor whispered in her ear, and her eyes widened in surprise.

"Wow. Will you teach me?" she asked.

"You bet," said Gregor. "And look here." He pulled out the travel chessboard.

"I found it in the museum. It's yours."

"For keeps?" asked Lizzie. "Jedidiah has a chessboard, but not a magnetic one."

"Yeah. He's going to be real jealous," said Gregor.

Boots tried to poke her nose in the backpack. "Where's my present?"

"Your present?" asked Gregor. He dug out the rest of Mrs. Cormaci's oatmeal raisin cookies, still wrapped in foil. "You get the cookies."

"Oh!" said Boots. "All for me?"

"Well, you'd better share at least one with Ripred," said Gregor.

Boots shared with everyone, even tucking two cookies in

Gregor's pocket so that he and Ares could have a snack later. Then it was time to go. Gregor pulled both of his sisters into his arms and held them tight. "You guys be good, okay?"

"Okay," said Lizzie.

"I am good," said Boots.

"I know. I love you. See you soon," said Gregor.

"See you soon," they both echoed.

Ripred had already given Ares directions to their position at the Plain of Tartarus. "Remember, Gregor, they think you're dead. So don't let them see you until the Bane appears."

"Got it," Gregor said.

"All right. Fly you high, you two," said Ripred.

"Run like the river, Ripred," said Gregor. And then Ares took off. They flew through the darkness that was no longer darkness to Gregor. While clicks and coughs produced brighter results, he concentrated on using his breathing to see. The images were not quite as clear but they were continuous, since he was either inhaling or exhaling as a matter of course. And the longer he relied on the breathing, the more distinct his surroundings became. In about an hour they had reached their destination. Ares landed on the floor of a small tunnel just before a wall made of a pile of large rocks. Beyond it, Gregor sensed emptiness. He dismounted cautiously and made his way to the wall. Hanging his head over, he let out a deep breath. His mind registered a cavern so vast he could not find the other end of it. The walls sloped up at a steep angle. Far below him, the floor was occupied by the single largest gathering of rats Gregor had ever encountered. There must have been well over a thousand, sleeping, fidgeting, nursing their wounds. Ordinarily Gregor would have been more concerned with them catching his scent. But the air was heavy with the smell of rotten eggs, which he remembered from his first journey, when Ripred had dragged them all through dripping caves, soaking them in sulfurous liquid to conceal their natural odor. This time, the smell seemed to be coming from a mist that rose out of a foul river winding its way along the side of the cavern. Even at this distance, Gregor was pretty sure that there was nothing alive in that water.

"So this is the Plain of Tartarus?" Gregor whispered to Ares.

"Yes. You can see it?" the bat whispered back.

"Yeah. Ripred finally knocked echolocation into my head," said Gregor. "I have to admit, it's cool. You see the Bane anywhere?"

"No. He must be nearby, though. He is the reason they have come here," said Ares.

They settled themselves down to wait. Gregor passed Ares a cookie and ate the other. If he did end up dead, he was glad the last taste in his mouth came from Mrs. Cormaci's kitchen. But he was no longer so resigned to dying. Not after what Ripred had said. Then it occurred to him that he was not alone; he was only half of a team, and it might be important for Ares to know Ripred's thoughts as well.

"Hey, Ares, can you keep a secret?" said Gregor.

"I would say it is one of my few talents," said Ares.

"Ripred doesn't believe in the prophecies. He thinks Sandwich was a crazy fool, and that we're all running around trying to make what he said come true," said Gregor.

Ares was silent for a while. "I would be a liar if I said similar thoughts had not crossed my own mind," said the bat.

"Why didn't you say so?" asked Gregor. Were there other Underlanders who had their doubts?

"Because everyone treats his words with such reverence. But who was he, really? Not a kind or wise man. His words are full of doom and only terrorize us into killing one another," said Ares.

"You know, when I first got down here, I didn't believe in his stuff at all. Then, as things happened, it seemed like it was coming true. But what if we did just make Sandwich's words fit? Take 'The Prophecy of Gray.' That whole thing about me leaping and then Henry dying. I could have died and the prophecy would have still made sense. So maybe the only really remarkable thing that happened that day . . . was that you decided to save my life," said Gregor.

"I was not thinking of Sandwich's words. I was thinking of what was right," said Ares. He crunched down on his cookie. "Do you know, when a prophecy does not fulfill itself in a coherent manner, we always say it was not yet its time. And we blame ourselves for not realizing it."

"I'm beginning to think the main thing we ought to be blaming ourselves for is letting Sandwich boss us around

271

instead of doing what we think is right," said Gregor. "Using him as an excuse to kill one another. At the end of the day, we're the ones holding the swords."

"There must be better words to follow," agreed Ares.

"Sure there are. You and me, we could make up better words in our sleep," said Gregor.

Suddenly Ares lifted his chin, his ears twitching.

"What? What is it?" asked Gregor.

"It has begun," Ares said.

They rose and looked out over the rock wall. At first, Gregor could detect nothing new, only the army of rats sleeping fitfully in the gaping cavern. Then a faint ripple of air hit his cheek, and the scene in front of him exploded.

It was a well-coordinated attack and unlike anything Gregor had ever seen. The ripple he'd felt came from the beating of a thousand wings as a wave of humans flew through the darkness toward the rats. The bats were carrying large unfamiliar packages of some sort in their claws. When they were over the rats, they released their cargo. The packages exploded into small bonfires when they hit the ground. They must have had plenty of fuel because they continued to burn brightly after they landed.

The rats' warning system was not working well. Ripred had probably sent in soldiers to kill their scouts ahead of time. Gregor had heard a few cries of alarm, but they had not been enough to rouse the Bane's army. So the rats were still sleeping when the firebombs were dropped, and the swords and claws began to assault them.

At the same time, other adversaries were attacking from

all sides. Cockroaches and mice were pouring in from the left and right. Spiders — who had apparently decided to join with the humans — began to drop from the ceiling. And then Lapblood's rats appeared from the tunnels behind the rat army, essentially cutting off any possibility of retreat. They had dipped their tails in some kind of glow-in-the-dark coating, something phosphorous maybe, so that their allies could distinguish them from the enemy.

Awaking under these conditions, the Bane's army panicked. Some were on fire, others had already received mortal wounds. The human/bat teams and the rats carried the bulk of the fighting, but the smaller creatures were inflicting a lot of damage, too. The mice and cockroaches targeted wounded rats, swarming them and finishing them off. The spiders would drop suddenly on unsuspecting rats, sink their poisonous fangs into their bodies, and whiz back up their silk lines before their victims knew what had hit them. But the Bane's rats were hardened soldiers, and after the initial shock, they pulled themselves together and fought back.

Silently, from their perch high above, Gregor and Ares watched. By the time the ground fires died down, torchbearers had lit the area sufficiently so that Gregor didn't need to use echolocation to see the hell unfolding below him. The battle soon lost any sense of organization and deteriorated into a killing frenzy. Everywhere, every second, creatures were dying. Human, rat, bat, mouse, cockroach, and spider bodies accumulated on the ground, until those who still survived were fighting on a carpet of corpses. Panic and confusion reigned. Fighters had to be wary even of their allies. A human ran a sword through a nibbler, a rat blinded a rat on the same side, a torchbearer set a spinner on fire. The clear purpose that had taken the soldiers into the battle was becoming muddied in the turmoil.

Remote and safe for the moment, Gregor had a hard time making sense of the picture. It seemed unreal, as if he were watching a movie on television and he could make it stop by clicking to the next channel. This couldn't really be happening, this carnage, this waste of precious life. Who would do something like this? Why would they do it? What could they possibly accomplish? They were killing, killing, killing one another and then at the end they would have diminished one another's ranks but . . . what would have changed? The whole thing suddenly seemed like a ridiculous game that could easily have been replaced by another game, a hand of cards, a chess match, a roll of the dice. A game from which everyone could have gone home alive.

"Gregor! There! Above the river!" Ares said.

Gregor unglued his eyes from the battle and scanned the wall above the river. In the distance, they found Nike's black-and-white-striped wings fluttering in the mouth of a cave or tunnel — Gregor couldn't tell which — as she fended off a rat on the shelf of rock before her. About twenty yards above her, a digger's claws were widening a fresh hole in the steep wall. A stream of rats was emerging from the hole and half- climbing, half-sliding down toward Nike.

"What's she doing here?" asked Gregor. She was supposed to be with Boots and Lizzie, far from the battle as Solovet had promised. If Nike was here, where were his sisters? Stuck somewhere with only Temp, Hazard, Reflex, and Heronian for protection? And why didn't she just fly off? She wasn't big enough to be taking on that rat without a human teammate. What was she —?

And then Gregor saw something that stopped his heart. A thin beam of light shining out of the opening behind Nike. It was flashing in a pattern that Gregor recognized. Played on the bedroom wall, tapped out with a fork on the kitchen table, the flashlight signaling . . . dot-dot-dot-dash-dash-dash-dot-dot-dot . . . dot-dot-dot-dash-dash-dash-dot-dot-dot . . . SOS. SOS. SOS.

"Lizzie," he whispered. Then he began to scream. "My sisters! My sisters are in there!"

CHAPTER

24

Gregor vaulted onto Ares's back. "Go!" he shouted. "Go!"

Ares didn't object, but he did remind Gregor: "They will know now! That you still have life!"

Ripred had told Gregor to lie low until the Bane arrived, but that seemed of little importance now. He hardly noticed — or cared — that his appearance was a huge shocker for the rats, who began to howl his name the second he and Ares left the cover of the rocks.

Gregor ignored them. He would deal with the Bane later, if the white rat even showed up. Now he had a far more urgent mission. And he wasn't going to make it. He wasn't going to. He had flown on Ares enough now to gauge the amount of time it would take him to travel a certain distance, and they were too far. The rats would beat them. Nike could not fend them off. His sisters would be torn to pieces and —

Suddenly he saw a form streaking up the side of the cavern wall toward Nike. It didn't seem possible that any creature could scale such a steep incline with such speed. But one could. The one Gregor would have chosen. "It's Ripred!" he told Ares. "If he gets in, we can attack the rats from behind!"

Nike fell back out of sight as the rats from the digger's hole began to rain down onto the shelf of rock and lunge in after her. At least twenty had made it when Ripred reached them. Not stopping to fight, he raced over the backs of the enemy rats and was swallowed by the darkness beyond. Seconds later, Gregor and Ares dove in and threw themselves into the battle. It was like old times for Gregor, like when he had first become a rager and the adrenaline rush had obliterated his awareness of his actions. But he was so afraid, so deeply terrified for Boots and Lizzie that he could not contain himself. Every stroke of his blade was a death stroke, every movement designed to kill. He hacked and sliced and plunged his blade into rat after rat, oblivious to all else.

Ares had to arch back and crack Gregor in the face with his head to get his attention. "Gregor!"

"What?" Gregor snarled back. "Get in there, Ares!" His bat was drawing him away. "I have to kill those rats!"

"Try this one!" Ares said. The bat swung around and there was the Bane, right in his face.

To Gregor, who had been absorbed in the fight to save his sisters, it seemed as if the Bane had materialized out of nowhere, as if he had simply sprung out of the ground to exact his revenge. Ares veered sharply to the side just as one of the powerful clawed paws whistled by Gregor's ear and then scraped down the side of the cavern, unleashing a magnified sound like nails on a chalkboard.

"We must have more space!" said Ares. They couldn't fight the Bane trapped up against this wall. They needed room to maneuver.

"But my sisters — !" Gregor began. Then he knew he had to let them go. To trust Ripred and the humans and bats who had flown in to save them. Because wherever Gregor was now, so was the Bane. "All right!"

Ares swiftly flew back toward the heart of the battle, drawing the Bane after them. But Gregor had a few moments to assess his opponent. Boy, the Bane was a royal mess! He was scarred and hurting from their last encounter. The stump of his tail was capped with a huge ball of bloody spider silk. Losing the tail seemed to have done something to the Bane's sense of balance, because he moved unsteadily, almost as if he were intoxicated. But the real change was the look in the white rat's eyes. One glance told Gregor he had crossed over the line from damaged to demented.

The Bane came crashing across the plain toward them as the other creatures desperately fled to escape him. Bodies on the ground burst open under his feet. Anyone in reach of his claws was shredded.

"This isn't like before," thought Gregor. "I'm fighting a whole new opponent." For a moment, he felt a shudder of fear deep inside him. Then he pushed it down. "Where'd he come from?" he asked Ares.

"The tunnel to the right," Ares replied. "I know it. It leads farther into the rats' land."

"Is there much room?" asked Gregor.

"Yes. A large tunnel, then more caverns," said Ares.

"Take it," said Gregor. "Let's make him work for us." A chase would hopefully wear the Bane out a bit and keep him from killing anyone else. It would also give Gregor a less distracting place to fight. He wanted quiet. He wanted one-on-one.

Ares shot down the tunnel, and the Bane was right behind them, bouncing off the walls, roaring. The torchlight was gone, but Gregor's breath was coming in pants and he had no trouble seeing. The tunnel led into a rocky cavern that soared high into the air. Ares flew up higher but the Bane followed, making seemingly impossible leaps up boulders and onto ledges as he followed behind. At first, Gregor could sense other rats in the area, but soon they fell away, either unable or unwilling to pursue them. And still Ares flew higher, finding a strange tunnel with dripping rock formations, and finally coming to rest on a plateau that seemed a million miles from anywhere. He was able to land for a minute and rest. They listened to the sound of the Bane, bellowing in rage and pain as he struggled toward them.

"Will this place do?" Ares asked.

"It's perfect," said Gregor.

As the Bane took one last giant leap onto the plateau, Ares took to his wings. The chase had been a good idea.

The Bane was drained, gasping for air, thick foam hanging from his mouth. Several wounds had reopened on his face. The spider silk bandage had ripped off somewhere and blood ran from the stump of his tail.

"Alone at last," Gregor said. But they weren't.

"Take a minute," said the soothing voice. "Calm yourself before you destroy him."

"Twirltongue," Gregor said to Ares. "Where'd she come from?"

"I do not know," said Ares. "She was not with him on the Plain of Tartarus."

The Bane must have picked her up somewhere along the way. She leaped off of his back now, onto a pile of boulders. A nice safe place to observe the match. Gregor could see she was unmarred, not a wound on her anywhere. Her silver coat was flawless and unruffled.

It was all Gregor could do not to take her out right then and there. She was the one who had made the plans and groomed the Bane into this deranged creature. She'd probably ordered Twitchtip's death, too. Twirltongue and her silken voice. How he hated her. "You're looking good, Twirltongue," Gregor called. "A little too good. Seeing much action? Or you just sending the Bane in to lose his tail and such?"

"My tail? My tail?" said the Bane. He began to move in circles, trying to locate it. "My tail!"

"A king does not need a tail," said Twirltongue.

"He's not going to be king," said Gregor. "Are you, Pearlpelt?"

The name distracted the Bane from his tail. "I am king. I am king now! The rats follow me!"

"Then how come they're out there attacking you? Plus the spinners, the crawlers, the humans, the fliers, the nibblers," said Gregor. "Hey, that whole nibbler thing kind of blew up in your face, didn't it?"

"Twirltongue says I'm the king!" said the Bane.

"Yeah? Is that how it looks to you?" said Gregor. "Because from up here, it looks like she's getting you killed so she can take over."

"What? What?" The Bane was so far gone that that was all it took. He turned to Twirltongue, his eyes narrowing into slits. "You will not take over. I'm the king! I'm the king!"

"Of course you're the king. Who would follow a nothing like me?" said Twirltongue with a light laugh. But she was backing away. "He's lying!"

"If he's lying, then why are you untouched and I am like this?!" hissed the Bane.

"Because kings are bold and brave fighters. Your scars are badges of your might. No one would follow someone as untried and feeble as myself," said Twirltongue, edging along a boulder.

"No. You're right. No one will follow you. No one will ever follow you again!" The Bane sprang and, in one bite, ripped Twirltongue's head from her body. It hung in his mouth, teeth bared in a final grotesque grimace, before the Bane flung it at Gregor and Ares, almost hitting them. It smashed into the ground with an awful, hollow sound. The

281

Bane stroked his paws over his eyes a few times, then looked up in confusion. "Where's Twirltongue?" he said forlornly. "Where did she go?"

Neither Gregor nor Ares replied.

The Bane nosed along the ground until he found the head. "Twirltongue? Twirltongue? She's dead. . . ." he began to whimper. "She's dead. . . ." And then his distress transformed back into rage. "You killed her!" he spat at Ares and Gregor.

"Man, he really believes it!" Gregor said in a hushed voice.

"Just like you killed my mother!" said the Bane.

Whether the Bane had just thought that one up on the spot or Twirltongue had planted it in his brain along the way, Gregor had no idea. He only knew that twelve feet of rat was coming at him and the long-anticipated fight had begun.

Ares dodged the rat's first attack. By the time the bat had spun back around, Gregor's rager state was at its peak. But he was not overcome by it. In fact, he could control his actions with a deadly accuracy that left him heady with power. This was a new feeling. This strength. This lethalness. This must be what Ripred felt all the time.

"Go for his face!" Gregor said. This strategy had worked well before and now the Bane had no tail to retaliate with.

But if the Bane had been a challenge back in Regalia, there had been at least some sense to his movements. Now his motions were erratic and unpredictable. He wasn't concerned with his own state, only that Gregor end up dead. The Bane swiped at them again and again, not bothering to block Gregor's attacks, ignoring his own wounds as his claws found Ares's wing, Gregor's arm, Ares's ear.

"Pull back!" Gregor shouted and Ares whipped out of the Bane's reach.

"We need a new plan," said Gregor, trying to twist the sleeve of his shirt into a sort of bandage over a gash on his left arm.

"He has lost his balance," said Ares.

"Use it," said Gregor.

Ares began to dive in wild circles around the Bane. The rat soon became disoriented, lurching from side to side, but was still fighting bitterly. Gregor did some damage to his paws, but that was all that his sword could make contact with.

"I've got to get in closer if I'm going to take him out!" said Gregor.

"Hang on!" said Ares, and suddenly they were spinning over and over, and Gregor found himself directly under the Bane's foreleg. He plunged his sword into the soft flesh. The Bane gave a strangled cry and jerked backward, freeing Gregor's blade.

"Get out!" Gregor cried. "Get out, Ares!" He had a terrible sense of dread. Something was wrong about their position, their proximity to the Bane. Even before his bat opened his wings, Gregor knew there was no way they could clear the claws. He thrust his sword in the Bane's direction but it was too late. "Ares!" Gregor cried. "No!"

Everything seemed to move in slow motion as the rat caught Ares's wing, spun him around so they were face-to-face, and pulled him forward. Gregor dropped Solovet's dagger and wrapped both hands around the hilt of his sword. As the Bane sank his teeth into Ares's neck, Gregor's blade pierced the rat's heart. For a moment, they hung there, interconnected, supported by teeth and swords and claws. Then the Bane made an unearthly sound and rammed his free paw into Gregor's chest. Gregor lost his grip on his sword as he flew back into the air and slammed onto the stone floor. His hand went to his breastbone. The claws had torn aside his armor and opened a hot wet hole in his chest. His fingers pulsed with the rapid beating of his heart.

Above him, Ares still dangled from the Bane's jaws. The rat opened his mouth and the bat fell, lifeless, to the ground. The Bane pawed at the blade in his chest, trying to dislodge it. Then he became still and slowly sank down to four legs, onto his side as if to curl up, and rolled onto his back.

He knew they were dead. Both Ares and the Bane. Because only one creature was breathing. And it was Gregor.

Despite this knowledge, despite the pain, he dragged himself across the floor to his bond. Ares lay on his back, his wings bent at awkward angles. The entire front of his neck had been torn off. Gregor pressed his face into the bat's blood-soaked chest, hoping in vain for a heartbeat, a chance to revive him. "Ares? Ares? Don't go, Ares, okay? Don't." But he had gone. No one could survive a wound like that. "Ares?" Gregor's right hand reached out and found Ares's claw and latched on to it.

Ares the flier, I bond to you.

The words went through his mind but he couldn't speak them. Not anymore.

Still clutching Ares's claw, Gregor rolled over onto his back and found himself cradled by the bat's wing. The blood was leaving his body fast. Seeping out of his chest and mingling with Ares's blood, then running onto the ground to join the Bane's.

"This is it," thought Gregor. "This is the end." The blood was flowing too quickly and no one who could help even knew where he was. Sandwich was right. He was right after all. The Bane would die, Gregor would die, and they could even throw in Ares for good measure. This is where they would eventually find them, already buried in this sunless hole far beneath the earth's surface.

"It's okay," Gregor whispered to himself. "It's okay. Think of the knight." He remembered the calm, smooth face of the knight in the Cloisters, a face free of all earthly pain, and a feeling of peace slowly descended on him. He realized his death was not only okay, it was for the best. He was never going back to New York, anyway. That had been some laughable dream. How could he go back after all that had happened? After what he had become? Where would a twelve-year-old kid, a warrior, a killer, ever be at home? Not in the Overland. And the Underland? No, he'd eventually end up like Ripred. Like Ares. A dangerous character. Suspicious. Scraping out a life in some desolate place. Because no matter how much the humans loved him during a war, who would want him around on a regular basis? There was no place for Gregor. Over, under, or in between.

He wasn't really so different from the Bane. Both of them were pulled into this whole mess without having any real understanding of it. Both of them were used — the Bane by the rats, Gregor by the humans — to play out this war. And both of them were paying with their lives. To have them dead would be a relief to everyone.

Except maybe Gregor's family . . . but they had no idea who he had become . . . how much he had killed . . . and he hoped they never found out. . . .

The images of the cavern were dimming. His breathing became shallow. He could feel the world slipping away. "It's okay," he whispered to himself. "It's okay."

Far away, a pure, blue light appeared. It must be the light people talked about. The ones who'd had near-death experiences. You went down a tunnel. There was a light. People you'd loved who had already died were reaching for you. "Maybe Ares is there," thought Gregor. "Maybe he's waiting for me."

The pain left his body and Gregor had the sensation he was traveling. He was gliding closer and closer to the beautiful blue light. In a few seconds he would reach it. He wanted to reach it. To dissolve into the blueness. He was almost there.

Then everything went black.

CHAPTER
25

Something sprinkled across his forehead. Sand maybe. Was he at the beach, awaking from a long, warm nap in the sun? There it was again. People needed to be more careful. Kicking sand around. He should have picked a better spot. But when he'd died in that cave he'd been thinking more about — Wait! When he'd died in that cave? Where was he?

Gregor's eyes flew open. Above him, the hospital ceiling was brightly lit by torches. Boots's face slid into the frame. She took a bite of a cookie, showering crumbs down on his face. "Hi, you!" she said.

Something must have gone terribly wrong. He was still alive.

Boots took another bite of cookie and he shut his eyes to avoid the fallout. "You slept a long time. I got tired waiting." She did seem slightly put out.

"You're getting crumbs on him, Boots," he heard Lizzie whisper.

They were both alive. Ripred had gotten them out somehow.

"Gregor?" said a voice he had never hoped to hear again. His dad leaned over him, his face worn, older. "How you doing? How's my little guy?"

His dad? What was his dad doing here? What was going on? Why wasn't he dead? Where was the blue light? Who could possibly have found him in that forsaken place?

"Can you understand me, Gregor?" asked his dad. Gregor could see the concern in his eyes.

"Yeah." His voice was rusty and almost inaudible. "Hey, Dad. You're here."

"I came down just as soon as I could," his dad said. "Come to take you all home."

Gregor slowly became aware of his body. With great effort, he managed to wiggle his toes. Why was he so weak? How long had he been here? He struggled to move the fingers on his right hand but found it impossible. His left arm jerked up in a panic and pain spiked through his arm, his chest, oh, man, his chest! He dropped his arm back quickly. The pain ebbed but was still there. It was better if he didn't move.

"So, you have decided to wake up?" Howard's smile was so warm that Gregor couldn't help smiling back. The muscles on his face felt stiff and unused.

"What happened?" Gregor asked.

"You were rescued from the Dead Land by a pair of

daring adventurers, who risked all to carry you back to our doctors," said Howard. "At least, this is how they tell the story. Some, myself included, feel it had less to do with a love of you and more to do with a love of cake."

"Cake?" said Gregor. And suddenly it became clear to him. "Not the fireflies."

"Oh, yes. Our old and dear friends Photos Glow-Glow and Zap," said Howard.

That explained it. The beautiful, blue light wasn't from another world; it was from Photos Glow-Glow's butt. Gregor couldn't help laughing, even though it hurt like crazy. The whole thing was so absurd.

"They have spent the last two weeks gorging themselves in a room off of the kitchen. You see, it is quite impossible for them to leave until they are assured of your recovery. And Luxa indulges them for her own reasons," said Howard. "So, Gregor, just how bad do you feel?"

"Very," said Gregor. "Whole body hurts."

"Good. Then your nerves are working. Drink this," said Howard, lifting his head to help him swallow some medicine and a little water.

"I can't move my fingers." Gregor glanced down at his right side, where he hoped he still had a hand.

"Yes. Well. They will work by and by," said Howard. His face was sober as he gently lifted Gregor's hand into his line of sight. Locked in his fingers, cemented with blood, was Ares's claw. "The shiners were unable to release your grip. Zap managed to gnaw his claw free. We have not wanted to force your hand open, for fear of breaking bones. We can soak it . . . but you will have to let him go yourself."

Ares. The last horrible moments of his bat's life replayed in Gregor's head and he squeezed his eyes shut tight. Howard asked him more questions, but he couldn't respond.

"In his mind, all of this happened only minutes ago. We must give him time," said Howard to his family. "He must rest."

"Girls, you go up to the nursery. Give Dulcet some help with those mouse babies, okay? I'll sit with your brother," said his dad.

Gregor heard his own voice in his ears. *"I've got to get in closer if I'm going to take him out!"* Wing snagged. Bane drawing them in. Locking his jaws on Ares's throat. Sword in heart. Chest ripped open. Falling. Dying. *"Don't go, Ares, okay? Don't."* Lying in blood. Soaked in blood. Dying. Dying.

The darkness began to close in around him again. But through it he heard his dad's voice. "It's going to be okay, Gregor. You don't think so now. You don't see how it ever could be. But one day, I promise, it's going to be okay."

When he woke again, Mareth was sitting in the chair next to his bed. His dad was asleep on a cot. A couple of nurses propped Gregor up a bit with pillows and brought him some broth. Mareth volunteered to feed him, and the nurses accepted and dashed off.

"The hospital staff is still working around the clock," said Mareth. "Come, you need some nourishment." The soldier spooned broth into his mouth and filled him in on the last couple of weeks. The minute the fireflies had brought word of the Bane's demise —along with Gregor's unconscious body — to the Plain of Tartarus, the Bane's forces had fallen to pieces and been easily defeated by the humans and their allies. They were already weakened psychologically, having by that time figured out that the Code of Claw must have been cracked. Lapblood's armies fighting against them had been a significant blow, too. The Bane's death had just been the final straw that had broken their spirit. There would be an official surrender in the arena soon. Terms would be agreed upon.

As for his loved ones, Vikus was recovering but had lost much of the use of his right side. Just as Ripred had predicted, everyone was turning to Luxa for leadership. Her uncle, York, was going to come down from the Fount for the surrender as well. He would bring Gregor's mother with him.

"She's better, then?" asked Gregor.

"Yes. But still very weak," said Mareth. "Your family will have much healing to do."

"Who else was lost?" asked Gregor.

"Many," said Mareth. "Better perhaps to think of who still lives. Your family. Luxa. Hazard. Aurora. Nike. Howard. Nerissa. Vikus. All of the code team survived."

"And Ripred," said Gregor. "I've got a lot to tell him."

Mareth stirred the broth, avoiding his eyes. "No, Gregor, he did not make it."

"What? But everybody got out of that cave," said Gregor.

"It was a tunnel actually. A short one that ran between

the Plain of Tartarus and another cavern beyond the walls. The rats attacked from both sides. Ripred was able to fight a path out the back, enabling Nike to flee with your sisters, Hazard, Temp, Heronian, and Reflex. But he was overcome, his body flung into the abyss below. We sent a rescue team when word came. When they arrived, he had already been devoured by the swarms of flesh-eating mites in that nest there. You know the ones. We met up with them on the Waterway."

"The mites who killed Pandora," said Gregor.

"The same," said Mareth.

"Then you never actually found Ripred," Gregor said stubbornly.

"We found rat skeletons. Three of them. One, a large male who had evidently survived the fall and dragged himself some twenty yards before the insects overcame him," said Mareth. "The rescue team saw only this much, as they were forced to flee. But ask yourself, who but Ripred could have managed such a feat?"

"No one," said Gregor softly. Still, it did not seem quite real. That Ripred had died. Ripred couldn't die. He was invincible. A rager. Then he remembered Ripred's words. "Even a rager can be outnumbered, Gregor. I start to crack at about four hundred to one." There would have been more than four hundred mites in a nest. There would have been thousands and thousands.

"Beyond that, we have had no word of him. It is unlikely, having been so instrumental in this war, that he would be silent in the aftermath," said Mareth.

"Yeah," said Gregor. To his surprise, he felt as devastated by Ripred's loss as he had by Ares's. His bond at least knew how Gregor felt about him. He had never showed any gratitude toward Ripred. Never really thanked him. Never once told the rat how much he admired him. Maybe even loved him. It was not the kind of thing they discussed.

"I didn't expect . . . to have to deal with this. Up until that last morning, I was sure I'd be dead. Then Ripred —" Gregor stopped. He wasn't supposed to tell about how Ripred didn't believe in Sandwich's prophecies. Did it make any difference now the rat was dead? Maybe Ripred would want everyone to know his position. And there was proof now, because he had been right about Gregor surviving the war. But who could Gregor tell this to? Luxa? Vikus? He was too weak to go into it now. "Ripred gave me a pep talk. Told me I could beat the Bane."

"And you did," said Mareth.

"Not by myself," said Gregor. His right hand contracted around Ares's claw, not wanting to let go. But he had to let go. Ares wasn't coming back. Holding his claw wouldn't bring him back. It should be buried with the rest of him. "Howard said I could soak my hand."

"He left you a basin," said Mareth. He placed it at Gregor's side and then guided his hand into the water.

"You don't have to stay, Mareth," said Gregor. "I know they need a lot of help right now. I'm fine."

Mareth seemed to understand that Gregor did not want company just then. "I will check on you by and by," he said, and left.

The water was warm and comforting. Slowly, Gregor loosened his grip. The blood that glued him to the claw dissolved. One by one, his fingers peeled away and he extended his stiff fingers. The claw broke away from his hand and floated beside it in the basin.

Somehow Luxa was beside him with a towel. She solemnly removed the claw and wiped the remaining blood from it. When it was clean, she wrapped it in a white cloth and laid it on the table beside him. Then she sat on the side of the bed, lifted Gregor's hand, and carefully dried it. "It does not seem to be injured. How does it feel?" she asked.

"Empty," said Gregor. Luxa entwined her fingers with his. Her skin was warm, like the water, but alive. "That's better."

There were probably a million things they should be saying to each other, but they just stayed like that for hours, not talking, until his dad woke with a start from a nightmare, and Gregor had to reassure him that everything was going to be okay. "Maybe if we just keep telling each other that, one day it will be true," he thought.

For the next few days there was not much Gregor could do but sleep and let people feed him. He was so weak it was an achievement when he sat up himself, a small miracle when he could walk across the room again. It wasn't until he took his first bath that his condition really hit him. He was so skinny, shaky, and beat up. The wound on his chest was unreal. They had painstakingly stitched closed the stripes left by each individual claw mark. When it healed, Gregor could see there would be five scars to remind him of the Bane's final attack. How would he explain that to someone in the Overland?

His dad kept talking about their new life in the Overland. And Gregor didn't know how to tell him that he didn't want to move to the family farm in Virginia, didn't even want to go back to New York. That the boy who had fallen down the air shaft on a hot summer's day was gone, replaced by someone who could never find a home anywhere. But there was his dad going on about planting extra tomatoes so they would have plenty to fry up green, and going fishing, and how Gregor could join the school band again.

The school band? It took him a minute to even remember what instrument he had played. "Saxophone. I ran track, too. I liked science class. At least, he did. That other kid from that other time," Gregor thought.

And what about his sisters? Boots would be fine. She was only three. Eventually she'd stop talking in Crawler and probably forget all of this, which was sad in a way, a blessing in another. But Lizzie . . . Lizzie would forget nothing. She would just keep turning it over and over in her mind. She hardly talked since the war had ended. She just sat with her legs tucked up under her in a chair, her face thin and sad. Half the time she didn't even hear people when they spoke to her. Ripred's death had hit her hard.

One night, when their dad and Boots were asleep, Gregor asked her about it. Why Ripred had even brought the code team so close to the battle.

"Because of me. He didn't say it, but I knew he wanted to

keep an eye on me. To protect me the way he couldn't —"
Lizzie cut herself off.

"The way he couldn't protect Silksharp," Gregor finished for her.

"How did you know about her?" asked Lizzie.

"Heard you guys talking one night," said Gregor.

"It was my fault he died, Gregor," said Lizzie. "If I hadn't been there, he'd still be alive."

And there was nothing Gregor could say to convince her otherwise.

"Oh, yeah, let's move on down to Virginia and plant those tomatoes," Gregor thought. "That's going to fix everything." But he couldn't say something like that to his dad.

By the end of the week, Gregor was taking walks around the hospital. Luxa spent as much time as she could with him, but she was already being consumed by her new responsibilities. With the council members and Solovet dead and Vikus trying to learn to feed himself with his left hand, everyone turned to her for answers. More than a third of the human population had been wiped out, Regalia was a wreck, and the entire nibbler nation was homeless. In public, Luxa was steady and strong, but sometimes when she was alone with Gregor, she would bury her head in her hands, repeating again and again, "I do not know what to do." And he would put his arms around her and hold her, but he had no idea what to tell her. In his mind, Gregor knew how to kill things, not bring them back to life.

At least Luxa had a strong support system: Aurora,

Mareth, Perdita, Howard, Hazard, Nerissa, Nike, and several mice helped however they could. York advised her in letters from the Fount. And Gregor had to smile when he saw her in deep conversations with Temp. But ultimately, all of the decisions were landing squarely on her shoulders.

Looming over her was the day of the surrender. Although the Bane's forces had thrown in the towel when they had learned of his death, this was the official acknowledgment of the rats' defeat. But what was to be done with Lapblood and the rats who had sided with the humans in the end? Would they all be lumped together with the enemy rats? That wouldn't be fair, but as some pointed out, Lapblood's armies hadn't fought to save the humans, they had fought to save themselves from the Bane. Besides, there was so much hatred between the species now that anything was possible. Everyone knew the surrender was merely a gesture that would be directly followed by the question "What will happen now?" And Luxa, as the head of Regalia, would be expected to have answers about who would control what lands, and how the living would now pay for the acts of the dead, and if rats could be divided into friends and foes. It was very complicated stuff.

Gregor once walked in on Luxa and Nerissa trying to unravel the last stanza of "The Prophecy of Time" . . .

WHEN THE MONSTER'S BLOOD IS SPILLED,
WHEN THE WARRIOR HAS BEEN KILLED,
YOU MUST NOT IGNORE THE RAPPING,
OR THE TAPPING, TAPPING, TAPPING.

IF THE GNAWERS FIND YOU NAPPING,
YOU WILL ROT WHILE THEY ARE MAPPING
OUT THE LAW OF THOSE WHO GNAW
IN THE CODE OF CLAW.

. . . but they stopped abruptly when they saw him. He wanted to tell them it didn't matter. Couldn't they see that? Wasn't he living proof that the prophecy was wrong? That Sandwich was a fraud? But he didn't know how to convince them to change their minds about Sandwich. They had lived by his words for too long.

The night before the surrender, Luxa was eating dinner with his family in the hospital room, when Gregor's mom walked in. She was way too skinny and unsteady on her feet, but she walked in and opened her arms without a word. They all ran to her and wound up in one big embrace. Boots, who was too little to get in on the main action, began to squawk, "Me! Me! Kiss me!" and his dad scooped her up and everyone covered her in kisses, which only made her giggle and call for more.

After a minute, Gregor noticed Luxa, standing alone by the door, watching his family reunite. He couldn't help thinking of how once she'd had so many people to love her who were no longer here. He reached out a hand for her to join his family, but she just gave him a small smile, shook her head, and slipped out the door. And for the first time in forever, Gregor remembered why he was lucky.

The next morning, Gregor met Luxa before the surrender. She was dressed in a gorgeous gown with a jewel-studded tiara on her head. "Wow, you look so grown-up in that. At least thirteen," he said.

That made her laugh, although he could tell she was pretty nervous. Gregor was just wearing a plain shirt and pants. And his swords. He felt naked without them. Back in the Overland, he couldn't wear them, of course. He had separation anxiety just thinking about it.

His sisters and dad had already flown ahead to the arena, but Gregor had promised Luxa he would walk through the city with her. When the platform lowered them to the ground, Gregor could see the road was lined with people. No one cheered. Rather, they bowed as Luxa passed. A lot of people had tears running down their cheeks. Luxa acknowledged the crowds, nodding, occasionally lifting a hand. She spoke only once when they came to a crossroads where four streets met. She stopped and surveyed the wreckage around her. The rats, with the help of the diggers, had turned buildings into rubble. The paving stones beneath their feet were stained with blood and scorch marks from the fallen torches. A little girl missing an arm stared at them with empty eyes.

"Look at my city, Gregor," said Luxa. "Look at my home."

When they got to the doors of the arena, Luxa paused. Gregor reached out and gave her hand a quick squeeze. Then she took a deep breath and headed in. Gregor followed a few steps behind. The place was packed with delegations from every species that had played a principal role in the war: crawlers, spinners, diggers, nibblers, fliers, gnawers, and humans. Gregor even noticed Photos Glow-Glow and

Zap sitting on a bench. He hadn't seen them since the rescue, hadn't even thought to thank them. He would try to remember to after the ceremony.

Even though a path had been left for them, it was hard to make a dignified entrance because the floor of the arena was so pitted with the tunnels the diggers had made. But Luxa swept around them gracefully while Gregor sort of hopped along after her. At the center of the arena was an empty circle. Three rats waited before it.

When Luxa stepped into the circle Gregor hung back at the edge. Aurora fluttered down and landed just outside of the circle as well. Nearby, Gregor could see his dad and Lizzie. Mareth, Perdita, York, and Howard stood in a group. Even Nerissa had pulled herself together for the event. Somewhere in a bunch of cockroaches he spotted the tops of two curly heads and knew that Boots and Hazard were watching, too.

As Luxa took her place, what little conversation there had been in the arena ceased. If she was still nervous, it didn't show. She held herself with dignity and her voice was clear and steady. "Greetings, all. We have gathered here to mark the end of an unhappy and costly war. I have come to accept the surrender and present the terms of the defeat. Gnawers, who speaks for you?"

One of the rats stepped forward to reply when there was a commotion. Small stones and dirt began to fly out of the mouth of one of the diggers' tunnels. A general ripple of alarm ran through the arena. Everyone was still so jumpy from being under attack. Then the bedraggled creature nosed its way out.

He was almost unrecognizable. Half of his fur and a good portion of his skin had been eaten away, leaving bloody, oozing places. One of his back legs was useless, trailing behind him. His face had received another diagonal slash, which crisscrossed with the existing scar. But his voice was unmistakable.

"I do," said Ripred, dragging himself into the circle. "I speak for the gnawers."

CHAPTER

26

The stunned silence in the arena was broken by Lizzie's squeal of joy, "Ripred! Ripred!" She pushed her way out of the crowd and threw her arms around his neck. "I thought you were dead."

"I told you, it takes a lot to kill me. More than a few bugs, anyway," said the rat.

"But they found your skeleton," said Lizzie.

"That must have been Cleaver's. I dove under his body as soon as we landed and then ran. The mites had to chew him up before they got to me so it bought me some time. Not a lot, but enough to get away. Funny, I always despised Cleaver, but I can't help thinking warmly of him now," said Ripred.

"How did this happen?" asked Lizzie, reaching up to lightly touch the new slash on his face.

"Oh, a rat cut me. It's nothing. Now up you go." He nudged Lizzie up onto a patch of fur on his back.

"I'll hurt you," she said.

"No. You'll remind me why I'm here," said Ripred, and locked eyes with Luxa.

"And why is that, Ripred?" Luxa said icily.

"I told you. To speak for the gnawers. Or did you think I spent years risking life and limb so that you could dictate our future?" asked the rat.

Now the creatures in the crowd found their tongues, and everyone was turning to their neighbor in either dismay or confusion. Most of the rats had long considered Ripred an enemy. And he'd been fighting with the humans and their allies for so long, even they'd begun to take his allegiance for granted. But taking Ripred for granted was a big mistake. Gregor had the feeling that he had always been working toward this moment. Maybe he hadn't expected to be dealing with Luxa, maybe he'd thought Solovet or Vikus would be there to negotiate with him. It didn't really matter who he was up against, as long as he stood for the rats.

Luxa raised her voice above the hubbub. "Is this true, gnawers? Does he speak for you?"

The rats were clearly as amazed by Ripred's appearance as anyone else. They shifted around, whispering among themselves, trying to reach some kind of consensus.

Then a voice rose, clear and forceful, above the others. "Yes! I say he speaks for us!" Lapblood and her two children made their way out of the crowd. If Ripred had always been an object of suspicion, it was clear that Lapblood was trusted among her own kind. She had been chosen to find the plague cure and had had the influence to lead the dissenters against the Bane. A moment after her declaration, the rats united with her and began to call for Ripred to act as their representative.

Gregor could see the tension in Luxa's shoulders. It was hard enough to have to lay out the postwar plan in front of the entire Underland. But to do it with Ripred standing by to challenge her every move? Ripred? She was out of her league and she knew it. Who wouldn't be out of their league with Ripred?

To make matters worse, Nerissa suddenly cried out, "Oh, Luxa, see you the mark on his face?"

Luxa scrutinized the rat's face. "It is but another scar among many."

"But look! It forms an *X*! The mark borne by the peacemaker!" said Nerissa.

"Many of us have scars that cross!" York strode out of the crowd.

"Think of the words," said Nerissa. And the arena quieted to hear her recite the poem from the prophecy room in her quavering voice:

> ON SOFT FEET, BY NONE DETECTED,
> DEALING DEATH, BY MOST REJECTED,
> KILLED BY CLAW, SINCE RESURRECTED,
> MARKED BY X, TWO LINES CONNECTED.
> FINALLY, THEY INTERSECTED,
> TWO LINES MET, ONE UNEXPECTED.

304

"Do you not see?" insisted Nerissa. "It describes Ripred exactly. Slipping in undetected, deadly, hated, thought lost, but brought back to life. And the *X*! One half was given by a human. One half by a gnawer. Two lines intersecting. And now the human line and the gnawer line meet in the flesh as well. In Luxa and Ripred."

The arena went nuts but Luxa remained unmoved. She waited for the commotion to die down, then said, "Do you fancy yourself the peacemaker, Ripred?"

"Well, I don't like to blow my own horn, but it does make a lot of sense, what Nerissa's saying. And if I am, there's really nothing I can do about it one way or the other, is there?" said the rat.

Gregor could hear everyone murmuring to one another that this was true, that the prophecies were written in stone. But the rat was looking at Gregor, smirking and rolling his eyes ever so slightly as if to say, "See what I mean?"

While he had no way to prove it, Gregor was suddenly convinced that Ripred had given himself the second wound. It would be a small price to pay for being designated the peacemaker.

"Good. Then you should have no problem peacefully leading your fellow gnawers into the Uncharted Lands," said Luxa.

This surprised even Gregor, although in retrospect, maybe it shouldn't have. When she had started the war, Luxa had told Gregor, "We may as well get it over with. Have the war that will answer the question of who stays and who goes." But he had thought, with all that had happened during the war, that she might have changed her mind. Apparently not.

With her proposal, everything became ugly and hard.

"Yes, I do have a problem with that, Your Highness. So much so that I flatly refuse to do it," Ripred spat at her. "What do you say to that?"

"I say that you may go peacefully or by force; it is your choice!" said Luxa.

"If it is another war you are looking for, then believe me you shall have it!" growled Ripred. "But I wonder how you will fare, with your limping army and your broken city and me at your throat instead of your back!"

"I do not need you, Ripred. I have Gregor!" said Luxa.

"Do you? I wouldn't count on it. Even if he stays, I'll wager he finds your measures too harsh. Perhaps he will even remember past kindnesses and take my side instead!" retorted Ripred.

Gregor's mouth dropped open in disbelief. What were they talking about? What were they both doing? Could they actually be going back to war? And did they plan for him to join them?

"We will leave it to him to decide," Luxa said, and then turned to him. Everyone in the whole arena turned to him, wanting to know where he stood.

"You're really going to do it, aren't you? You're really going to go back to war?" Gregor said. He could feel something boiling up inside of him. "So, we'll just forget about what happened. The jungle, the Firelands, the Bane." His voice was rising and he could feel the rager side of him taking

306

over. "Forget about everybody who's dead! Tick and Twitchtip and Hamnet and Thalia and Ares! And your parents, Luxa! And your pups, Ripred! Let's just forget about everybody who gave their lives so that you could have this moment where you could — could make things right again! So you could stop the killing! We were fighting for the same thing, remember? You two owe each other your lives! You owe me your lives! And now you stand there and ask me to choose between you? To help you kill each other?" Gregor yanked Sandwich's sword from his belt and swung it so violently that even Luxa and Ripred stepped back. "Well, guess what? The warrior's not fighting for either of you!"

And with that, Gregor took the sword blade between his hands and slammed it across his leg with such force that it snapped in two. He flung the pieces aside, one toward Luxa, the other toward Ripred. Fresh blood was running from his empty hands as he held them up. "There. The warrior's dead. I killed him."

"And so 'The Prophecy of Time' is fulfilled!" said Nerissa breathlessly.

Gregor shook his head. Would they never shut up about those prophecies? But he only said, "Whatever. Now what are you two going to do?"

"What, indeed, after such a display?" said Ripred to Luxa. "Although the boy does make a point about the perversity of starting a new war while the blood is still drying from the last one. Especially when the cutters are amassing at our borders." The crowd reacted, and Ripred circled around to make sure everyone could hear him. "Oh, didn't I mention that before? Now I'm not saying they're taking this opportunity to finish us all off, but you have to admit it'd be an excellent time. With them so strong, and us so weak. Of course, if things were different between us . . ."

"Yes, I see. We might deter them," Luxa said sharply.

"We have done it in the past," said Ripred.

"The past is gone. How do we know we can trust you now?" asked Luxa.

"Trust us? You just tried to banish us to the Uncharted Lands! I think if anyone needs a little reassurance, it's the gnawers!" answered Ripred. "So — I don't know, write up a treaty or something."

"No one trusts treaties. They go up in a flash," said Luxa.

"Then you decide, Luxa. Friends or enemies. Trust or no trust. Between you and me. Between our species. You decide how it is to be," Ripred said.

It was the moment of truth. Gregor could see Luxa's internal struggle playing out on her face. Flickers of Solovet's hardness interchanging with Vikus's desire for understanding. All of the old hatreds and sacrifices and debts and hopes swirling around inside her as she tried to decide the fate of the Underland. War or peace. Battle or compromise. Solovet or Vikus. It was the very decision that had destroyed Hamnet. Made him go mad, then flee, then die in battle.

Finally Luxa's expression solidified. "There will be no treaties," she announced. "They have always failed us in the past."

Gregor's heart slammed somewhere down around his feet. But she had not finished.

"There will be no treaties!" Luxa repeated. "But I offer this." She stepped forward and raised her right hand to Ripred.

The crowd let out a gasp at what she was proposing. Even Ripred was initially taken aback. But he recovered quickly. "A bond?"

"A bond between all humans and gnawers. A vow to defend each other to the death. I offer it. Do you dare take it?" asked Luxa.

"Do I dare?" said Ripred. "Yes, I do." He lifted his paw up and pressed it against her hand.

After a moment, Luxa began:

Ripred the gnawer, I bond to you,
Our life and death are one, we two.
In dark, in flame, in war, in strife,
I save you as I save my life.

To which Ripred replied:

Luxa the human, I bond to you,
Our life and death are one, we two.
In dark, in flame, in war, in strife,
I save you as I save my life.

Then the rat dropped his paw and gave a big stretch. "Don't we get a feast now?"

"Let it be as he says," said Luxa. And the whole arena broke into cheers.

"Your grandpapa is going to be so proud of you," Gregor heard Ripred say to Luxa.

"And my grandmama is rolling in her grave," replied Luxa.

"She was always too hard to please," said Aurora. Luxa put her arms around her neck, and the bat enfolded her in her golden wings. "It was the best thing to do," Aurora said.

"If you think so, then I can survive it," answered Luxa.

"What about me? Don't I get a hug?" Ripred asked.

"Ugh, you are teeming with infection. Lizzie, get off of him before you catch something vile." Luxa lifted Lizzie off of Ripred's back. "You had best get to the hospital," she told Ripred. "And then I suppose we must meet to determine the specifics of this historic day."

Ripred sighed. "I suppose so. You and I seem to end up doing everything. Shall we say four members for each delegation?"

"Why not?" Luxa said. "Four can be as stupid as ten. No need to crowd the room."

Ripred laughed. "You know, I think you and I are going to get on famously."

"And you, Overlander," said Luxa, turning to Gregor finally. "You are bleeding, too."

"Well . . . I did kill myself," Gregor said with a smile.

"I do not suppose we left you much choice," said Luxa. "Come, then. I will walk you two down to the hospital. I want the pleasure of telling Vikus what happened. I need one human to genuinely approve of what I just did."

"You've already got that," said Gregor. He collected the broken pieces of his sword and they headed for the hospital.

As they walked into Regalia, Luxa said, "You should have made that cut a little deeper, Ripred. It may leave no scar at all, and then where will our peacemaker be?"

Gregor laughed. Ripred hadn't fooled her one bit.

"I have no idea what you're suggesting," Ripred said loftily.

"Bet there aren't any cutters on the border, either," said Gregor.

"Well, there might be," said Ripred. "It's their border, too. And may I add that I think it's very ill-mannered of you two to be doubting me. Particularly my new bond."

"I expect you will get used to it," said Luxa. The rat did not deign to reply.

Lizzie went with Ripred to be treated, but Gregor wanted to see Vikus first. The old man was sitting, propped up in bed. The right side of his body was impaired by the stroke. But his left eye brightened and his good hand reached out when Gregor and Luxa came in. Gregor clasped his hand with his bleeding one. "Hey, Vikus, how you doing?" Vikus couldn't really speak yet. "Look, I just wanted to return this to you." Gregor held up the pieces of Sandwich's sword and laid them on the bed. Vikus raised his eyebrow for an explanation. "Luxa and Ripred were recruiting me for a new war, this time against each other. So, I retired the warrior. Killed him off really."

Vikus's face was registering alarm.

"Do not worry," Luxa said. "Yes, Ripred is alive and leading the rats, but there is to be no war. Do you not wish to keep the sword, Gregor? For memories' sake?"

"No, thanks. I've got more memories than I can handle." Gregor removed Solovet's dagger from his belt and put it with the sword. "Besides, my mom won't even let me have a pocketknife," he said.

Vikus gave him half a smile. With great effort, he worked a word from himself. It was difficult to distinguish, but Gregor thought he knew what Vikus wanted to say. "Hope?" Gregor asked. The old man nodded and pointed at Gregor's chest. "I give you hope?" Vikus nodded. "Well . . . just wait until you hear what Luxa did." Gregor leaned down and kissed him on the cheek. "Take care, Vikus."

Gregor left so that Luxa could tell Vikus about what had happened in the arena. Besides, he was dripping blood everywhere. He found Ripred and Lizzie in a room. A team of doctors was trying to put the rat back together, putting his leg in a cast, cleaning and bandaging his mite-eaten flesh. For somebody who was so tough, Ripred was putting up an awful big fuss. But not as big as it would have been if Lizzie hadn't been comforting him.

By the time Howard had bandaged Gregor's hand, the meeting of the delegates was about to begin. Lizzie wanted to go to be near Ripred, so Gregor went, too, to keep an eye on her. It was held in a room with a large, round table. Gregor and Lizzie sat up against the wall, but four delegates of each species, humans, rats, bats, mice, spiders, cockroaches, and moles gathered around the table. There were twenty-eight in all, but it was soon clear that Ripred and Luxa planned on doing most of the talking. For a couple of characters who had just bonded, they sure didn't agree on much. Not land division, not restitution, not military control. Other voices chimed in and soon the conversation had moved away from the future and back to the past evils they had done to one another. Things looked like they might actually turn physical when Ripred jumped on the table and shouted, "Don't feel superior! Don't anyone in this room feel superior! We have all inflicted unspeakable evils upon one another! Let's admit that or we're just sliding backward!"

"Hey, like in the prophecy," interjected Gregor. "Time is turning back."

"Shut up!" Ripred spat at him. The rat climbed off of the table and no one knew where to pick up the conversation.

Then Lizzie timidly spoke up. "I have an idea." She wasn't really supposed to talk, but everyone respected the code-breaker.

"I am sure we would all welcome it, Lizzie," said Heronian encouragingly.

"I think there are too many of you. I think each group should only get one delegate." Lizzie licked her lips. "And that that delegate should be chosen by the other species."

There was a long pause while everyone considered this. Of course, everyone liked the idea of choosing the others' delegates. But to let the others choose theirs . . .

"We make no headway here. I believe we should give Lizzie's suggestion a try," said Luxa.

"Well, I'll just leave now, shall I?" said Ripred, giving Lizzie a wounded look.

"Oh, stop sulking! It is not as if I will be invited to stay," Luxa snapped.

"Well, I wouldn't vote for either of you," put in Gregor. They both glared at him but that only made him grin.

The delegates were chosen. The seven were Mareth, Nike, Temp, Heronian, Lapblood, Reflex, and a mole whose name no one could pronounce.

"Oh, look, all the reasonable delegates are left," said Gregor as he left with the rejects.

"All the weak ones, you mean," muttered a spider who Gregor didn't know.

Gregor looked into the room. "No," he said. "There's nobody weak in that room. Good luck, you guys." He took Lizzie's hand. "And good idea, Liz."

"It's kind of like the logic puzzle about the cheese. Only you turn it inside out. So there's one cheese and seven creatures have to share it. The trick is, you have to figure out who are the most likely to share," said Lizzie. Then she added sadly, "But now Ripred's mad at me."

"On the contrary," said Ripred, tugging on her braid. "Ripred's very cranky that no one voted for him, but very pleased that he can go to the feast now. Hop on," he said, and Lizzie scampered up onto his back. "It's ideal really. They will come up with a plan. No one will like it. Everyone will feel they have been treated unfairly, but will be happy that their neighbors feel the same. And that is the nature of compromise. Now let's go eat an awful lot."

Gregor and Luxa lingered in the hall as the others went to the feast.

"When must you go?" asked Luxa.

"My mom wants to go today. In a few hours, maybe," said Gregor. "My dad convinced her it was important for us to stay for the surrender. But she wants to get to Virginia as soon as possible."

They collected a basket of food from the kitchen, and Aurora carried them out of Regalia to Ares's old cave. Then she flew out around the lake, leaving them alone.

"We finally can have that picnic," said Luxa.

"Yeah," said Gregor. But neither of them could eat. They just sat with their arms around each other.

"Where is Virginia?" Luxa asked.

"A long way from New York. Hundreds and hundreds of miles," said Gregor.

"We shall never see each other again," said Luxa.

Gregor found himself wishing Sandwich had been able to cough up a few more prophecies about the warrior. "Probably not. Won't even be able to write."

"Will you be glad to be home?" asked Luxa.

"No," Gregor said. "I can't even imagine being back. Anyway, Virginia isn't my home. It's just a place I've visited."

"It will be easier for you. Here there will always be talk of you. In the Overland, who but your family even knows my name? And they will not want to dwell on your times here. It will be quite simple to forget me," said Luxa.

"Never," said Gregor. "I'll never get rid of you, no matter

how hard I try." It was no longer an effort to say the words. "I love you."

"I love you, too," said Luxa.

And after that, there was nothing left to say.

Tick, tick, tick, tick, tick, tick, tick, tick, tick, tick, tick, tick, tick, tick, tick. . . .

In no time, horns were blowing from Regalia. Aurora fluttered in. "They are calling us back," she said.

Gregor had trouble believing it was really happening. The quick flight back. His family waiting on the docks, ready to go. His few possessions from the museum already neatly packed in a bag. There were hugs and good-byes but only Boots said, "See you soon," as she showered Temp with kisses.

Ripred made a point of giving Gregor some last-minute rager advice. "Watch yourself. That rager thing isn't going to magically disappear. It's part of you. There won't be anyone you can't take. And you've killed enough that you don't have to think twice to do it. Remember, it's a lot easier to lose your head than to keep it."

The words made Gregor's blood run cold. "I'll remember," he said. He'd better remember. Or who knows what he might do? "Run like the river, Ripred."

"Fly you high, Gregor the Overlander," said the rat, and then turned his attention to Lizzie, who was crying her eyes out.

Nike and Aurora flew his family and Luxa over the Waterway and dropped them at the stairway beneath Central Park. Gregor said good-bye to the bats, then held

Luxa's hand while his dad pushed the rock aside. Cool night air rushed in.

"Come and look, just for a second," said Gregor. But Luxa would only climb up to where her head and shoulders were aboveground. It was a clear night. A few stars were visible and the moon was magnificent.

"This is where I will think of you," she said. "You know where I will be."

Gregor kissed Luxa good-bye and climbed out into the park. Then she backed down a few steps and they held each other's gaze until Gregor's dad slid the rock in place, parting them forever.

CHAPTER
27

It was late. Two-fifteen by the clock on the taxi's dashboard. The driver was tired, uncommunicative, and didn't seem to wonder what they were doing hanging out in Central Park at that hour.

When they got to their building, the elevator was broken, so they took the stairs up to their apartment. Gregor's mom had to rest every couple of flights. His dad finally gave him the keys and told him to take the girls on ahead. When Gregor opened the door to his apartment, he couldn't believe how small and cramped the place looked. He and Lizzie slumped back on the couch while Boots immediately dumped a basket of plastic animals on the rug and arranged them in a parade. When she came to a little black bat she'd gotten last Halloween she held it up happily. "Look! Ares!"

Gregor could think of nothing to say as she flew the bat around her head.

His parents came in about ten minutes later, and even though she was dropping from fatigue, his mom went right in to check on his grandmother. That's when Gregor realized she didn't know that Grandma wasn't there. His dad had been waiting until they got home to break the news. "It's her heart, Grace. She's in the hospital. We'll go see her first thing tomorrow," his dad said.

They went straight to bed. Gregor didn't even bother with pajamas. He just stripped down to his Underland briefs and crawled between his blankets. They had a dusty, familiar smell. A siren went by. Music from a car radio blared then faded. A toilet flushed. The old comforting sounds of New York City lulled Gregor to sleep. . . .

The tunnel was dark. The flashlights long dead. Gregor was relying solely on echolocation. It had been stupid to go this way. Ripred had told him that but he hadn't listened. Now they had found him. As he ran he could feel the rats panting so he turned and swung, slashing open several faces, splattering himself with blood. But then something happened to his sword. It became rubbery, melting in his hand. He tried to run again but the floor was crumbling beneath his feet and then he was falling, falling, falling into a black pit. He screamed for Ares but there was no Ares and he could see the sharp rocks as they rushed up to meet him, feel the agony as they pierced his chest!

Gregor bolted up in bed, heart pounding, sweat-soaked, his right hand clutching his throbbing chest. Had his own voice woken him? No one came running in. No one called his name. The screams must have stayed in his dream.

The falling nightmares that had plagued him growing up had stopped when he'd had Ares. Now they were back again, filled with rats and blood.

Dawn was just breaking over the city. He'd been in bed only a few hours. He knew he should go back to sleep. But the nightmare had been too real. He sank back on his pillow and watched the sunlight brighten until it stung his eyes.

Gregor cracked open his window and took a deep breath of the exhaust-scented air. What day was it? What month was it? He had no idea. He hadn't been home since Hazard's birthday. That had been in the dead of summer. This air was crisp. Suddenly he had an urgent need to know how much time had passed, to ground himself in some kind of reality. The calendar in the kitchen would be worthless, but he could turn on the TV. . . . No, that would wake everybody. . . . He could go down to the corner and check the date on a newspaper. He flung off his blanket and froze as he got his first look at his body in sunlight.

"Oh, geez," he said. He knew he'd gotten beat up pretty bad in the Underland, but things healed up and you moved on. Only he hadn't accounted for the accumulation of scars that dated all the way back to his earliest visits. Marks left by squid suckers, vines, pinchers, teeth, claws. Then there were the wounds he'd made on his hands when he'd broken Sandwich's sword less than a day ago. His skin was like a map where you could trace all of the terrible things that had happened.

The Underlanders had given him more of that fish ointment. Maybe it would help. But some of these things . . . like the five claw marks the Bane had left on his chest . . . They were going nowhere fast. They were part of him forever. How could he ever explain them? Say he'd been in a car wreck? Fallen through a plate-glass window? Wrestled a pack of tigers? If he couldn't explain them, he'd have to hide them. Forget the beach, forget gym class, and forget even going to the doctor unless he was on death's doorstep. A doctor wouldn't accept some lame excuse. He'd want answers and the truth would land Gregor in a mental ward.

Gregor dressed in a long-sleeved shirt and pants, both of which seemed too short. He'd done quite a bit of growing in . . . in however long he'd been gone. He put on his socks and his only Overland footwear, a pair of dress shoes he'd gotten for the spring concert. His toes felt cramped and they looked stupid with his outfit. He wanted those great sneakers Mrs. Cormaci had sent him but they'd been ruined in the war.

He left quietly, but as he passed Mrs. Cormaci's apartment, the door opened. She had always been an early riser. "So. You stayed in one piece," she said, looking him up and down critically. "Your pants are too short. Want some French toast?"

Gregor followed her into the kitchen and sat at the table while she made breakfast. She filled him in on his grandma's condition. "She's not doing too well, Gregor. She's in intensive care. If your mother has some idea about taking her on a road trip to Virginia, well, that just isn't going to happen."

She piled the thick slices of challah bread fried in egg batter on Gregor's plate and placed a platter of bacon in front of him. "I don't see how we can stay here," he said, pouring syrup on the toast. "Maybe she'll just take us kids." It would be awful breaking up the family again, though. They'd just gotten back together.

"Maybe. So, what's been going on with you, mister?" Mrs. Cormaci asked.

Gregor thought about all that had happened since he'd last been home. All he'd seen and done. He couldn't form any of it into words.

"Cat got your tongue?" asked Mrs. Cormaci. "It's okay. You don't need to tell me or anyone else about it unless you feel like it." She dipped a piece of bacon in his syrup and chewed it thoughtfully. "You know, Mr. Cormaci fought in a war. He didn't want to talk about it, either. I knew there'd been some terrible things, though. That man had bad dreams until the day he died."

"One woke me this morning," said Gregor.

"It won't be the last," said Mrs. Cormaci. "Want some juice?" She poured him a glass without waiting for him to answer. "It's like this. You spend your whole childhood hearing about being nice to other people and how hurting someone's a crime, and then they ship you off to some war and tell you to kill. What's that going to do to your head, huh?"

"Nothing good," Gregor said.

"You'll be all right, though, Gregor," said Mrs. Cormaci.

"I don't know. In my dream, I fell to my death," said Gregor. "I used to have falling dreams before, but this was the first time I hit bottom."

"Don't worry. If you hit bottom, there's a whole lot of people here to help you up," said Mrs. Cormaci.

"Help me up?" Gregor thought. "Wipe me up is more like it. Nothing left to help once you hit those rocks." And even if people wanted to help, Gregor was alone in his dreams. No one could help him there.

While he ate, Mrs. Cormaci found a pair of old sneakers that had belonged to one of her sons about twenty years ago. They weren't exactly in style but they fit pretty well and looked better than the dress shoes.

"You're going to need new clothes for school," she said.

"Has it started already?" he asked.

"Weeks ago," she said. "We're halfway through October, Gregor."

"I didn't know," he said.

The morning was spent watching his sisters while his parents and Mrs. Cormaci went to the hospital. While Lizzie and Boots ate breakfast, Gregor stood at the kitchen window watching the neighborhood kids go off to school. He thought of his friends Larry and Angelina and wondered what they must make of his disappearance. Did they think he had moved? Was sick? Part of him wanted to see them badly and another part never wanted to see them again. He had been through so much, changed so much, that the idea of hanging out with them and pretending everything was back to normal seemed impossible.

His parents got back around lunch. The visit had been a shock to his mom. No one could say when his grandmother would be able to leave the hospital, and even then she'd probably have to go to some kind of nursing home with full-time medical care.

"Can I see her?" asked Gregor.

"Not now, son. Maybe when she's stronger," said his dad.

"What are we going to do now?" asked Gregor. "About Virginia?"

"I don't know. We'll work it out," said his dad.

"I don't want to go to Virginia," said Lizzie, and they all looked at her in surprise.

"But you said you did, Lizzie," said their mom. "You were the first one packing when I mentioned it."

"I don't want to go anymore. This is our home. I don't want to run away," said Lizzie. "Ripred says if you run from things that scare you they just chase you."

"What about you, Gregor?" asked his dad.

Gregor tried to imagine living in Virginia. Tried to imagine staying here. "It doesn't matter. I don't care where we live," he said. It would be awful wherever he was. He pulled his jacket off of the hook by the door. "I'm going for a walk."

He hadn't had a destination in mind when he'd left, but in a few blocks he knew where he wanted to go. He checked his pocket. Thirty-five bucks. That would be plenty. He hopped on the subway and headed to the Cloisters. He had to see the stone knight who had gotten him through these last weeks. Maybe that would help him make sense of things.

The day was cool and sunny. The trees were starting to turn. But Gregor kept thinking of another world, one without sunlight and precious few trees, that he seemed to belong to now. What if he'd told his parents he wanted to go back and live in the Under-land? Where he was not such a freak? Where he had friends? Where he had Luxa? They would never let him go. And did he really want to go? He didn't know. He only knew that he felt like a stranger in what used to be his home. And he felt very alone.

The woman at the booth hesitated when he tried to buy a ticket. What did she see? Some kid in mismatched clothes showing up alone in the middle of the school day. Weird bandages on his hands. And Gregor couldn't remember the last time he'd had a haircut. He tried to cover. "I have to do a school report. We're supposed to write about the coolest building in New York. I picked here. Do you have any information or anything I could look at?" She was still wary, but she let him in with a couple of glossy brochures and a warning not to touch anything.

The place was almost empty. Gregorian chants were being piped in, which were sort of eerie and calming at the same time. The Cloisters reminded Gregor of Regalia, with the carvings of strange animals, the tapestries, the stone walls, floors, ceilings. He wandered through a couple of rooms before he found the tomb. The knight was just as Gregor had last seen him, lying beneath the window, his hands resting on his sword, sleeping away eternity. Thinking of this knight had gotten Gregor through some tough times. He had made the trip today because he expected to find some comfort in the stone figure. But now, he realized it was no longer of use to him. He had spent the last months learning how to die, and now he was going to have to learn how to live again. The knight couldn't help him with that.

It was late afternoon when Gregor got home and he wasn't one step in the door when his mom descended on him. "Where on earth have you been? Do you know how long you've been gone? You had the whole family worried sick!"

Boy, she was upset! Her eyes were red as if she'd been crying.

"I'm sorry," Gregor said. "I just went for a walk."

His dad laid a hand on his shoulder. "It's okay. You've just got to get used to having parents again."

"I'm sorry," Gregor repeated.

His parents went in the bedroom to talk. Lizzie and Boots were playing some game with the plastic animals on the floor. Gregor turned on the television and flipped through the channels. He stopped on the news. A bomb had blown up in a marketplace somewhere, killing forty-nine. There were body parts and smoke and relatives wailing. The next story was about refugees dying on the road, driven from their homes by an enemy army. The news anchor was just starting to show a grainy video of a soldier who had been taken hostage when his mother reached in and switched off the television. She looked so sad. "I think you've seen enough, Gregor."

It had all looked pretty familiar. The bodies, the fear, the desperation. These things had always been here in the Overland, he supposed, but he had never really paid any attention to them until now.

"Why don't you take your sisters out to the playground?" said his dad. "They've been cooped up in here all day."

"Are we moving to Virginia or staying here?" Lizzie asked.

"We're still working that out," his dad said. "You kids go on out and play a while."

When they reached the playground, Boots immediately ran off to build castles with some little boy in the sandbox. Lizzie wandered around alone with her hands deep in her jacket pockets and her eyes on the ground.

Gregor sat on a bench. He had walked a lot today and all of his injuries were hurting. Seeing the news had made him think. He was safe for the moment, here in the playground, but people all over the world were suffering, starving, fleeing, killing one another as they waged their wars. How much energy they put into harming one another. How little into saving. Would it ever change? What would it take to make it change? He thought of Luxa's hand pressed into Ripred's paw. That's what it would take. People rejecting war. Not one or two, but all of them. Saying it was an unacceptable way to solve their differences. By the look of things, the human race had a lot of evolving to do before that happened. Maybe it was impossible. But maybe it wasn't. Like Vikus said, nothing would happen unless you hoped it could. If you had hope, maybe you could find the way to make things change. Because if you thought about it, there were so many reasons to try.

One tugged on his jacket and lifted up her arms. "Hold me." Gregor pulled Boots up onto his lap and snuggled her inside his jacket. She rested her head on his shoulder and studied his face. "You feel sad," she said.

"A little," said Gregor.

"You miss them," said Boots.

"Yeah, I do," Gregor said. "But I've still got you." He remembered all of the times he'd thought he had lost her, and tightened his grip around her.

"Here." Boots dug in her pocket and pulled out the little black plastic bat. Ares. She put it in his hand. "You can have this, Gregor."

"Thanks," he said. They leaned back and watched as the streetlights came on.

Suddenly Gregor smiled. "Hey, Boots," he said. "Hey. You can finally say my name."